W9-BCI-427

5/16/23

6/10

THE TREE OF KNOWLEDGE

Daniel G. Miller

HOUNDSTOOTH
BOOKS

Copyright © 2021 Daniel G. Miller
Published by Houndstooth Books, Dallas, Texas
Edited and designed by Girl Friday Productions
www.girlfridayproductions.com
Cover design: Bailey McGinn
Project management: Bethany Davis
ISBN (paperback): 978-0-578-75320-1
ISBN (ebook): 978-0-578-75321-8
ISBN (hardcover): 979-9-518-02227-0
First edition

To Mom and Dad for allowing me to dream and teaching me how to bring my dreams to life.

Of Man's first disobedience, and the fruit
Of that forbidden tree whose mortal taste
Brought death into the World, and all our woe,
With loss of Eden, till one greater Man
Restore us, and regain the blissful sea . . .

—John Milton, *Paradise Lost*

PART I
DISCOVERY

The serpent said to the woman . . .
For God knows that in the day you eat from it your eyes will be opened,
and you will be like God, knowing good and evil.

—Genesis 3:4–5

CHAPTER 1

Wally McCutcheon eased into the creaky chair at the security desk. He treasured the stillness and peace of working night security at the Bank of Princeton. There were rarely any visitors, and the bank hadn't been robbed since he started, which was a long, long time ago. Wally listened to the steady rain pattering on the roof and settled in for a snack. He opened his scuffed green army thermos and poured himself a piping hot cup of coffee. The soft aroma filled the room. He unzipped his travel cooler and smiled. Nancy had packed a piece of pecan pie—his favorite—into his dinner this evening. The dear woman was a saint.

Wally dove into his first bite of pie and savored the sweet molasses. He closed his eyes and listened to the rain.

A persistent tapping on the front door of the bank interrupted him.

He peered through the glass door of the stone building. Outside the main entrance of the bank stood a wiry figure in a black trench coat and fedora holding an umbrella shimmering with droplets of rain. Probably another Princeton alum who took a wrong turn, thought Wally. He considered ignoring the stranger to focus on his pie, but begrudgingly heaved his frame out of the chair and made his way to the entrance.

Wally flipped the lock, opened the door, and said as pleasantly as he could manage, "Bank's closed, but if you take a left out of the parking lo—"

A fierce kick shook Wally's kneecap and dropped him to the ground.

He grunted in pain and struggled to stand up, but the stranger's gloved hand grabbed his throat, crushing his windpipe and stanching the flow of oxygen to his brain. His cheeks burned and his eyes strained to escape his skull. His mind whirred. *He should grab the hands—no, get a look at the face—*

Through the pounding in his ears, he heard the assailant whisper three simple words: "Safe-deposit box."

There was something terrifying in that raspy voice.

Wally lifted his quivering arm and pointed to the thick walnut door at the end of the hallway.

With two swift moves, the stranger ripped the key card off Wally's belt and forced a soaked rag over his mouth and nose. Wally tasted the chemicals flowing past his throat into his lungs, choking the consciousness from his body.

These might be his last moments. He thought of Nancy, of never seeing her again.

Frantically, he clawed at the intruder's trench coat, tearing at the pockets, hoping to escape the chemical fog that seeped through his brain, but the stranger's grip was too strong. Realizing this could be his last breath, Wally looked up at his killer.

It was a woman. Her eyes were onyx with flecks of gray-orange, like the wolves Wally used to hunt when he was younger. She removed her hat, and he cried out as her straight dark hair tumbled down her back. He squinted and searched her face, silently pleading with her to stop. Her hand stayed firm. The silhouette in front of him faded first to red, then to gray. Then all went black.

CHAPTER 2

A lbert Puddles was sweating.

He stood at the front of a spare mathematics lecture hall at Princeton University, about to embark on his first class of the academic year. The room was silent except for the occasional squeak of a student shifting in their chair. Albert marveled at how the experience of silence could shift from peaceful to terrifying depending on your circumstance.

Today it was terrifying.

He looked out at row after row of eager scholars sitting at their desks, fingers poised, ready to write down every word that spilled from his mouth. It reminded him of how the neighborhood bullies used to look at him back in Minnesota. Each student was an unknown quantity to him.

He organized them in his mind. He couldn't help it. Seventy-four students. One hundred seats. Forty-eight men, twenty-six women. Sixteen wore glasses. Fifty-eight didn't. Twenty wore jeans. Forty pants. Fourteen dresses or skirts. Fifty-four looked at their laptops, notebooks, or phones. Twenty stared directly at him.

He assessed them assessing him. *Did they think his tweed suit was too stuffy? Did they notice the drops of sweat collecting around his brow?*

His glasses sliding down his oversized nose? Did he look too young to be taken seriously? Too old to be cool?

That was the trouble with people. They had never made much sense to Albert. He had been a professor at Princeton for five years, and with every turn of the calendar and every new batch of undergraduates that shuffled into his classroom, he felt like he was starting over. People were unpredictable, irrational, emotional. Emotion implied the absence of logic, and logic was Albert's cool, comforting refuge against the hot, emotional chaos of the world. Logic was precise. Certain. Absolute. It didn't change with the times or adjust for the latest fad. It was everything life should be, and so rarely was.

Nevertheless, it was his duty to bring order to the chaos, so he straightened his immaculately tied bow tie, brushed back a tuft of brown hair hanging down in his face, and steadied himself. He grabbed the bright-blue Expo marker from its gray metal tray. With a shaking hand, he wrote on the enormous lecture hall whiteboard:

Introduction to Logic

He pivoted back to the class. "Good morning, everyone. I am Professor Puddles, and this is Introduction to Logic."

He scanned the room for the few students who would inevitably smirk at his last name. Albert had noticed a high correlation between students who chuckled and those who eventually dropped the class. Of course, correlation did not imply causation, but it was interesting, nevertheless.

"Let me begin by thanking you all for enrolling in my class. I am keenly aware that Introduction to Logic is not, at first glance, the 'sexiest' class on the Princeton syllabus."

He cracked a smile and looked around the room, holding back a sigh when he saw no answering grins.

"However, I will submit to you today that logic is, indeed, sexy. Logic is fact in a world of fiction, truth in a society of lies, and light in the shadows. Logic will never betray you, deceive you, or disappoint you. It will guide you and illuminate your path ahead. Logic provides the loyalty, confidence, and friendship that many of you hope to find in a spouse someday. What could be sexier than that?"

Albert noticed a slight movement out of the corner of his eye. The lecture hall door crept open, and his graduate assistant, Ying slid through the opening. She carried a notepad and an uncharacteristically grim expression. *Something was wrong.*

He pushed the thought from his mind and turned to the class.

"In this class, I'm going to teach you how to think like a logician. What does thinking like a logician mean? Well, let's start with a simple case. Raise your hand if you would torture someone?"

The students stopped typing and exchanged confused glances. No one raised a hand.

Albert raised his hand and took a few steps forward. "Nobody? Nobody here would torture someone?"

He raised his voice for dramatic effect. "I would."

More confused glances.

Albert called on a scruffy faced student in the back.

"You, sir. Why wouldn't you torture someone?"

The student squinted and looked to his classmates for support. "Uh, because it's wrong."

Laughter.

Albert smiled and glanced around the classroom. He had their attention now, which was always a challenge when teaching logic. "Because it's wrong. An admirable sentiment. But let's play this out. Imagine a serial killer kidnapped your family and planted a bomb that would kill them if you didn't find them in time. But now, you've found the killer, and the only way you can find your family is to torture him into giving their location. Would you torture him?"

"Well, yeah."

"Ah, so you *would* torture someone?"

"I mean, in that extreme case, yes."

"Exactly. As would most of us, although I'm sure we wouldn't be happy about it. And that is the difference between thinking emotionally and thinking logically. Our emotional selves tell us, 'Oh, I would never torture someone. It's morally wrong.' But if we put emotions aside and think logically, the uncomfortable truth is 'It depends.' And that is what logic is all about, putting our emotions, traditions, morals temporarily aside and making decisions through the cold lens of cause and effect and cost and benefit rather than good or bad, right or wrong."

Ying waved from the side of the room.

He paused.

"Yes, Ying? Did you want to add your thoughts to this grim subject?"

"I wish I could, Professor, but I actually need to speak to you for a second," she said in her lilting voice.

That was odd. Ying wasn't just his graduate assistant; she was a PhD candidate and one of the brightest people on campus. Like Albert, she had won the junior mental calculation world cup when she was younger. She knew the first class of the year was a priority for him. If she was interrupting, it had to be important. *But what could be so urgent?*

"Sure Ying. What's up?"

Ying looked nervous, now. She pulled her cardigan close and gazed around the giant lecture hall. Albert could see the gears in her brain turning. She raised her eyebrows, and said cautiously, "It would probably be better to talk about this outside."

He glanced at his watch. His lecture was already one minute behind schedule, and he would never get back on track if he left the class. He ran all the permutations of what could necessitate this interruption through his mind. *A call from a family member. An angry colleague.* None of them constituted a good reason to halt the class. He scanned the faces of his students. They appeared as eager to know what was going on as he was. He pressed on.

"Ying, it's fine. You can just tell me."

Ying looked around once more, shrugged her shoulders, and in the most upbeat tone she could muster, said, "A police officer is here to see you."

"A police officer?"

A murmur rose from the class. Albert watched as they leaned over from one desk to another, whispering to each other. His heartbeat accelerated. *Had something happened to his mom? His dad?*

"What does he want?" Albert asked, unsure of whether he wanted to hear the answer.

He watched as Ying hesitated.

"Well, he says . . . he says that there was a murder last night and . . ."

She trailed off and swallowed hard.

"...and that you might know something about it."

CHAPTER 3

Albert excused himself and slid out of the lecture hall, with Ying following close behind. The pair strode the ancient hardwood floors of Princeton's Fine Hall toward his office. The building's name had been changed to Jones Hall, thanks to a beneficent donor, but he preferred to think of it by the name it had carried during its glory days. Fine Hall was a source of calm in an otherwise disordered place. Every time Albert walked the enormous, sterile white hallways, he pictured the giants of mathematics at work. He saw Einstein holding court on his theory of relativity; John Nash working the chalkboards at the library late into the night; the great logician Alonzo Church carefully erasing the blackboard in his classroom until the last speck of chalk was gone before beginning his lecture.

Yet, on this day, the tightly cinched knot in the bottom of Albert's stomach choked his ability to appreciate his surroundings. His mind sparked with calculations. What could this tragedy have to do with him?

A murder?

I might know something about it?

I don't even know any police officers. I've never done anything illegal in my life.

What could this possibly have to do with me?

"What else did the officer say?" Albert asked Ying.

"That was about it." Ying looked over at him earnestly. "I explained that you were teaching and could go to see him after the class, and he said that a security guard had been killed during a burglary last night, and there was some evidence that they thought you might be able to shed some light on."

"Evidence?"

There must be a mistake. They must be confusing me with another faculty member. Yes, that must be it ... a mix-up.

With that soothing thought in his mind, Albert gingerly opened the solid oak door to his office.

In front of his desk, in one of the tiny chairs that his students usually occupied during office hours, sat the massive frame of a police officer. The sight of this mammoth man squeezed into a chair meant for a considerably smaller individual would have been comical had it not been for the circumstances. Albert wondered how a single man could so drastically shrink his previously roomy office.

At Albert's entry, the police officer extricated himself from his seat, extended one gigantic hand, and gave Albert a warm smile.

"You must be Professor Puddles," said the detective. "I'm Detective Michael Weatherspoon, Princeton Police Department. It's a real pleasure to meet you."

Albert eyed the detective to see if he could glean his intent, but he wasn't giving any hints. Weatherspoon resumed his seat, inviting Albert and Ying to join him. He cleared his throat. "I'm sorry to bother you, Professor, but there was a burglary last night."

"Oh, I'm sorry to hear that, Detective. Where?"

"At the Bank of Princeton," chirped Ying, sliding forward in her chair.

"That's right, ma'am," said the bemused detective, running his hands through the gray remains of what looked to have once been a world-class Afro.

Ying attempted to stifle her mischievous grin. "Sorry, I just feel like I'm in an episode of *Law and Order.*"

Detective Weatherspoon chuckled and shook his head. "If only we were, I could be sure we would solve this. Unfortunately, we don't have much to go on, and the security guard on duty was killed attempting to stop the thief."

The detective removed a picture from his file and handed it to Albert. He recoiled as he saw the prostrate body of Wally McCutcheon on the floor. Wally was a gentle-looking older man, and Albert couldn't help thinking of his grandfather.

"Who would do this?" asked Albert.

An unwelcome spasm of emotion ran through his gut.

"We don't have any leads yet, but we know from the security feed that, before he died, the guard ripped a sliver of paper from the assailant's coat pocket."

The detective removed a copy of the paper and placed it on Albert's well-ordered desk.

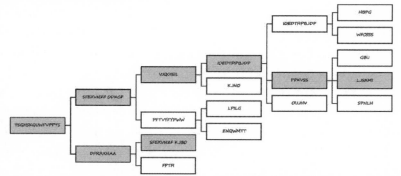

"At first, we thought it was a scientific formula, so we took it down to the chemistry department, but they said that it was some kind of decision tree and that you'd be the man to talk to. What do you make of it?"

Albert studied the piece of paper as Ying sidled up beside him. The two exchanged glances and nodded.

"Well, this is clearly a decision tree or game tree," said Albert. "Mathematicians, logicians, and computer scientists use these in rudimentary problem-solving, computation, and decision analysis to ensure that their thinking is perfectly logical or MECE."

"I'm sorry, MECE?" asked the detective.

"Yes, mutually exclusive and collectively exhaustive. To properly consider any problem, it's critical to weigh all the options. For example, say your in-laws are in town."

The detective rolled his eyes at the thought.

"You would want to logically assess which hotel you should have them stay at, so that you'd be confident you weren't overlooking a good option. That's the collectively exhaustive part. Then, once you had your list of hotels, you'd want to make sure that the lists didn't overlap. That's the mutually exclusive part."

Weatherspoon's furrowed brow conveyed a combination of confusion and irritation.

Albert continued. "For example, if you initially broke down hotels into two categories—hotels with rooms and hotels with parking—that would be collectively exhaustive because all hotels have rooms, right?"

Detective Weatherspoon nodded.

"But it wouldn't be mutually exclusive because there are some hotels that have both rooms and parking, so they would sit in both categories and muddle your thinking. To be fully logical, you would have to start with a different categorization of hotels that was completely MECE, such as hotels within Princeton city limits and hotels outside Princeton city limits. Every hotel on earth would fit into these categories, so it would be collectively exhaustive, but none would overlap because they are either in Princeton city limits or they're not, so it's mutually exclusive. Once you've settled on those base categories, you then add additional branches to the tree until you've settled on your answer."

Albert walked to the small chalkboard next to his desk and sketched a decision tree depicting the hotel decision-making process:

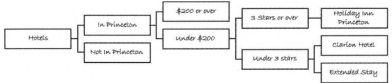

"It's quite fun, isn't it?" Albert said, with a twinkle in his eyes.

Weatherspoon coughed. "I don't know about fun, but it's certainly enlightening, and it will help the next time the in-laws are in town. So, what does this decision tree mean?" he asked, pointing to the scrap of paper. "I'm assuming it's not about where the criminal will vacation?"

Albert had been so caught up in the joyful world of decision trees that he'd forgotten the task at hand. Resuming his serious posture, Albert returned his gaze to the tree before him.

The tree in question was rudimentary but, because of the use of random letters rather than words within each box, difficult to understand. In addition, the use of the words "prima facie" at the top of the page implied a multi-scenario analysis of which he had only one page.

Albert shrugged. "Honestly, Detective, at first glance, I can't tell you much. Judging by the size of the tree, the analysis is relatively basic, but because it is just the base case, there could be more to the analysis. The shaded boxes show the path of decisions made by the tree's maker. Until I know what the letters symbolize, I can't possibly tell you what the tree means. The letters almost certainly represent some type of cipher or code, but I can't be sure until I look at it in more depth. Give me some time, and maybe I can identify a pattern."

"OK, Dr. Puddles. You work on that. I'm going to make a couple of calls. The detective rose from his chair and lumbered toward the door. But do me a favor. Don't take too long, because this is just about the only evidence we've got on the killer. We got lucky."

Weatherspoon opened the door to exit.

Albert nodded. "Oh, Detective, just out of curiosity, what did the thief steal?"

Weatherspoon sighed. "Nothing special. The bank logs say that it was just something in a safe-deposit box. We're trying to get in contact with the owner as we speak. But I'd remind you that there's a woman who lost her husband of forty-five years last night, and she's depending on *you* to figure out this problem. Like I said, don't dawdle."

CHAPTER 4

Eva set her red-ribboned fedora down on the entry table of her lavish Malibu home. She had loved this place from the moment she'd toured it. It was the first and only home she had lived in since leaving her mother's house, but she had never wanted anything else.

The open, high-ceilinged space provided transparency and order, while the carefully appointed minimalist décor suggested elegance and modernity. Dove-gray upholstery and marble offset steel appliances, white walls, and light wood. There were no pets, no plants, no clutter. The floor-to-ceiling windows and wraparound deck overlooking the Pacific Ocean spoke to her of limitless possibilities. Beyond the aesthetic trappings, however, her Southern California enclave represented something even more inspiring: freedom. This was the only place where Eva could be alone and be herself.

She unbuttoned her double-breasted black pinstriped blazer and opened the sliding glass door to the balcony. The cool ocean air slid past her damp skin, bringing the smell of salt and marine life. She stared out at the glittering water and relaxed. Outside this house, everything was a test or a mission. Only here, alone, could she let go.

"Not your best work, soldier," hissed a voice on the balcony behind her.

Eva whirled, startled.

"General?" She swallowed hard and resisted the urge to snap at him to get out. That this was her private sanctum. But that would betray an emotional weak point—something those in the Society should *never* do. She took a moment to steady her voice before asking. "Why are you here?"

The general eased forward. Tall and lean, with a bullet head and a nose that jutted forward like the prow of a ship, he was an impressive figure. Smoke drifted up from his tan-filtered cigarette and across his face. His voice was soft but still commanding as he said: "Tell me, what is the third rule?"

Eva stared at him impassively. Anger beating in her ears. *He had invaded her sanctum for this, to ask questions they both knew the answers to?*

But he continued to advance, backing her up against a railing.

"What is the third rule of the Society?" he asked.

She swallowed hard to control both her anger and the sudden worry that something had gone terribly wrong. "Our reasoning is only as strong as our information." She stood taller and straightened her shoulders to retake the offensive. "General, what's the problem? The mission last night was a success."

The general stared past Eva out at the Pacific and took a long drag from his cigarette, exhaling smoke through pursed lips like a blow dart. "Not entirely."

"I retrieved the information without being apprehended. What else was there?"

He turned and leaned in closer to Eva, practically pushing her against the railing. She could smell the nicotine on his breath as his tongue slid across his lips.

"Then why is there a dead security guard in the lobby of the Bank of Princeton with a logic tree in his hand?"

"What? What are you talking about?" Eva reached into her blazer pocket and rifled through her notes inside. "I just drugged him. I didn't kill him."

The general's face grew red, and a powerful vein bulged from the center of his forehead underneath his cropped, receding silver hair. He pulled a folder out from under his arm and slapped her chest with it to punctuate each sentence. "If you had properly researched the security guard, you would know his name is Wally McCutcheon." Slap. "He had a heart condition, which is why the Sevoflurane killed him." Slap. "And he is also a former state wrestling champion, which would explain how he pulled that piece of note paper from out of your pocket." Slap.

No, no, no. Eva ripped through the pages.

"Oh, God. What time is it? Five p.m. That means the police have it."

The general clasped Eva's shoulder with his long, bony hand, his thumb digging into her clavicle. She could hear the waves crashing behind her.

"As you well know, Eva, the Society frowns on murder. It is impractical and expensive. Now, I have to deal with the police, the media, and several other nuisances that I have *zero* tolerance for."

"I know." She suppressed the urge to swallow nervously or to point out her previously spotless record. "I'll fix this."

"You had better, or the security guard won't be the only dead body I'll be dealing with this week."

And before she could answer his threat with one of her own, he was gone.

CHAPTER 5

"So, are we going to crack this cipher, or what?" said Ying. Albert raised an eyebrow and shook his head at his smiling colleague. "*We* aren't going to do anything. *You* are going to the lecture hall to inform the class that we'll resume our session tomorrow, and I am going to see if I can break down this cipher."

"Oh, come on," implored Ying. She pushed her thick-rimmed glasses up her nose and blinked her big brown eyes. "You know that it's probably some type of Caesar cipher, and we'll be able to do it much faster together than if you do it on your own." She smiled and her cheeks formed two shiny round balls that kept the glasses from sliding down again.

Albert sighed. Ying had grown up in Singapore with four older brothers. He had spent enough time with her to anticipate she wasn't taking no for an answer. He removed his glasses and massaged the bridge of his nose. "OK, Ying, go tell the class that we're done for the day and that we will resume tomorrow."

"Yaaaaay," Ying exclaimed as she scampered out the office door.

"Tell them to finish the first two chapters of *Introduction to Logic*," he shouted after her.

"I will," she called back over her shoulder.

Alone in the office, Albert stared at the cipher and sighed. He hated to admit it, but Ying was right: they would solve this much more quickly together. He reminded himself that wanting to solve the puzzle alone was vain—a pointless piece of self-indulgence that would only slow down the investigation.

"What's a Caesar Cipher," asked Weatherspoon, reentering the room from the hallway. "I couldn't help but overhear."

Albert waived the detective in.

"It's a cipher that dates back to the Roman Empire. Emperor Julius Caesar used it. It's a basic substitution cipher in which we substitute each letter of the alphabet with the letter three places down in the alphabet. For example, we replace the letter A with the letter *D*, the letter *B* with the letter *E*, and so on."

"Isn't that pretty easy to crack?"

"It is, but it proved extremely effective in its own era. The vast majority of the known world was illiterate, and knowledge of linguistics and codebreaking was in its infancy. While it's quite basic, it would provide enough security to keep most people from understanding a code at first glance. My friends and I used to use them to pass notes in high school back in Northfield, so it's as good place to start as any."

"Sounds like you and your high school crew were a wild bunch," said Weatherspoon, grunting his approval.

Albert pulled a piece of scrap paper toward himself and, despite the situation, felt a smile grow on his face. It had been years since he had performed any decryption. As a teenager, he had loved trying to decode mathematical puzzles and cryptograms, but he no longer had the time to do so. The demands of modern professorship were constant: publishing new papers, teaching, attending faculty meetings.

"Just start trying things to get your mind moving," he murmured to himself, an echo of his father's constant advice to him when he was younger.

His father, a world-class teacher and mathematician in his own right, referred to the paralysis that students often felt when tackling a math problem as "the freeze". He taught his students, and Albert, that starting anywhere and "talking the problem out" would "thaw" the brain and allow a solution to present itself.

The thought of his father always brought with it a complicated wave of emotions, but the advice comforted him.

The letters in each box were a random jumble. Then he spotted something. In the shaded box, second from the right, was a code with not one but two repeating letters in it: "PPKVSS."

He turned the paper toward Weatherspoon.

"This could be a vulnerability."

"How do you figure? Because of the repeating letters?"

"Exactly. In the ninth century, al-Kindi, an Arab linguist, analyzed the Koran and discovered that certain letters occurred with much greater frequency than others. He published a book documenting what he found, and, for the first time, cryptographers could look at a cipher and, by identifying symbols that occurred with greater frequency, crack the code.

"I take it that put an end to our friend the Caesar cipher."

"Yeah, linguists in other countries soon discovered that these differences in the distribution of letters existed in all languages, so Caesar ciphers were never again used in serious communications."

Albert returned his focus to decoding the cipher.

Let's assume that each letter is just substituted for one letter down in the alphabet. A would be B; B would be C, etcetera.

Albert performed the analysis and stared at the result with a sigh: QQLWTT.

"OK, I'm pretty sure that's not it," he said to Weatherspoon.

He was tapping his fingers on the desk, scanning his brain for any words that began with two of the same letter, when Ying returned from telling the class the good news.

"Any progress?"

"Nope," said Weatherspoon.

Albert ignored the detective's pessimism. "I tried a simple substitution, and unless 'QQLWTT' is a word I don't know about, I'm pretty sure we need to try something else."

Ying laughed and came to look over the logic tree. She pushed her glasses up her nose. "You know, I've been thinking about it, and I really don't think this cipher can be that complicated. The code is done by hand and on a pretty simple game tree, so I just don't see the thief using anything too advanced. Should we try a brute-force attack?"

A brute-force attack was cryptography slang for solving a cipher by trying all variations according to a hypothesis. While inefficient with more complex ciphers, it was doable for the Caesar cipher, as the codebreaker would simply rewrite the cipher twenty-six times for each potential number of shifts in the alphabet.

"Yeah, that makes sense." Albert stood and pushed his chair to the side to make room for Ying. "I'll take the first thirteen letters; you take the second."

Ying smiled and clinked her pen against his in a *cheers* motion. Albert could not help but smile. The office was always a little cheerier when she was around.

Together, they rewrote the cipher, each time shifting down one letter of the alphabet. Albert began by making the *A* into a *B*, the *B* into a *C*, and so on, but that produced nothing. He then made the *A* into a *C* and continued, but still nothing. After fifteen minutes, he and Ying had completed their respective tables. The two combined the tables and hunched over the finished product, hoping to see something of meaning:

Shift	Translation	Shift	Translation
1	QQLWTT	14	DDYJGG
2	RRMXUU	15	EEZKHH
3	SSNYVV	16	FFALII
4	TTOZWW	17	GGBMJJ
5	UUPAXX	18	HHCNKK
6	VVQBYY	19	IIDOLL
7	WWRCZZ	20	JJEPMM
8	XXSDAA	21	KKFQNN
9	YYTEBB	22	LLGROO
10	ZZUFCC	23	MMHSPP
11	AAVGDD	24	NNITQQ
12	BBWHEE	25	OOJURR
13	CCXIFF		

Albert stared in disbelief at the jumbled list of letters in front of him. He scanned twice, and then three times, before groaning in defeat.

"Are you kidding me? I can't believe that this is more than just a basic substitution cipher."

"I know. It seems like a lot of effort to go through to hide a decision tree," said Ying.

"I hope this is a Vigenère cipher, because if it's not, then it's probably unbreakable unless we have the keyword, which we don't. Ying, will you do me a favor and hop on the computer? There's a guy at MIT who's created an automated program for cracking a Vigenère cipher. I'm not sure if it will work, since each cipher in each box of the game tree is so short, but it's worth a shot."

Ying hustled over to the computer on Albert's desk while he stood in front of the chalkboard, thinking of alternatives. He found the chalkboard calming and illuminating. The feel of the soft, powdery chalk. The clear, dark blackboard like the endless expanse of space.

"Didn't the confederacy use a cipher like this in the Civil War," said Weatherspoon.

"They did indeed, Detective. Albert grabbed his familiar eraser and slid it back and forth across the board until the last particle of chalk was gone. They actually used the key 'complete victory' until the union cracked it."

"How does it work?"

"It's pretty straightforward. The Vigenère cipher uses a Caesar cipher, but instead of a constant substitution shift, such as three letters to the right, the shift changes at each position according to a keyword. If the keyword is as long as the text of the message itself, then the code is considered unbreakable."

Weatherspoon laughed. "So, we've got an unbreakable code on our hands. Sounds like I need to call it a day."

The Detective grabbed his bag and threw it over his shoulder. He made his way over to Albert and handed him his business card.

"Puddles, Ying, I'm going to head on back to the station, but you give me a holler the second you find something, OK?"

Albert put down his chalk for a moment and shook Weatherspoon's hand.

"OK, Detective. We'll do our best."

"I know you will, Professor." He slapped Albert on the back, nearly knocking him over, and left the office.

Albert turned to Ying. "I just can't accept that this is that complex a cipher. I mean, think about it. You're a thief about to break into a bank. You're a freakishly logical thief with some training in mathematics, so in preparation for the theft, you create a decision tree—by hand, mind you—that requires a complex encryption. That seems so illogical and tedious given the incredible unlikelihood that it's going to wind up in someone else's hands."

"Yeah, and you can tell by the way it's scribbled on the paper that the thief sketched it fast. When I was in Professor Turner's cryptography class, he said that if we ever wanted to encrypt something by hand quickly, we should just use a Trithemius cipher," said Ying.

Albert chuckled. "He said the same thing when I was in his class."

Professor Turner was an institution at Princeton. He had won every mathematics prize ever invented, had taught nearly every aspiring mathematician of the last half century, and had launched the very Mental Calculation World Cup that Albert and Ying had each won when they were kids.

Albert's eyes brightened at the thought.

"That's it! It's a Trithemius cipher."

Johannes Trithemius was a German abbot in the late fifteenth and early sixteenth centuries. During his lifetime, Trithemius published numerous works on history, language, and cryptography. In 1499, he completed his most famous work, *Steganographia*, the first book ever published on cryptography. To the layperson, *Steganographia* appeared to be a work outlining a system of angel magic. However, in a clever inside joke, the author encoded the text on magic, and upon breaking the code, it showed itself to be a book on cryptography and steganography. The book included what is now known as the Trithemius cipher, a more practical but less secure predecessor to the Vigenère cipher.

The Trithemius cipher used what the inventor titled a "tabula recta", which was a square table of alphabets, with each alphabet shifting one to the right. Using the tabula recta, a person could decode a message by moving down one row of the table for each letter in the message. This enabled the message writer to encrypt the message easily by hand while enabling an amateur to decode the message.

Albert quickly grabbed his well-worn copy of *Introduction to Cryptography* from his alphabetized bookshelf and flipped through the pages until he came upon the legendary tabula recta. He ripped out the page featuring one of the most well-known images in cryptography, posted it on the chalkboard, and translated the cipher.

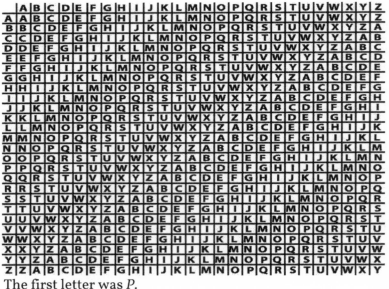

The first letter was *P*.

The next letter, *O*.

A good sign. "PO" could be the start of a word.

Albert continued. *P-O-I.*

His throat tightened. There were very few words in the English language that started with *P-O-I*.

Ying recoiled as Albert finished the word in front of them.

P-O-I-S-O-N.

CHAPTER 6

The Princeton police station anchored the main street through town like a sofa in a living room. Everything about it oozed small-town charm and stability. The brick facade and careful yet understated landscaping said to the passersby, "Things are quiet here, and we like it that way."

Unfortunately for Detective Weatherspoon, the recent murder had fractured the everyday quiet and soothing boredom of his normal police work. Instead of investigating which one of the neighborhood kids sprayed "don't" on the stop sign on Spruce and Chestnut, the former All-State offensive tackle was spending night and day investigating a murder. His dark-brown skin seemed to be gaining cracks by the hour, and his large, square head seemed to be losing hair by the minute. He imagined that he'd get up tomorrow morning and be a bald, wrinkled prune of a man, one of those useless old fellows his wife, a nurse, liked to make jokes about.

And I got squat for evidence, thought the detective as he climbed the steps to the station and massaged his aching knees.

"Barb!" Weatherspoon shouted to his assistant as he entered. "Get me someone over at that defense company who knows something about codes."

"You mean Fix Industries?"

"Yeah, Fix."

While the detective waited for his treasured assistant to hunt down yet another egghead, he thought about all the dead ends that he had run into so far.

No witnesses.

No video surveillance, other than the ten seconds it took the perp to put down the security guard.

No description.

No license plate.

All he had was one ripped sheet of paper with some letters and boxes he didn't understand. The detective chuckled, thinking about the curious professor he had talked to today.

What kind of a name is "Puddles" anyway?

Weatherspoon liked Professor Puddles, even though he thought he looked like a kid in his dad's suit. Unfortunately, Puddles hadn't given the detective much cause for optimism about his ability to translate the paper. Even if Puddles translated it, it probably wouldn't give him anything useful.

Weatherspoon flipped through his barren police report. He squinted at the name on the safe-deposit-box registry.

"A. Turner."

Who is that?

"Line one, Dr. Belial from Fix Industries," shouted Barb.

"Hello, Doctor, I'm wondering if you can give me a little info on a case I'm working on," boomed the detective as he put the phone to his ear.

"It would be my pleasure to help in whatever way I can," replied Belial in a nasal voice.

"Great. Well, you see, I'm following up on a burglary, over here. The thief left behind a scrap of paper, but it's got some kind of cipher on it. I've got a guy at Princeton working on it, but we don't know what the symbols mean, yet. Anyway, he didn't seem optimistic that he could solve it, so I thought I'd get another pair of eyes on it."

The cryptographer paused. When Belial finally responded, Detective Weatherspoon thought he could sense some nervousness or anxiety. It sounded as if Belial's throat were constricted in some way.

"Yes, ah, I can look at the code for you. I doubt I'll be of any help, though. You know, these codes can be quite complicated."

Weatherspoon sighed. "Hmm, I spoke with one of your colleagues who seemed to think that you could break almost any code."

Belial's voice quavered. "Well, of course, I . . . well, I'll look into it."

Weatherspoon squinted his eyes as if to stare down Dr. Belial through the phone. The cryptographer's evasiveness framed every word.

"Alright, Doctor. I'll send a copy of the sheet over to you. This is confidential, of course."

"Of course, Detective . . . One quick question . . . Who did you give the tree to at Princeton? Talking to him may give me some insight."

"A guy named Puddles in the Math Department."

Another long pause. "Hmm. Don't know him. Good luck, Detective."

Weatherspoon hung up the phone and turned to his computer. *Something isn't right about that guy.*

* * *

As Weatherspoon absorbed the disconcerting call, Dr. Belial picked up the phone and dialed. He tried to steady his high-pitched voice. "General, I just received a disturbing call from the police. They gave the tree to Dr. Puddles at Princeton. I didn't give the detective any information, but Puddles will crack the cipher. Someone needs to clean this up before it spreads."

CHAPTER 7

Eva gazed out the window of the first-class section of Delta flight 457 from Los Angeles to Newark. She had spent the last thirty minutes attempting to fend off inane conversation with the whiskey-breathed, married businessman next to her. Why was it that men—who were typically so rational—lost all ability to reason around a beautiful woman? The businessman had been leering at her chest and attempting to seduce her with winning lines like "I like your black shirt" and "Where are you from?"

Did that ever work?

If I were a balding, overweight, married businessman—in an ill-fitting suit—and I saw a good-looking twenty-something woman next to me, I would rationally assess the situation and say to myself, "There is no pickup line in the universe that is going to enable me to have sex with this woman." That's what I get for not flying private.

To prevent what would surely be another lame salvo, she pulled out her tablet, opened her *Economist* magazine app, and focused on the screen.

"A Queen or a Democracy in California?" read the headline.

Leaders | The Economist
A Queen or a Democracy in California?
Cristina Culebra's uplifting campaign belies a worrying drive toward authoritarianism
At first glance, Cristina Culebra appears to be everything that voters say they want in a candidate. She's staggeringly smart, having graduated with a PhD in mathematics at 25. She has been successful in every venture she has undertaken, including creating a global business empire, writing a bestselling business book, and raising a successful child. Her campaign oozes efficiency and optimism as evidenced by her slogan "Government that works for you" and her logo of a tree in full bloom. She even has movie-star good looks. For these reasons and many others, the 53-year-old Ms. Culebra holds a commanding fifteen-point lead in the race to be California's governor, despite campaigning under the banner of the newly created Reason, Enlightenment, and Democracy (RED) Party.

However, upon closer examination, Cristina Culebra's cause takes on a more sinister air. In addition to running a campaign, Ms. Culebra has quietly channeled millions of dollars to an organization that supports a controversial citizens' initiative to restructure state government. Of course, in California, they frequently pass citizen referendums with little fuss, but what makes this referendum so disturbing is that its sole purpose seems to be to subvert the democratic process and give Ms. Culebra nearly dictatorial powers.

Initiative 471, or the "Make Government Work" initiative, would temporarily suspend the state's House of Representatives and Senate and replace them with an advisory board. This board would have no formal power but would merely serve as a counselor to the governor, thereby freeing the governor to take immediate, unilateral action on the state's most pressing problems.

Proponents of the initiative say they need this measure to break the legislative gridlock, and history is on their side. The California legislature has failed to pass a budget in the last two years, while squabbling and infighting among legislators are at unprecedented levels. The state is almost bankrupt, and the current governor, Evan Adams, has been reduced to the role of referee. Meanwhile, California faces crumbling infrastructure, record unemployment, and a housing crisis that is among the worst in the nation.

While it is tempting to take Ms. Culebra and her supporters at their word, we at *The Economist* have seen this movie a few too many times. Nearly every foreign dictator in recent memory has used government inefficiency or ineffectiveness to justify the "temporary" suspension of the democratic process. However, once this power is concentrated in a single pair of hands, it becomes nearly impossible to remove.

Fortunately, for the citizens of California, their likely governor controls a state, not a country, and as a result has no military to use against them once they grow weary of her reign . . .

If they only knew, thought Eva.

Eva finished the article and swiped her finger across the tablet's screen. Just as she had hoped, a new email popped from her inbox.

"NEW ASSIGNMENT: HAIRCUT"

The title of the email sent a curl of anticipation and excitement through her body. She had been a victim of her own ego with the last mission, both in her mistakes and in her anger at the general for pointing them out. As the general always reminded her, there was no room for ego in this business.

This new assignment would give her a chance to remind them all of what she could do.

The Society believed that individuals needed regular assignments to stay motivated. Simply giving someone a position and a set of responsibilities was far too amorphous, leading to atrophy. The process of reason demanded steady, unrelenting progress, achieved through the disciplined delegation and monitoring of tasks. While others chafed, Eva loved the system because it broke her work up into new, exciting, and discrete challenges as opposed to a monotonous ongoing "job".

Whenever members of the Society made mistakes, there would inevitably be loose ends that needed to be cut. These loose ends could be people or things, but their common characteristic was that they provided a link back to the Society and its plans. These links must be eliminated, and the Society term for such eliminations was a "haircut".

Biting firmly on her lower lip, Eva opened her new assignment. Her eyebrows pinched together as she gazed upon a picture of a young, bookish-looking man before her.

Could it be?

Eva's brain swam through memories as her eyes slowly scrolled down the page.

PROFESSOR ALBERT PUDDLES, the email announced.

"Dilbert...?" Eva whispered.

"Hmmm?" said the businessman next to her.

Eva shoved the tablet into the seat pocket and looked out the window. Thoughts swirled and crashed, threatening to overturn the fragile equilibrium she had rebuilt after her failure. This haircut was happening because of *her* mistake. It was her responsibility to clean up the mess she had created.

But she had never imagined *this* man being the target of her assignment. Her hands clenched into fists and her eyes drifted closed as she allowed herself one moment of despair: *Why me? Why should I, of all people, have to do this mission? I never wanted to see him again.*

CHAPTER 8

Albert blinked again and again, hoping the image in front of him was nothing more than a figment of his imagination. But the sinister decision tree stared right back at him.

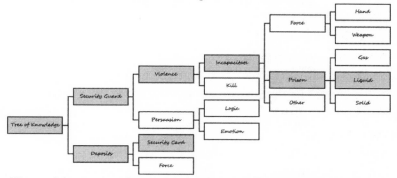

"Does this mean what I think it means?" asked Ying.

Albert looked sadly at Ying. He appreciated her boisterous optimism and hated to see that sadness in her eyes. Albert also feared that, in this case, ignorance was indeed bliss.

"Yeah, I'm pretty sure that this is a decision tree detailing the thief's approach to the theft," he whispered.

Ying sighed, adjusted her glasses, and gazed at the tree.

"So, if I'm reading this right, the thief thought that there were two major obstacles to securing the Tree of Knowledge: the security guard and getting access to the storage room. Access to the storage room was simply a matter of obtaining the security card, which, of course, was held by the guard. That's why you see that branch of the tree ends there and the box is shaded."

Albert massaged his forehead, removed his glasses, and rubbed his eyes. He carefully ran his finger along the spine of the game tree. Albert executed every movement with the same care and precision as a man walking an endless tightrope. "I'm afraid so. The most disturbing part to me is that, judging by the tree, the thief evaluated dealing with the security guard through force and persuasion equally. There's literally no acknowledgment that using violence is wrong or more costly. The two concepts are presented as equally valid, and the thief ended up choosing violence."

The thought made him queasy. He searched the diagram for some sign of compassion, but there was nothing.

"One part of the tree is wrong, though," said Ying, pointing to the box titled "incapacitate".

"What do you mean?"

"According to the tree, the murderer didn't mean to kill the security guard. You see how the tree branches off at 'incapacitate'? It looks like the murderer just intended to incapacitate the guard with some poison."

Albert got up from his chair and looked out his office window. He watched the students roam across the campus quad, laughing and texting. The sun shone brightly, painting a glorious contrast between the school's emerald-green lawn and the multicolored stone buildings. It reminded him of how far removed his life here at Princeton was from the raw brutality of the "real world".

"What an honorable thief," said Albert sarcastically as he continued to gaze out the window. "The problem is that we don't know that for sure. These are just notes and it says, 'prima facie' so there could be other versions."

"You're right. That's not necessarily the route the thief finally chose."

"More important, it doesn't give us any insight into who the thief is or what they stole, and I have no idea what 'Tree of Knowledge' means. I have a feeling that Detective Weatherspoon won't find our observations particularly useful."

"Are you sure about that, Professor? If you think about it statistically, we can probably narrow it down. I mean, how many people can there be who both have the familiarity with decision trees and the cryptography to make this?"

"That's a fair point, but anyone with an interest in logic and cryptography could do this. Even someone who just took a couple of intro college classes or went down an internet rabbit hole. Just think how many people have taken Turner's cryptography class—"

Albert swiveled around from the window and grabbed the cryptography book that he had laid on his desk. "That's it! Turner. Turner's the only guy I know who uses Latin in his work. Remember?" Albert paged through the book. "He used to call his first efforts at anything 'prima facie' and his second '*secundus fortuna*'."

"Yeah, second chance," replied Ying. "Every other person in the field uses the term 'scenario one' or 'base case' or something normal for their original analysis."

"He loves the ancient philosophers. Whoever made this must have been a student of Turner's. Nobody else would have ever put the words 'prima facie' on this tree."

Albert grabbed his leather shoulder bag and stuffed the satchel with the books on his desk.

"Ying, what do you say we pay Prof. Turner a visit?"

"You took the words right out of my mouth."

While Ying ran into the main office of the Math Department, Albert picked up his phone and removed Weatherspoon's business card from his wallet. He dialed the main line of the Princeton Police Department.

"Hello, could I please speak with Detective Weatherspoon?"

The assistant on the other end of the line blandly replied, "Detective Weatherspoon's out of the office but should be back shortly."

Albert pulled his fingers through his hair. "OK, will you leave him a message? Tell him Albert Puddles called and that he's solved the cipher."

CHAPTER 9

E va felt a pang of wistfulness as she walked through the gates of the Princeton campus. Besides her house in Los Angeles, this was the only place that had ever felt like home. She surveyed the students as they meandered across the walkways of the grounds, their backpacks bursting with textbooks and laptop computers. She could still remember how intimidated she had been by kids like these when she attended the school.

Like her mother, Eva had been a mathematical savant from the beginning. By the age of fourteen, she had conquered her high school's mathematics curriculum, so her mother enrolled her in classes at Princeton. Not every family had the pull *or* the funds for such a thing, but Eva's father had set up the family well; it was one piece of his legacy that she still appreciated every day. Walking through the gates of the campus, the young girl had felt as though she were in the presence of giants—and not just metaphorically. Still short, and without the confidence to signal that she was an adult, she found the other students towering over her.

The classroom magnified her intimidation: high, echoey ceilings and rows upon rows of chairs filled with students who looked at her in either disdain or bemusement. Of the two, Eva strongly preferred the former; disdain she could prove wrong.

The professors were tolerable, but they were old and fossilized from the years in academia, hardly the comforting peers for whom Eva had desperately longed. She was afraid she *had* no peers, no one who would see her as more than an oddity.

Only one student had the kindness to welcome her not as a charity case or a babysitting project but as a fellow student, a friend. On the second day of Professor Turner's class, when she thought she couldn't sink any lower, Eva realized she had forgotten her notebook. The student had noticed, torn a piece of paper out of his notebook, and handed it to her without her having to ask. It was a simple act, offered with his usual distracted half smile, but to Eva, it felt like someone had thrown her a life preserver. As they left the classroom that day long ago, he joked, "I've found that it's a lot easier to do math when you have paper." Eva remembered giggling and then being mortified as a snort jumped out of her nose, but he had only blinked owlishly and smiled, pleased at her reaction.

She had nicknamed him Dilbert. His short brown hair sat atop his head with a cowlick that always made it stick up a little, reminding her of the cartoon character. Every day, he wore a tie and jacket to class as if he had just rolled off some sort of prep-school assembly line, and his shirt was always perfectly ironed. All that was missing was a big red crest on his chest pocket.

From that moment on, she always tried to sit next to him in Professor Turner's class. She cringed now to think how absurd she must have seemed to him, like a little puppy following him around. But he never showed an ounce of impatience or condescension. He always greeted her with a kind, if distant, "Hey, there," and patiently helped her whenever she had a question.

Before her fifteenth birthday, however, it had all gone wrong. Eva had begged her mother to allow her to invite Dilbert to her quinceañera.

She still remembered her mother's condescending sigh. "Evi, he's not a teenage boy. He's an adult, a university student, and he doesn't have time to go to your quinceañera."

Eva had screamed at her mother and told her that she didn't understand, and that Dilbert was her friend and that he wanted to come. After days of alternating between her daughter's sulking and screaming, her mother finally relented and told Eva that she could invite him.

The next day after class, as Dilbert packed up his bag, Eva, eyes trained down and voice wobbling, invited Dilbert to her quinceañera. The words floated out of her mouth, coated in hope. A hope that evaporated as soon as Eva saw Dilbert's confused reaction.

"Oh." Dilbert hesitated. "Thanks for the invitation, Eva, but I've got a lot going on this weekend, so I probably won't be able to make it." He hurriedly packed up his bag and walked toward the lecture hall's exit. "Have fun, though. Don't eat too much cake." And then he was gone. She hadn't needed any special abilities of clairvoyance to see that their fragile friendship had burst like a soap bubble.

That moment was still seared in her brain: the stony silence of the room, the crushing return of the alienation she had felt with all the other students. And...the rejection. She had loved Dilbert and invited him to the most important event in her life: the moment when she would officially become a woman, and he had discarded it with a smile as though she had been handing out coupons at the supermarket.

Standing stock-still, Eva had waited until every other student had left, and then she wept. She pressed one hand over her mouth and cried in silence, not daring to break the solemnity of the enormous, empty lecture hall. She sobbed until her chest hurt and her shoulders ached from the shaking. After every tear had gone, she removed a tissue from her bag, wiped her eyes and nose, and resolutely turned a determined stare toward the ceiling.

"Never again," she had whispered to herself. "Never again."

Now, Eva physically shook the memory from her head. The Society did not believe in nostalgia.

Rule Seventeen: Time is the scarcest resource that one has, and it should not be wasted on considering the past unless it improves one's ability to predict the future.

Eva brushed past two administrators on break, entered Jones Hall, and made her way quickly to the Math Department office. The gangly student behind the desk was busy with his cell phone. She coughed discreetly.

The student's eyes bulged as he gazed upon the striking woman in black before him. His voice cracked as he asked, "How can I help you?"

Eva suppressed a smile as she pictured how easy it would be to manipulate this poor boy. But now was not the time for pranks.

"I'm here to see Professor Puddles."

"Oh, uh...he just left." The boy looked awkward, sad to disappoint her, then brightened. "I could see if I can find you his cell phone number."

"That would be lovely. I'm an old friend of his, but we've lost touch. Do you know where he went?"

"I think they were headed to Professor Turner's hou—"

Eva didn't let him finish the sentence. She leaped behind the desk and looked out the window onto the quad.

There he was: a man in a suit, walking next to a woman even shorter than Eva had been when she was last on campus. Even from this distance, Eva could see how eagerly Albert moved, full of life and purpose. He had always delighted in solving puzzles.

And she could *not* let him solve this one.

CHAPTER 10

Angus Turner resided in a beautiful, old brick home just a five-minute drive from the main campus. The crushed-rock driveway arced in a gentle circle up to the front of the Tudor house and then away again. Trees towered around the circle's entrance and gently tapered off toward the house, giving one the feeling of traveling through a dense forest to find something magical on the other side. Albert eased the car into Turner's driveway and smiled in admiration as the sun sparkled off the brick facade and slanted roof.

This is a man of order, a man of tradition.

"Well, isn't this a pleasant surprise," hummed the professor's familiar tenor as he greeted the pair at his front door, walking stick in hand. He wore a dark-brown cashmere sweater vest over a light-blue gingham shirt that oozed academia. Albert and Ying couldn't help beaming, like high school students around a movie star.

"To what do I owe this great honor, Dr. Puddles and Ms. Koh?" Turner had gone on sabbatical at Oxford years ago and had adopted a hint of an English accent, a source of much amusement to his students. Upon greeting Albert, his warm eyes never left his former student's face, and Albert felt again that inchoate emotion

Turner always inspired in him—that he would follow this man anywhere.

Trying to contain his excitement, Albert said, "Well, Professor, we've been handed a problem that we think you might be able to help us with."

"How exciting!"

Turner ushered Albert and Ying into the house. "Please come in. I can't wait to hear all about it." The living room was just as Albert remembered it. He recalled the delightful evening chats that Turner would host with his top students every Wednesday night. It had felt like being in some rarefied secret world. A world free of the messy practicality of "real life". A world of order and ideas.

"Ms. Koh, it's delightful to see you outside of the classroom," Turner said, turning those magnetic eyes on the young woman. "Can I interest you both in a glass of my signature homemade lemonade?"

Ying smiled and turned bright pink. "Yes, please."

"I'm alright for now, but thank you, Professor," said Albert. He had sworn off sugary drinks as being an inefficient consumption of empty calories.

Turner, however, was not dissuaded. "I'll get you some, just in case," he told Albert with a wink.

Five minutes later, the three of them sat around the Colonial-style living room with its warm draperies, old leather, and polished wood, sipping lemonade. The Turner living room functioned almost like a narcotic. Whatever stress the outside world exerted on a person's body faded away amid the yellow lamplight, soothing colors, and quiet creak of the den.

Turner took a sip of his lemonade with obvious pleasure. "Well, Dr. Puddles, do tell."

Albert pulled the paper from his pocket and laid it out for the professor next to a spectacular marble chessboard. Turner was a world-class chess player and loved an impromptu game. Albert was convinced that Turner left the board out in its conspicuous grandeur to lure unsuspecting victims into a match. Albert and Turner had certainly fought their fair share of battles.

Leaning over the chessboard, Turner placed his glasses on his leathery face and scanned the document.

Albert began, "Last night, there was a burglary at the Bank of Princeton. The security guard was killed, but in the struggle with the thief, he managed to grab this paper. As you can see, it's a decision tree encoded with a cipher. Ying and I cracked the cipher, which revealed these words. We believe the thief plotted out the crime using a decision tree and that these were his notes." Without thinking, he took a sip of Turner's lemonade. The icy sweetness relaxed him.

"Oh, dear," said Turner, clearing his throat. Albert thought he detected a note of fear in Turner's voice—something he would never have associated with the professor.

"Anyway, the reason we came to you is that the thief used a Trithemius cipher, which, Ying reminded me, you have always recommended as a quick and easy way to make a relatively complex cipher."

Ying added, "And the thief also used the term 'prima facie,' which I remembered you used because I didn't even know what you meant when you first wrote it."

Professor Turner smiled at the young woman, but Albert could see there was something like pain in his eyes.

"That is undoubtedly true, young lady. Anything else I should know?"

Ying paused. "No, that's about it. We were just wondering what your thoughts are. Do you think this could have been a student of yours?"

Angus Turner sighed, removed his glasses, and sat back in his chair. He swirled the iced lemonade in his glass. He looked tired, even frail. "I'm afraid that a former student of mine indeed created this tree . . . and I know just who the student is."

CHAPTER 11

Who?" Albert leaned forward eagerly in his chair, his elbow nearly knocking the lemonade glass off the table.

Turner looked between Ying and Albert as he sipped his lemonade; Albert sensed he was not drawing out the moment for dramatic effect but was instead reluctant to share his knowledge. Turner tapped the side of his glass and said finally.

"What I'm about to tell you, fewer than ten people in the world know. Everything I tell you now stays here. You understand?"

Ying and Albert nodded.

Turner paused, and all that could be heard was the creak of his wooden chair as he settled in and gave a sigh.

"As you know, I have always been passionate about the power of logic. Early in my academic career, I dedicated myself almost exclusively to studying logic and reasoning, and how we could apply it in a variety of arenas. At first, because we were in the midst of the Cold War, I researched how logic could be more effectively applied to cryptography. What I found, of course, is that by using logic, we can crack most of the ciphers on this earth."

"Yeah, but you would need a lot of time," added Ying.

Turner rose from his seat and paced the room.

"Exactly. Some codes were so complex that for a human being to crack it by hand could take months, by which point the cipher would have served its function. This led me to extend my study of the potential impact of computers on logic. It was at this point that I created the game tree or decision tree. As you know, computers are nothing more than incredibly complex decision trees consisting of a series of either-or scenarios." Turner paced the room, and his hands conducted the story like a symphony.

"Is that when you started doing the testing with board games, Professor?" said Albert.

"Yes. My goal was to design a program that could beat any human being in a common game. I started with tic-tac-toe because of the relative simplicity of the game. Immediately, I was astounded by how complex the game was."

"Yeah, I used to play with my mom back home in Singapore," Ying said. "I had really bad scoliosis when I was a kid, so I had to wear this terrible back brace. I couldn't play half of the games the other kids played outside, and when I did, they would just make fun of me because I moved around like a robot. So, while they were running around playing outside, I just sat inside. I would get so bored that I would mess around and try to figure out all the tic-tac-toe combinations. I thought it would be so easy, and then it wasn't. I think I read once that tic-tac-toe has twenty-six thousand eight hundred and thirty possible games."

Turner nodded. "Which makes it a relatively complex programming challenge, especially when you consider the technology I was working with at the time. Picture a computer the size of this room. However, after spending an obscene amount of time on the problem, I designed a rudimentary tic-tac-toe program that was unbeatable."

Ying gave him a mischievous smile. "You haven't seen me play."

Turner smiled. "Of course, I'm sure no program could beat you, Ms. Koh. That said, having conquered tic-tac-toe, I moved on to my true love: chess. We created chess decision trees, but we quickly realized that the complexity of chess was almost unknowable."

"Isn't the number of chess moves something like ten to the one hundred and twentieth power?" ventured Albert.

"Yes, and to give you an idea of how complex that is, the number of atoms in the known universe is only ten to the eighty-first power. While I knew that I couldn't design a chess program that would beat grandmasters with the computer power that was available, I could design a program that could beat amateurs. I knew it was only a matter of time before a computer would beat a grandmaster.

"At around the same time, a chess grandmaster named David Levy made an audacious prediction. He said that there wouldn't be a computer program developed in the next decade that could beat him in chess."

Ying and Albert laughed.

"I privately scoffed as well, thinking that it would be only a matter of a few years. But sure enough, ten years later, Levy played a game against Chess 4.7, the strongest computer program, and easily defeated it.

"Of course, the reason for this is that chess is a game tree with a practically infinite number of branches. A computer program must churn through each of these branches one by one to make the right decision, while the human mind can, through a combination of creativity, intuition, and logic, quickly identify the branches of the tree that matter. It was then that it struck me ... the human mind was the most powerful decision engine that the world has ever known, but up to that point, we had just been using it for the societal equivalent of tic-tac-toe."

Turner's worry had faded away. He was animated now, caught up in the memory of his discoveries.

"I, like my colleagues, had overlooked the *actual power* of decision tree analysis, which was in the interaction of *humanity*, not computers. Once I realized the awesome capabilities of this confluence...well, I realized that the 'tree of knowledge' that the Bible refers to was not merely a metaphor; it was a reality. If I could use game trees in real time, in real life, then I would possess the same divine power for both good or evil as the metaphorical tree of knowledge from which Adam and Eve first plucked the apple."

He looked at Albert and Ying expectantly. His hope—that one of them could grasp the power of the revelation—was palpable.

Albert cleared his throat awkwardly and gave a quick glance at Ying. He was pleased that she looked equally underwhelmed. He hated to disappoint one of his idols, but he could not yet see how this was anything more than the standard decision-making matrix anyone might use for studying tactics or even computer science. "I'm not quite sure I'm following you, Professor," he said cautiously.

He had forgotten the other man's love of teaching. Turner loved a challenge, and especially the challenge of explaining a complex concept. Now, Turner's face lit up with a smile.

"Think of it this way," he said, leaning in a bit. "In the game of chess, each player has a simple goal: to capture the other person's king. This is equally true in real life. Every individual is motivated by a goal at every moment of the day. When you wake up, you are motivated by the desire to go to work and make money. When you blink, you are motivated by a desire to moisten your eyes. When you eat, you are motivated by the desire to quench the hunger in your belly. Consequently, the functioning of 'society,' as we call it, is nothing more than the interaction of competing motivations or goals in much the same way that chess is an interaction between the competing motivations of capturing each other's king. If we see the world in this light, then it becomes clear that, with the proper tools and analysis, we can manipulate people's actions in life in the same way we can manipulate them on a chessboard.

"For example, in chess, it is not your opponent's goal to lose their bishop. However, given the right incentives, your opponent may surrender their bishop to save another piece. Similarly, at a restaurant, it is not the chef's goal in life to make you a cheeseburger. However, if the restaurant pays him enough money, he will happily do so."

"But aren't there a lot of people who have known this?" said Ying cautiously. "Couldn't *anyone* do this?" One bewildered glance in Albert's direction said that he had the same questions.

Turner gave a knowing smile. "There are many people that can shoot a basketball, but there are but a handful of people in the world who have the ability to do it with such precision that it becomes valuable. So it is with the tree. The only people in the world that can realize the potential of the tree in real time are the so-called mental calculators like ourselves. But even for people like us, it's not enough to perform multiple calculations in one's head, you have to *practice* putting those calculations into action. Do you follow?"

Albert and Ying both nodded cautiously.

"Good. So, once I considered that every person, including myself, has a motivation at all times and that my fate, as well as everyone else's, was determined by how these competing motivations interact, I experimented to see to what extent I could logically map out and then manipulate the motivations of the individuals around me. In doing this, I mimicked the way I think about chess. I drew a game tree outlining potential scenarios. 'If I do this, he will do this,' 'if I do that, he will do that,' and so on. I would have meetings with people and could anticipate the entire give-and-take, steering it where I wanted it to go.

"At first, it was time consuming—I could spend a whole day planning just one fifteen-minute interaction. But it became more natural to me to visualize the branches a tree might have. Just as I had theorized, I found that I could achieve any goal if I could determine the motivations or goals of the person with whom I was dealing—my opponent, as it were. I'm ashamed to say that I found this new power of manipulation quite intoxicating. I can't possibly explain to you what a powerful feeling it is to know that you can manipulate any individual to your whims."

Turner fell silent for a moment, going to the window and gazing out at the street. Albert and Ying watched him. Sadness had gathered around him like a cloak.

When Turner spoke next, his voice was faraway, remembering. "In the spring one year, an exceptionally beautiful and intelligent student of mine fell in love with me, and I with her."

Albert cleared his throat as quietly as he could manage. Though he respected Turner immensely, the idea of the man having a flirtation with one of his students unsettled him. Looking over at Ying, he caught a flash of something that almost seemed to be disappointment as she gazed at Turner. She looked down at her lap and picked at her nails, her jaw set.

Lost in memory, Turner had not noticed their discomfort. "She had these incredible eyes that held little flecks of bright yellow surrounded by dark brown. As you might imagine, every man at Princeton was in love with her, and I remember feeling so blessed every day that she spent time with me, because it felt like she chose me above everyone else. She exuded such a powerful combination of youth, vibrancy, ambition, and intelligence that you just wanted to cling to it in the hopes that it would rub off on you." He cleared his throat.

When he turned back, both Albert and Ying watched him with carefully neutral expressions.

"We would talk for hours every night," Turner told them as he came back to his seat. "We would stay up until the early morning speaking of life, love, mathematics, economics, chess, and the world. She hung on my every word and soaked up information like a sponge. At first, it was intoxicating—even more so than it had been to realize the power of the Tree of Knowledge.

"Then...it became a trap. She was so hungry for new ideas that I worried I would one day run out of knowledge to give her, and she would leave me. Eventually, I *did* run out of knowledge. She would ask me about topics such as politics and war that were far outside my area of expertise, and I would do my best, but...I could feel her pulling away from me more and more each day. In desperation, I brought her into my confidence and told her about the Tree of Knowledge."

Turner's smile was sad now; he looked every bit his age. "At first, she greeted me with the same healthy skepticism with which the two of you are greeting me right now. However, as I explained how information combined with game tree analysis could allow you to manipulate people, her interest soared. I was no fool, you know. I ran the calculations. I knew she might abuse the Tree...but I let my heart win." Quietly, he added. "Or, perhaps, that makes me more the fool.

"Whatever the case, when she had drained every piece of useful information about the Tree from me, she left. No goodbye or thank you. I just returned home from class one day, and she was gone. It devastated me. I often joke about being 'married to my students', but in reality, it was her ... I was devoted to her. She married another man soon after, but I never forgot her."

Ying reached forward and patted Turner's shoulder. "I'm sorry, Professor," she whispered. Albert could see that her own emotions, no less complicated than his own, also held sympathy for the man. He supposed that she, too, knew the loneliness of feeling apart from everyone else. Both she and Albert had rare mental capabilities—and Turner outstripped them both. How much lonelier would it be for him? How much greater would the temptation be to keep his one true equal by his side—even if that woman were using him for her own ends?

Turner took a long drink from his lemonade, looked off into the distance, and then a lonely smile crept across his face.

"For fourteen years, I tried—and failed—to forget about her. Then, in the fall one year, a young high school student walked into my classroom. I took one look at those coffee-colored eyes with the yellow flecks, the wolf eyes, and I knew it was her daughter. She was just as smart as her mother and had the same tenacious desire for knowledge. She was a championship chess player, and within weeks, she, too, asked me about the Tree. By teaching her I felt like I had a connection to her mother again."

Albert frowned. The description of those eyes—it couldn't be…

"As her knowledge of the Tree and its powers increased, this young woman explored the branch of the Tree that I had for so long ignored: violence. She would ask me to practice using the principles of the Tree for violent means. "

"What do you mean when you say using the Tree for violence, Professor Turner?" said Ying. "Like in combat?"

"Yes. The Tree of Knowledge can be both a tool and a weapon. Person-to-person combat is just the tip of the iceberg. The Tree can be used to defend yourself, incapacitate and harm others, and even kill. It can also be used in war strategy and other forms of mass violence. Interestingly, when you use the Tree, what you find is that the most common uses of violence are the least effective. For example, bank robbers most often rob banks using guns. This is absurdly ill-considered because it does not incapacitate your enemy unless you shoot everyone in the bank—and it does nothing to protect you. It's the equivalent of taking your queen out in chess with no means of protecting her. A much better approach would be to simply gas the entire bank as you enter and wear gas masks. This incapacitates your enemy and protects you. If you were hell-bent on using guns, it would be much better to procure a secure location across from the bank and use long-range snipers to take out the people in the bank and then rob the bank. Again, this would remove your enemy without risking harm to yourself.

"Another example is poison. Poison is grossly underutilized. Why kill someone in public with a gun when you could simply offer them a stick of gum laced with poison and be done with it? She was curious about all of this and more: how to use it in hand-to-hand combat, in security, even in war. I told her I would teach her if the information stayed between the two of us and if she promised not to use it on anyone else. She promised, but again, as I predicted from using the Tree, I suspected it was a promise she wouldn't keep." Turner passed one shaking hand over his brow. "You must think me a fool—especially now, when you know where it all led. I just couldn't stand to let her go. I had seen her mother walk out of my life, and I didn't think I could take it again."

"And you think that's why the thief killed the security guard at the bank," Albert said slowly. "Because she was your student, and you had discussed similar situations before."

"Yes," said Turner. "And that is why I know she was behind this. But, Albert, you're still not grasping the power of the Tree, and she does. You've seen how she operates: logically, with no room for sentiment or morality. You *need* to get to the police before Eva realizes what she's done."

CHAPTER 12

The tires of Albert's white sedan spun in the gravel of Angus Turner's driveway as he pulled out of the circle. A cloud of gray dust floated up around the front of the home like a dark mist. As he screeched onto the main road, Albert replayed the scene inside Turner's house. Turner's bearing gnawed at him. He remembered the last time he'd seen that helpless, broken expression on someone's face.

Until the age of eight, Albert's life had been perfect. His loving parents had raised him in a beautiful three-bedroom house in a small college town in southern Minnesota with the modest name of Northfield. The bright-white paint, set off by the house's green shutters, gave the impression of Southern gentility in a northern Midwestern town. The backyard had fruit trees a boy could climb; the front yard, carefully tended flower beds. Both his parents had been professors of mathematics at the two colleges in town: Carleton and St. Olaf. His mother taught at Carleton, which was the more prestigious institution, and his father instructed at St. Olaf. Both believed passionately in the power of education and, more specifically, mathematics to solve the world's problems. For much of his life they insisted on homeschooling Albert so that he could get the benefits of "higher-level" instruction.

While this was highly unusual in Northfield because of its strong, college-influenced school system, Albert loved it. He adored his parents and eagerly anticipated his morning lessons. His mother would teach him Monday, Wednesday, and Friday, and his father Tuesday, Thursday, and Saturday. Albert reveled in the distinct teaching styles of his mother and father. His mother was a tactician who believed that the essence of mathematics was technical skill and proficiency. She would push Albert to solve problems according to certain rules, to show his work, and to do it at greater levels of speed. He especially enjoyed Fridays when his mother would give him a set of one hundred problems and time him to see how fast he could do them. When he did well, she would take him down the block to the local ice-cream shop, and the two of them would enjoy root beer floats. He could still feel the warm sun and see the soft smile on his mom's pretty face and the sleek, dark wave of her hair as the two of them savored their desserts.

His father, on the other hand, believed in the magical and creative power of mathematics. Instead of focusing on mathematical rules or problem-solving speed, he would encourage Albert not just to solve a problem but to understand its core nature. He would always give the example of multiplication tables, which he thought were a destructive influence. "Cages for the mind," he called them, as he paced around the room, his tall, stork-like figure throwing off energy, his narrow face alight with feeling. "Any idiot can memorize seven times eight is fifty-six," he would say, "but until you understand at a gut level *why* it is fifty-six, you don't understand math." Albert would just giggle, watching the old man get upset about multiplication tables.

His father loved logic puzzles and games. The two would play chess on Sunday mornings, at which Albert always excelled. His father would then tell him fantastic tales of mathematical concepts and their almost religious connection to nature. He would instruct

Albert on the Fibonacci sequence, a string of numbers that appeared in the most fascinating natural settings, from the flowering of the artichoke to the arrangement of a pinecone. They would take long walks through the woods behind the campus and pick up pinecones to see how the spirals grew according to the famous sequence. His father would point out spiderwebs, pond ripples, clouds, moss on tree bark, and explain how mathematics described their patterns. The boy learned about numbers; he also learned to look carefully at everything around him. He reveled in these walks with his father and often hoped they would never end.

But they did end.

One morning, Albert stumbled down the creaking stairs of his house in search of his usual bowl of Cheerios. As he breezed through the living room, he saw both his parents sitting together on the living room couch. The image struck him as odd because neither of his parents ever used that room. It was one of those decorative living rooms that went unused unless company was over. The colors of the room were dark—dark red and blue upholstery, dark wood, curtains pulled—and his parents, even his fair-complexioned father, looked dark as well. The jarring nature of the scene caused Albert to stop and lock eyes with his dad. His eyes were heavy; the boy could see he was exhausted. Scared, Albert turned his attention to his mother. The expression he saw on her face terrified him. The woman who had so boisterously taught Albert and loved his father had been reduced to rubble. Her eyes were dull, her face ashen. The only sign of life was the flicker as her gaze met his and a twitch of her bloodless lips that was more grimace than smile.

His parents could see the fear in Albert's eyes and wasted no time in delivering the news. They were getting a divorce. It wasn't Albert's fault. They both loved him very much, but they had grown apart, and it was time to move on. His father had decided to take a prestigious teaching job at a university in China. He would be leaving at the end of the month. Albert could fly out and see him whenever he wanted, but most of the time, he would be living with his mother.

Albert pleaded with his father. Tears streaming down his face, he begged and bargained to keep his dad from leaving. He would do better in math. He would clean the house every day. But his father just shrugged and said this was "something he needed to do". Albert then turned to his mom for help—help making his dad understand that he needed to stay. His mother just held Albert and looked at him with that face, that blank look of despair.

It was this same expression that Albert had seen on Professor Turner's face. He, too, looked crushed and abandoned. And what made the expression on Turner's face even more affecting was that, to Albert, Professor Turner had been an idol, someone who could not be crushed, defeated, or abandoned. Turner seemed to float above the challenges of life that impeded mere mortals.

And his despair had come over a woman and her daughter. *Eva? Could it be the same Eva?*

Albert thought of the scrawny little high school student with whom he had shared a class early in his college career. He had treasured her. She was a lovely young girl, with a smile and laugh that made you forget where you were and carried you back to a time when the world wasn't serious. He was twenty, but he still felt the draw of a little sister who made him feel young and important. Albert always felt slightly uncouth spending time with a fourteen-year-old. He was aware of how other students looked at him when the two of them would walk and giggle together after class. Even Professor Turner stared at the two of them with a parent's watchful eye. So, when at the end of class, she had invited him to her quinceañera, Albert realized he had to put a stop to it. As the words fumbled out of her mouth, he could see the love in her eyes and wanted nothing more than to be the hero of her quinceañera. But it just didn't look good. So, he did the "right thing" and told her he couldn't go. In the fourteen years since that day, Albert had thought of it many times and regretted it every time. Seeing the imprint that she and her mother had made on the giant that was Angus Turner made his regret even more piercing.

Albert angrily slammed down the accelerator as though he could outrun the pain of his past. In his youth, he had fought the battle between logic and emotion and had vanquished emotion, or so he'd thought. Now, as the car tore down the country road toward the Princeton police station, Albert sensed that emotion was back and chasing him. He turned his attention to the rearview and noticed a hulking silver sedan turn off a side road and accelerate behind him. The glimmering Rolls-Royce followed ten feet from his car's rear bumper and showed no signs of slowing.

Am I being tailed? Should I speed up? Slow down? His mind went into overdrive, his hands trembling on the wheel.

Albert's nerves calmed for a moment when the police station came into view. He took a sharp right into the parking lot. The Rolls turned in behind him. A stranger emerged from the car in a black trench coat and dark fedora.

He snatched Detective Weatherspoon's file off the passenger seat, exited the car with his head down, and prepared to bolt into the station. He looked up to see the stranger standing directly in front of him, blocking his path. Terrified, Albert glanced back to see if it was too late to jump back in his car, but before he could make a move, the stranger took off her fedora to reveal a stunning woman with rich black hair. Her smiling face and big white teeth gleamed in the sun.

"Dilbert! It's so good to see you."

CHAPTER 13

Angus Turner and Ying Koh sat in silence. The ticktock of Turner's grandfather clock pierced the quiet like the crack of a whip with each move of the second hand. Then, without a word, the professor jumped from his seat, eyes gleaming, and darted down the hallway to his study. Not knowing quite what to do, Ying sipped her lemonade and pondered her situation. *The Tree of Knowledge? Can it be real? What does this mean for me? For my family? For the world?* She could hear Turner shuffling papers in the back room but dared not disturb what looked like divine inspiration. Ying had been in academia long enough and had enough fits of intellectual fire herself to understand that there were times when just staying out of the way was the best move.

Germany. That was when it had started for her. That was when she realized she was different, but she also found out where she belonged. She stood on a small temporary stage in a simple brick building for the Junior Mental Calculation World Cup. The building smelled chill and dank like a wine cellar. The crowd was small, but all eyes were on her. The man that stood beside her sported a walrus mustache and glasses with a chain around his neck.

The final test was simple. On a screen in front of her, six five-digit numbers would flash for .4 seconds—just long enough for her to see—and they would ask her to add those numbers in five seconds. Ying adjusted her back brace. The doctors had removed her leg braces that August, but her back brace would have to stay on until she was fifteen. She looked out at the crowd expecting to see snickering faces, like what she received at school, but she saw the opposite. Just hopeful smiles. The warmth calmed her as she shifted her attention to the computer monitor in front of her.

The screen shone pure blue. In a matter of seconds, five-digit numbers would tumble forward one after the other, and her mind would have to memorize and add those numbers instantaneously. *Answer correctly and she wins; incorrectly, she loses.*

"Are you ready?" asked the moderator.

Ying focused and unfocused her eyes on the screen, taking herself to the place between presence and imagination. She nodded.

As the numbers flickered forth on the monitor, Ying slowed the world around her and blacked out the space. She froze each snapshot of digits and placed them side by side, cataloged in her imagination. Seconds later, she had organized them in her mind like books on a shelf with the last book being the answer. She ran her fingers across the smooth keyboard in front of her and typed in the number: 70,392. The moderator revealed the answer: 70,392.

Her parents and the rest of the audience burst out in applause and rushed the stage to congratulate her and shake her hand. Not one face held judgment or mockery like the kids at school. Just amazement and awe. Ying felt special. She was somebody.

But now, as she stood in Turner's living room, Ying wondered what type of somebody she would be, should be. She was proud of what she had accomplished. Getting into Princeton, traveling to the United States by herself. Entering the PhD program. Getting an assistantship with Professor Puddles. But was that it? Was this her life? To be a math nerd, gathering dust in academia. Something about this murder, and the mysterious logic tree that came with it, had sparked something in her. She was searching.

Ying turned on the local news hoping to see something about the murder. She clicked the wood-paneled remote to Turner's 1980s Zenith television. *Is this the first TV ever made?* she wondered. *Although, Turner having a TV at all is a minor miracle.*

Ying flipped the channels but was disappointed to see that all the major stations were running national news programs. She slid her thumb over the power button, intending to shut off the ancient device, but then something caught her eye.

On the screen stood a tall, striking black-haired woman surrounded by a sea of red-shirted supporters. The woman gripped an ornate wood lectern bathed in stage lighting in some type of arena. She wore a crimson suit, which contrasted with her dark eyes that burned like embers in a fire. The effect of the lights gave the woman a godlike quality as she thundered away to the audience. And the audience. The audience, dripping in bright-red T-shirts, hats, and jackets, appeared to move in unison like a monstrous red ocean bobbing and crashing with ecstasy. Young people lined the middle and outer rails of the convention hall, holding red banners with a modern tree symbol etched in black. The camera panned around the crowd, which numbered at least five thousand, and Ying could see the entranced faces of students, children, mothers, seniors, and workers as the woman spoke. When the speaker paused, Ying could hear a booming chant of "Cris-ti-na, Cris-ti-na" echoing throughout the chamber.

Ying leaned in to listen, joining the crowd in willing hypnosis. The speaker paused, and the roar of the crowd fell victim to the hushed silence of anticipation.

Cristina Culebra's voice echoed with haunting sincerity and power.

"As many of you know, I grew up in Chile."

She paused and smiled as the few Chileans in the crowd hollered out their support.

"Today, Chile is a wonderful place, but it wasn't always that way. When I was a child, my mother and father owned a beautiful farm about an hour outside of Santiago. It was a majestic piece of land. In the mornings, the sun would come up over the mountains, and the grapevines and lemon orchards stretched for what seemed like forever. My two brothers and I would walk the fields with my papa at dawn, occasionally sneaking a grape when he wasn't looking. He loved that farm, and he worked it every day. I could feel it when I held his hands, which were hard, cracked, and dry from the work. But underneath that tough layer of skin, I could always sense the tenderness that he felt for my brothers, Mama, and me. My brothers and I would work from sunup to sundown, racing to see who could pick grapes faster. They were older than me, so at first, they were faster, but soon I learned that with my small hands and a couple of different tricks, I could outpace them. When we finished our work in the fields, Papa, my brothers, and I would stumble into our home, exhausted and famished from the day's work, and Mama would hug us and tell us to clean up for supper, and then serve us a gigantic paella. We would scarf the food down like dogs while Mama scolded us for our table manners. Shortly thereafter, we turned in for bed. I shared a room with my two brothers, and I remember the three of us just staring at the ceiling with full bellies and the warm contentment of a good day's work and the love of family."

The crowd let out a collective nod as each individual recalled a personal family memory. The speaker's soothing words created a warm blanket of nostalgia over the willing audience.

"Then, when I was nine years old, everything changed," she said with a tone of heartbreak and anger. "Chile elected its first socialist president, who believed that the government should take land from those who had it and give it to those who didn't."

At this, the red crowd's nostalgia transformed into anger as they erupted in a chorus of boos and shouts of "Socialist!"

Cristina Culebra politely smiled and raised her hands to quiet the crowd.

"The government seized four-fifths of Papa and Mama's farm and gave it to four poor families who had never farmed before in their life. Despite my parents' best efforts, the remaining land was not enough to feed our family. For months, we attempted to survive on grapes and our remaining animals, but as we began to starve, my father decided that something had to be done. He and the other farmers went to the government and told them of our plight. He promised to help the poor families on our land if they would allow us to farm it.

"But it was all for naught.

"The government was practically powerless, crippled by a divided congress that could do nothing but squabble and bicker while their country crumbled and their countrymen starved. Eventually, my parents could no longer support our family, so they sold our land, had my brothers enlist in the army, and sent me to live with my aunt and uncle in Los Angeles. I never saw them again."

Ying watched in awe as the crowd stood ice-still.

The speaker paused and gathered herself for several seconds while the crowd's silence begged her to continue.

"I tell you this story not to earn your pity but to rouse your vigilance. Just like Chile back then, California stands on the brink of disaster. We have twenty-five percent youth unemployment, and our state is effectively bankrupt. Yet, just like my father and those farmers, we, too, are shut out while the politicians bicker and squabble."

The crowd again booed.

"But, as much as I hate to say it, just like in the case of Mr. Allende, it's not the politicians' fault. It's the system. We currently have a Republican governor, Democratic Senate, and Democratic House. Now, I ask you to imagine a company that had a CEO who believed in one set of ideas, but before the CEO could do anything, he first had to get not one but two groups of people who believe the opposite of what he believes to agree with him."

The crowd erupted in laughter.

Cristina Culebra smiled. "You laugh, but this is the comical system in which we ask our elected officials to operate every day. It's outdated, antiquated, and absurd.

"More than anything in this world, I want to make sure that no child ever has to go through what I went through. That no family is ever torn apart because of government bureaucracy and indifference. That every hardworking person can realize their dream and that their government will do everything it can to make sure that happens.

"But if we want to make that dream a reality, we can't keep doing the same thing with the same system." The speaker pounded the podium with her fist, and the crowd cheered. "We need a new leader. And we need a leader who can take action without wondering whether one hundred and fifty-five different legislators of different political parties agree."

At this, the crowd once again erupted in hypnotic support.

"And that is why I ask that on November 4th, you don't just vote for me for governor, but vote to temporarily suspend the legislature so that I can do what it takes to make sure all of us realize the dream that's within our reach.

"I believe we can make California the beacon of hope for America, and the world."

As the sea of red exploded in ecstasy, Turner returned to his living room with a stack of old papers in his hand to find Ying staring transfixed, her face inches from the TV screen.

"Ying, I've found some materials that we should review," he said excitedly.

Ying continued to watch Cristina Culebra as she came to the crescendo of her speech. *Was this what she had been looking for?*

"I believe that California can be the model of what a society can be."

"Ms. Koh, will you turn that off, please, so that we can get to work," Turner said with increased urgency and irritation.

Ying heard his words but didn't process them. The charismatic woman on the screen had her transfixed.

"I believe California can be that magical place where every child receives a world-class education and limitless opportunity."

Suddenly, Turner stormed over to the television, slammed on the power button, and shouted, "Turn that damn thing off!"

Ying snapped out of her trance. She blinked and looked up at the professor's face in shock. His cheeks were red, his fists clenched, and his eyes squinted in frustration.

"Oh, I-I'm so sorry, Professor Turner. I just turned on the TV to see if the murder was in the news and got kind of wrapped up in that speech."

"Yes, I know," Turner grunted as he moved away from Ying and toward the coffee table. "Ms. Culebra tends to have that effect on people."

"She's running for governor of California?"

Turner arranged the papers on the coffee table, his hands showing a faint tremble. "Yes."

"Do you think she'll win?"

"I'm afraid so," Turner mumbled as he put on his glasses and looked over his materials.

Ying let out a short laugh of disbelief. "You don't like her? She seemed pretty impressive to me. I mean, you have to admit that what she was saying has a lot of truth. Government in the US is kind of pathetic. One thing that I miss about Singapore is how well everything works. This is something I could get excited about."

"Yes, but that comes at a cost. If you speak out against the government in your beloved Singapore, you might get sued, caned, or imprisoned."

"But that's limited to people who agitate against the government," said Ying dismissively. "If you're a normal person, everything is better. The train system is clean and on time. The streets are perfectly paved. Housing and health care are cheap and plentiful. And all of that's because Lee Kuan Yew came in, took charge, and looked out for the people. I never could have come to America to study if it weren't for him. Maybe Cristina Culebra can do the same thing for California."

Turner glanced at Ying and rolled his eyes. "Believe me, she won't." He waved her over to the sofa. "Now, enough about Cristina Culebra. Come over here and look at this. Class is in session."

CHAPTER 14

Hello, Eva," said Albert sternly as their eyes met. He assessed her face. She was a gorgeous woman now, but she was still the Eva he had known. Her dark-brown, almost black, eyes still gleamed like onyx. Light freckles still danced on her cheeks, and her hair still cascaded perfectly around her face. Her gaze still displayed intelligence and curiosity.

Yet, despite all the similarities to the girl he had known, Albert realized that something was different. Her eyes that once shone with hope and imagination were now controlled and cynical; her once-joyful smile was now a cold, arrogant sneer. Albert found it both unnerving and attracting, like an electrical storm.

"Hello, Dilbert," she said with a seductive smirk, the old nickname bringing back memories of his college days, and his affection for the shy and brilliant teenager.

Albert wanted to let go and sink into that past—it was wonderful seeing her face again, even changed as it was—but he couldn't forget the picture of the dead security guard that Detective Weatherspoon had showed him.

"How could you do it?" he asked hoarsely.

Eva looked down, and for a moment, Albert thought he saw genuine regret, but as she tilted her head up, it vanished. "Ahh, you cracked the cipher. I knew you would, but I hoped that you and your chubby little girlfriend would take a bit longer to solve it."

"She's not chubby, and she's not my girlfriend," Albert blurted out, surprising himself with his anger and spontaneity.

Eva raised a hand to calm him. "I was just teasing. I'm sure she's a great girl."

"She's my colleague and—" Albert stopped, shook his head, and looked up at the sky in frustration. He noticed the clouds crashing together on the back of a growing wind.

How is she doing this? Why is she getting to me so much?

"Relax, Dilbert," said Eva. She lovingly brushed the chest of Albert's suit coat and picked off some of the lint and hairs on his shoulder. "I didn't come here to talk about you and your personal life. I came here to set the record straight."

Albert nodded, trying to slow his heartbeat and flush the red from his face. "OK."

"I want you to know that I never intended for that security guard to die. I'm sure you noticed that when you cracked the cipher. I was trying to pacify him. He had a weak heart, and it couldn't take the strain."

"OK. Fine. But what the hell were you doing sedating a security guard and robbing a bank?"

Eva began pacing. "As you know, my family is in the security and defense business." Albert nodded but squinted skeptically. "We have designed a virtually uncrackable security system. It will change how the world secures data, arms, everything. Unfortunately, a professor at Princeton made the same discovery and outlined the system in a journal and then stored it in the bank."

"OK. Why did you steal it? Couldn't you just buy it from him?"

"He would never sell it. But we feel that the benefits of this system are too great for society to keep locked away. Don't you see? It was for the greater good."

"Why do you care about what I think?" asked Albert. Strangely, he found himself hoping for a particular answer.

"Honestly? Because I hoped that if you knew the truth, you might reconsider what you're about to do and look the other way. I feel sick that the security guard died, but there's nothing you or I can do to bring him back. And putting me in jail isn't going to help anyone."

Eva looked at Albert and slowly blinked her big brown eyes.

"So, you want me to just do nothing? To pretend I couldn't solve the code in the decision tree the security guard took from you?"

"I was actually hoping you would just solve this code." She handed him a decoded decision tree scribbled on the same yellow notepaper. The tree appeared similar to the one that Wally had ripped from her jacket before he died, but instead of showing a bank robbery it showed a meaningless series of words. "You know me. You *know* I'm not a criminal. I was trying to do the right thing." With that, she slowly slid her small, cool hand into Albert's and glanced at him shyly.

For a moment, Albert was lost. Holding Eva's hand was like being transported into a utopian world where the two of them could live happily ever after. He smelled the ocean air as they sat holding each other on an imaginary Los Angeles beach. He pictured her bright eyes as they laughed over a home-cooked dinner. His mind raced as they discussed the great issues of the day while sipping chilled glasses of Chardonnay.

But after a brief second, his rational self yanked him back to the gray parking lot outside the police station. Albert tore his hand away from Eva's as if to break the connection and backed away. He handed the fake decision tree back to her. "I'm sorry, but I can't do that. I believe you had no intention to harm him, but the fact is that a man is dead, and I wouldn't feel right covering it up. If you're truly innocent, a jury should judge you, not me."

As the words tumbled from Albert's mouth, he could see Eva's shoulders and head fall. She looked like a judge who had just offered a man on trial one last chance at mercy but knew that she must execute a sentence.

"I'm sorry," repeated Albert as he pushed past Eva and walked toward the station.

"Where are you going?"

"Into the police station to tell Detective Weatherspoon the truth."

Albert reached the door of the police station and grabbed the handle.

"Dilbert," Eva cried with a raw urgency.

Albert stopped and turned, shaken by the sound.

"Dilbert, I know you think you're doing the right thing. And I respect that. But trust me. You have no idea what you're dealing with. I haven't forgotten what you did for me when I was younger, and because of that, I'm giving you one last chance. Please trust me. Give me the game tree, tell the police it was stolen from your office, and just walk away. I'm trying to save you."

She paused and gazed at him, shallow breaths heaving from her chest.

"If you turn your back on me now, you're on your own."

Albert stared into Eva's eyes. They were the same innocent, hopeful eyes that he had seen fourteen years ago in that Princeton lecture hall.

And just as he had all those years ago, Albert turned away.

CHAPTER 15

Albert entered the waiting room of the police station. A steel door and a large pane of bulletproof glass separated the room from the main office. He found it disappointing. On the way there, he had pictured an elegant wood-paneled police station like in the *Perry Mason* episodes his mom used to watch. This was more akin to a tow lot. The clock showed five minutes after five. Most of the police and administrative personnel had gone for the day. He caught the eye of one of the remaining officers and gave him a limp wave.

The officer waved him off. "We're closed. Use the dispatch phone." He pointed to the brown plastic phone on the wall.

"Excuse me, Officer. I'm wondering if I could speak with Detective Weatherspoon. It's a bit of an emergency."

The cop sized up Albert, vacillating over whether this was someone he should take seriously. The hair and bow tie said no, but the suit said maybe. "Alright, I'll grab him. Give me a minute."

***

While Albert navigated the police bureaucracy inside, Eva watched from the parking lot, through the glass door and prepared to make her next move. This would not be easy.

She closed her eyes and centered herself. She felt reality slow. Leaves rippled in the trees. A chime on someone's front porch sang in the distance. There were three objectives, each powered by a unique logic tree.

First, disable the police station.

She watched and waited for Albert to contact the officer at the front desk. As the officer went back to fetch Weatherspoon, she pulled a pistol from her coat and pointed it at the power line that fed into the station. Three shots tore through the power line, sending the building into darkness.

Now she controlled the chessboard. Speed chess. She had five minutes before the emergency generator kicked in and backup was called.

Eva enjoyed these five minutes. When her mind worked through the branches of the Tree, the future became scripted and her actions like those of an actor in a play. And like an actor, Eva didn't lament that she had only five minutes in a scene; she reveled in the performance. *Follow your blocking, deliver your lines.* The role was defined. The joy was in the execution.

Eva strode around the side of the building and stopped outside the rear entrance. There would be almost no one left in the station at this hour. The property room technician and maybe a couple of cops. Eva calculated how the tech would react sitting in that dark, windowless room with the power out. Investigate herself? Or alert her colleagues?

On cue, the tech opened the door and stepped outside. Eva wedged her foot in the door and slid behind her. She placed a gun to the technician's head and whispered, "What's your password?"

Trembling, the woman whined, "Whaaat?"

"What's your password? To the evidence database."

"Uh-uh."

"Now, or you're dead."

"Uh, it's Princeton2020."

"Thank you."

Eva placed a rag soaked in Sevoflurane over the woman's mouth, guiding her to the ground, then checked her breathing to make sure she was alive. She would not repeat the mistake she made with Wally McCutcheon.

Eva took the security keys off the woman. Peggy Jesme was her name. "It was a pleasure doing business with you, Peggy."

She opened the steel access door and crept down the rear hallway. Darkness covered the station. She had done her research this time. *No mistakes.* The Princeton police force had thirty-five officers and seven support staff. The support staff had gone home for the day, save the technician. Nearly all those officers should be done with their shift or on duty right now, but there could be a handful of stragglers. She had five minutes to disable a few officers and a property room technician without being seen. The property room tech was already down. Now, to the cops.

With the power out, all the entrances were locked. The variables had been reduced. The Tree's chain of decisions had been simplified. She placed her backpack on her shoulder, slid along the side wall of the rear entrance hallway, and edged around the corner. Two officers stood in the office bullpen. One officer was digging for his cell phone while the other reached for a radio.

Eva smiled as she remembered what the general had taught her: "To disable a cop, don't go for his gun, go for his radio. Their power is in their numbers, not in their guns." She pulled out two devices from her pocket. The first was a handheld electromagnetic pulse generator. The device issued high-frequency waves that fried any electronic equipment within a twenty-foot radius. Close enough to knock out the cop's cell phone, far enough way to spare the evidence room. She pushed the button and watched the first officer's phone screen flicker on and off in the darkness before finally settling to black. Next, she turned on a portable signal jammer and smirked with delight while the other officer's radio crackled with static.

Objective one was complete. The doors were locked; the power was out; the police communications equipment was disabled. Now it was time for objective two: *Remove suspicion.*

This would be more difficult. Police logged evidence both physically and virtually. Hard evidence was bagged and sealed in a property room, and pictures of evidence were uploaded to a secure database. The evidence was organized by case number. A case number that Eva didn't have. To find the evidence in the McCutcheon case by hand would take her hours. She needed the case number, and to find the case number, she needed access to the intake room computer, and for that, she needed the property technician's password. Fortunately, "Princeton2020" gave her all the access she needed.

Eva entered the intake room. A series of evidence lockers lined the right wall. In the darkness sat a lone steel desk and computer. The keys to the kingdom. She pulled out a portable charger and plugged the computer into it. The white screen jumped to life, brightening the room. Eva paused to see if anyone was coming, attracted by the light. Nothing.

In the password field, she quietly typed the password that Peggy had given her, "Princeton2020."

"Incorrect password" showed on the screen.

Eva's forehead creased as she retyped the password, "Princeton2020."

"Incorrect password."

Eva typed again, this time in all caps. "PRINCETON2020."

"Incorrect password."

Eva pounded the desk with her fist and whispered to herself, "Ohhhhhhh, Peggy, you bitch." She heard the footsteps of cops down the hall. They'd be coming soon.

Once again, she closed her eyes and steadied herself. She imagined a tree of passwords spanning out into infinity. The possibilities were limitless, but that was the power of the Tree . . . to take limitless possibilities and make them actionable probabilities. Eva calculated the probabilities.

Twenty percent of all passwords are simple. "123456," "Password," and the like.

She entered each password. "123456":

"Incorrect password."

"Password": "Incorrect password."

The footsteps were coming closer now. A few more guesses and the program would lock her out.

Sixty percent of passwords use personal information. Thirty-three percent incorporate a pet's name.

Eva jumped on Facebook and navigated to Peggy's page. She grinned. There in front of her was one of the fattest cats she'd ever seen and a post from Peggy: "Mr. Bubblesworth loves to cuddle."

She typed "MrBubblesworth" in the password field and watched with glee as a database of police files opened before her. *A little luck never hurts.*

The footsteps came faster now. *Whoever was coming could see the light.* Eva rose from the desk and slid behind the door. She heard a single cop enter the room. The smell of aftershave overwhelmed her. Through the crack in the door, she saw him enter. He approached the desk and assessed the computer screen glowing in the darkness.

Eva envisioned what he would do next.

He will check the cord to see how the computer is still on. He will look around to see who was here. He will check the hall. He will get backup. That can't happen.

The cop went behind the desk and looked at the computer. He fiddled with the cord to determine how a computer could be on in a powerless building. He reached for his radio, temporarily forgetting that it wasn't working. He stepped toward the hallway, oblivious of Eva's presence. She waited to see his neck enter her line of sight. The carotid artery and ten seconds were all she needed.

As the officer passed, Eva took one step left and wrapped her right arm around the officer's neck, driving her forearm into his carotid artery. The cop clawed at her black jacket. Eva secured her hold around the man's neck by placing her left arm behind his head, squeezing the blood flow to his skull. Five, four, three, two, one. His body went limp. She checked the cop's pulse to make sure he was still alive. He was. She deposited his body behind the door and resumed her seat at the desk. The backup generator would be on soon. She needed to hurry.

She searched the database for Wally McCutcheon and found the case number. She opened the attachments in the case. Just a few pictures of the dead body and an autopsy report. Nothing incriminating. Then she saw it: a picture of her notepaper in Wally's hand, evidence number 0127698.

Eva took Peggy's key to the evidence cage out of her pocket and opened the door. She scanned the boxes, looking for the details in the McCutcheon case. She opened the file and perused the evidence. There was almost nothing. Her notepaper with the decision tree she had used to break into the bank, some fiber samples, and notes on interviews with Albert and Belial. She grabbed the paper and replaced it with the more innocuous version of the decision tree that Puddles had touched outside. With a tweezer, she then grabbed the few fibers and hairs that she had swiped off Albert's coat and placed them in a bag.

Objective two was complete. It was time for the final act: *Neutralize Albert.*

***

Albert paced and whistled in the waiting room of the Princeton police station in darkness, completely oblivious to the goings-on inside. He had tried to exit through the front door, but the electronic locks were disabled, trapping him in the lobby. He wondered how long it would be before the power came on. How long it would be before Weatherspoon came out to meet him.

He peered through the glass divider separating the front waiting room from the main office. Stained-oak receptionist desks dotted the front of the open-office layout, and some type of command center stood guard in the rear. Through the darkness, Albert could barely make out two cops standing, heads down, futzing with their radios. They seemed to be having trouble with the signal.

And then he noticed something else. Tiptoeing behind them. A figure in the shadows. Lean and light yet somehow familiar. He stepped closer to the glass to see what he could make out.

The two cops continued to chat and play with their radios as the figure crept behind them. Albert pressed his hands against the glass. It was a woman. It was Eva! She was carrying something, a nightstick. Albert shouted and pounded on the glass, but the barrier muffled his voice.

The cops looked up to see what the ruckus was.

Albert shouted, "Look behind you!"

The cops strained to hear.

Albert banged his pointer finger against the glass, gesturing to Eva. But it was too late.

With two swift swings of the baton, Eva hammered the officers' skulls, dropping them to the ground. Her eyes met Puddles's. They shone in the darkness. She charged toward him.

At that moment, Weatherspoon stepped out from the side hallway, through the steel door, and entered the waiting room.

"What's all this about, Puddles?"

Albert rejoiced. "Detective, thank God you're here. She's attacking the station."

Eva continued to advance toward the waiting room.

Weatherspoon stepped toward Albert, his back to the office door.

"Slow down, Puddles. What are you talking about? Who's attack—"

But before the detective could finish, Eva burst through the steel door, leapt into the air, and plunged a hypodermic needle into Weatherspoon's neck. The giant officer cried out for a moment and then slammed to the ground. His body writhed, fighting against the darkness before finally succumbing.

Eva reached out two gloved hands toward Albert. In one hand was a nightstick; in the other, the needle.

"Hold these."

Without thinking, Albert complied.

"Wait, what happened? What did you do?" shouted Puddles.

Eva shook her head. "I didn't do anything, Dilbert. In fact, I was never here. You, on the other hand ... you just attacked a police station. And in a few seconds, the power to this building is going to come back on, and all these cameras are going to be recording you sitting in the front lobby with a nightstick in one hand and a needle in the other."

Albert backpedaled, suddenly aware of his precarious position. "Why are you doing this?"

Eva walked to the door. As the power flickered back on, she opened it, being sure to avoid the camera. She tapped on the door with her fingers and looked outside, avoiding his gaze. "You made me do this, Albert. I never wanted this," she said in a voice barely above a whisper.

"What *do* you want?" Albert begged.

Eva paused and looked out at the sky, now dark and rippling with storm clouds.

"I want you to run."

CHAPTER 16

The table of Angus Turner's living room was strewn with papers, each one containing a game tree sprawling out from a different goal.

Turner paced the floor of his living room as he opined on the true power of the Tree of Knowledge.

"Ms. Koh, what you have before you is a different way of seeing the world. It may be overwhelming at first, but you must understand that the Tree is nothing more than a modern extension of the work of the ancients."

"How so?"

"Have you had the opportunity of taking Professor Puddles's Classical Logic class, yet?"

"I haven't," said Ying with a blush.

"Ah, what a shame. The classics are my favorites, and Albert shares my passion. As you may or may not know, the founder of classical logic was our good friend, Aristotle, my personal hero."

"Really? Isn't he a little outdated, at this point?"

Turner gasped and touched his chest as though Ying had attacked a family member. "The man was the quintessential Renaissance man. He was the first to determine that the sun was larger than the Earth. He extrapolated the tremendous evolution of the Earth from the minor geological changes of his time. He was the first person to outline formal rules of logic. And, as a good friend of mine once said, 'It is doubtful whether any human being has ever known as much as he did'."

Ying's guard went up whenever she heard one old white man celebrating another old white man. "Yeah, but what does that have to do with your Tree?"

"Quite simply, Aristotle provided the intellectual foundation on which this Tree and all of modern logic and reasoning is built. You see, Aristotle outlined what he called the three laws of thought: the law of identity, the law of noncontradiction, and the law of the excluded middle. The idea behind these laws was to guide any rational discussion or inquiry."

Ying stood up and began wagging her finger.

"Yaaaas ... I've read this. It's coming back to me now ... The law of identity essentially says that something is indeed what you say it is. One must accept that before you can move forward with any rational discussion. For example, in order for us to discuss whether or not Albert Puddles is the tidiest man at Princeton, we must first agree that there is one Albert Puddles and he is who we both think he is."

Turner chuckled knowingly and nodded at her understanding.

"The second law is the law of noncontradiction, which means you can't say something that is both true and false at the same time. A classic example of a violation of this law is the statement 'Everything I say is a lie'. If it were true, then the statement would invalidate itself, but if it were a lie, then that would mean that at some point the person would have said something true." Ying drew breath like an auctioneer at a cattle sale. "And last but not least is the law of the excluded middle, which states that in order to proceed in a well-reasoned argument, something either must be true or not; there can be nothing in between. A classic example violating this law is the question 'Is the king of the United States bald?' Since there is no king of the United States, the question and any argument stemming from it are, therefore, invalid."

Turner nodded, impressed. "So, for our trees to be sound, we need to make sure that we build upon these three laws. Now, here's where we get to the good stuff—" At that moment, Albert burst through the door.

His face was pale, and cold sweat poured from his forehead and around his spectacles. His eyes were bloodshot, and dust covered his normally immaculate suit. His hands visibly shook, and his shoulders slumped under an unseen burden.

Ying jumped out of her seat with her hand on her mouth, her eyes straining with concern.

"My God, what happened to you?" cried Turner.

Albert placed his hands on his knees and gasped for air, attempting to collect himself. "Eva ... I ... I ..."

Angus rushed to Albert and grabbed him by the shoulders. "Eva? You saw her? Is she OK?"

Puddles wriggled from Turner's grip and took a step back. His cheeks regained some of their color, and his jaw clenched in anger.

"Yes, Professor. I saw her ... And she's doing well. My only regret is that I didn't get a chance to catch up with her before she framed me and took out the entire Princeton police station. By the way, I'm doing fine, thank you for asking."

"What!" cried Ying.

Albert grabbed Ying's lemonade glass from the table and sat down on Turner's sofa, gulping the cool liquid down in seconds. In his typically precise way, he took the spare moment to readjust his tie, wipe the spots from his glasses, and brush the dust off his coat and pants while catching his breath. Turner and Ying stood watching him as if he were a curious animal at the zoo.

When he finally felt comfortable that he had regained some of his typical immaculateness, Albert began, "I went to the Princeton police station to tell Weatherspoon about the Tree, just like you said, Angus. When I got to the station, before I could go inside, Eva stopped me in the parking lot."

"Oh, dear God," interjected Turner, staring at Albert with a knowing look.

"She wanted me to turn a blind eye. She said that the incident at the bank was an accident and that turning her in wouldn't do any good."

"What did you say?" asked Ying.

Albert resented the question and with one look made sure that Ying was aware of it. "I told her no and went into the station. And that's when she cut the power to the station, snatched up all the evidence implicating her, and planted evidence to frame me."

Both Ying and Albert turned to Turner. The older man's brow carried the weight of a man who has lost a child. He walked toward the kitchen and stroked his chin.

Softly, Turner asked, "How did you get out?"

"She let me out."

"Intentionally?"

"Yes."

"And what did she tell you to do?"

"She told me to run." Albert took another sip. "Shouldn't you have seen this coming, Professor, with your special 'Tree of Knowledge'?"

"The Tree is not all-knowing, Puddles. It is only as good as the information fed into it. I assumed Eva had no knowledge of the evidence she left behind. Clearly, I was wrong."

Seconds went by as Turner stroked his chin in a silence punctuated by the ticktock of his grandfather clock.

After staring at Turner for some time, neither Ying nor Albert could take it anymore, and the two simultaneously blurted out, "What should we do?"

"Ms. Koh. You need to return to your work and studies on campus. I couldn't possibly involve you in this. Forget what you've seen today. Puddles and I will be fine."

"Professor, there's a problem. Eva knows about Ying," said Albert.

"How?"

"She saw Ying and me leaving Princeton for your house. She knows Ying is involved. I don't think it's safe for us to just leave her here."

"Don't I get a say in this?" interjected Ying.

Turner looked at the two of them, rose from his chair, put on his sport coat, and said, "As I said, I'm only as good as the information I have. If Eva knows about Ms. Koh's involvement and told you to run. Then that is what we must do. If I know Eva Fix, the police will be here any minute, and she will ensure that they bring all three of us to account. Now is not the time for confrontation. Ying, I'm afraid you're going with us for the time being. Grab my papers and come. I know of a place where we can gather ourselves."

The sound of far-off sirens shattered the peace of Turner's living room.

Albert and Ying locked eyes in disbelief. How was it that this morning they had been preparing for the first day of class and now they were running for their lives? It was surreal. It was tempting to just refuse to believe it. But as the sirens drew closer, they realized they had to believe it. The logical choice was the only choice. They snatched up Turner's papers and followed him to the garage.

Seconds later, Turner's Buick rumbled out of the driveway and onto a side road, with Albert in the front and Ying perched in the middle of the back seat.

Two police cars, lights flickering and sirens blaring, raced by them in the opposite direction. Instinctively, the two passengers slid down in their seats.

"Where are we going?" screeched Ying.

"We are going to the countryside," said Turner. "I have some friends who may be able to help us."

The storm that had been crouching over Albert earlier in the day had now pounced, and a steady rain came tumbling down on the windshield of the aged automobile. He opened the window a crack and noticed how the soothing, warm air of this morning had morphed into a raw, wet, inhospitable world of gray. He smelled electricity in the air.

Albert's body ached as though that same raw chill had penetrated every aspect of his life, and it made him ill. Ever since he was a kid, Albert had longed for a deeper sense of purpose. He loved comic book superheroes, mystery detectives, and thriller tough guys—not for the powers they possessed but for the fights they fought. He, too, wanted to battle evil and villainy, not grapple with ambiguous and complex problems. To him, theirs was a life of purpose and passion, whereas his was a life of dry, abstract pursuits.

But now, as he stared out from the passenger seat of Turner's sedan, he did not feel purpose. He felt terror. His stomach clenched. His heart pumped at a furious pace. Waves of fear radiated from his temples and spread throughout his body, causing every limb and muscle group to curl inward. Instead of rising to the challenge, as he always hoped he would do, Albert wanted nothing more than to shrink from it. To go back to this morning in his office and decline the detective's request for help. Or take the decision tree and burn it. To go on living a life of comfort without meaning. But as the car splashed down the highway through the growing downpour, Albert knew that his life would have purpose . . . and meaning . . . and fear . . . and perhaps . . . a premature death.

PART II
AN EDUCATION

Then the eyes of both of them were opened,
and they knew that they were naked.

—Genesis 3:7

CHAPTER 1

Eva sat on the sterile gray swoop-back chairs of the John F. Kennedy International Airport and reflected on what she had just seen.

She had finally reconnected with Dilbert, her teenage crush. Even though it had been years since she'd seen him, she had occasionally thought of him and even dreamed of him. It was crazy that an old, momentary flame had stuck with her, but there he was. In her dreams, he was an idealization of himself, a modern-day Indiana Jones that no other man could match. At first, reality had disappointed. The man—and the experience of seeing him—seemed so much smaller, like touring the hallways of her former elementary school. But when she had finally spoken to him in that dreary parking lot outside of the police station and felt his earnestness—saw the kindness in the modest wrinkles around his eyes—she was fourteen all over again. The hard exterior that she had so carefully constructed over the years began to groan under the warmth of his presence; at that moment, she wanted nothing more than to give up the path of ambition, calculation, and competition—shed all that she had done, all that she had become—and just share in an ordinary life with someone. Not for any facet of that life in particular, but for the feeling of sharing . . . something, anything.

She pulled her phone from her jacket pocket and scrolled through her contacts until she arrived at General Isaac Moloch. She wondered how her life had ended up here.

For Eva, it began with a story and a moment. When she was a child, her mother often worked late into the evening. As children often do, Eva would burst into her mother's home office and nag her to play a game or watch a movie. To stop the nagging and buy herself some additional time to finish her work, Eva's mother would give her logic puzzles or riddles. Most of the puzzles Eva solved and discarded, but one puzzle resonated with the girl: the story of the lady and the tiger.

In the story, a beautiful princess falls in love with a commoner. The two of them court for months, but eventually, the king discovers the affair. He declares that the commoner will face a trial of fortune that will determine his fate. The king places the commoner in front of a crowded arena in which there are two doors. Behind one door is the most beautiful woman in the land, whom he will marry if he chooses correctly. Behind the other door is a tiger that will surely maim and kill him. As luck would have it, the princess discovers ahead of time which door holds the tiger and which the lady. The commoner knows the princess holds the keys to his life and looks to her before selecting a door. She tilts her head to the right. The question for the man is, knowing that the princess loves him with all her heart and loathes the other woman, should he choose the door on the right or the left?

As a child, Eva had puzzled over the answer to the question for hours, hoping to find as certain an answer as the other riddles had provided. When her mother finished her work, she asked Eva what she thought.

"I don't get it," she had shouted. "What's the answer?"

Her mother offered a warm smile. "That's the point, Evalita. There is no answer. It's an allegory about the power of passion and the difficulty of choosing between two equally unpleasant options."

At first, Eva had hated the story for its ambiguity. She wanted an *answer*. But as she thought about it more, she began to love it. She could see herself as the princess, overcome with love for this man, but racked with hatred for the woman he would love. It was then that she realized that she wanted to feel that same passion— for a man . . . or a cause. She wished she could unwind the clock and use her skills to overcome the struggles of the past. To conquer lands with Alexander the Great, to build Rome with Caesar, to lead a revolution with Washington. But those battles had already been fought and won, so what remained for her?

Eva pulled out her phone and called the general. As the phone rang her thoughts drifted. She had worked with him ever since she joined the Society for Reason, Enlightenment, and Democracy. It had seemed like the perfect partnership between mentor and mentee. Her intellect. His ruthless efficiency. But as the Society's influence grew, so, too, did the general's ambitions. They had done so much together. Built schools. Influenced policy. But now he was different.

"Fix. I was wondering if I would hear from you today," answered Moloch.

She shuddered at the sound of his voice but pressed on. "The job is done. I have the package, and I have smoked out Puddles and Turner."

She could see the general's big, yellow-toothed grin through the phone. She could almost smell his stale breath. "Superb. And his assistant?"

Eva sighed and thought of Albert's perky little bespectacled partner in crime, a far-too-cute interloper. "I don't think she'll be an issue."

"This was an excellent learning opportunity, don't you think?" Moloch asked her with his usual whiff of superiority.

Eva clenched the phone in her hand. "I don't appreciate your tone, General."

"What tone?"

She imagined his false naïveté.

"Your condescending tone. Not just today, but for the past week. Do I need to remind you that you and the Society would be nothing without me? When I joined ten years ago, the Society was just a cute little think tank that wrote letters to senators. I'm the one who made it matter. I'm the one who built RED schools in every state. I'm the one who raised billions for our charitable arm. I'm the one who built the RED army. I'm the one who made sure we had RED members in every major institution in this country. I'm the one who..."

She stopped herself. She realized that the more she climbed the Society's ladder, the more meaningless it all seemed. She was admired, feared, trusted. But she herself didn't admire, fear, or trust anyone. She didn't love anyone, except her mother, and that was a love in constant search of approval. Her ambition was a journey without end, an addiction that she could never quench. The Society had walled off all the opportunities of life that had beckoned her when she was fourteen. The lone path visible now was the one that she had already chosen, and she knew she had chosen poorly.

The general interrupted her thought. "Watch yourself, Fix. You've been valuable in building this organization, but RED is bigger than anyone of us. And I'm still in charge of this operation. You follow?"

"Yes," Eva said, unable to summon the energy to feign sincerity.

"You follow?"

"YES."

"Good. We will see you back at headquarters tomorrow."

The general hung up.

Eva shoved her phone back in her pocket and stared at the tarmac. Planes roared across the runway against a bright blue sky. She had joined the Society for the freedom and power that it offered, but bit by bit, the Society's leadership had encroached on that freedom. She was no longer a rookie. Something needed to change.

CHAPTER 2

A s Turner's Buick sped along I-95, Albert and Ying attempted to get a grip on the rupture in their lives.

After providing the details on his experience and history with Eva, Albert turned his attention to Turner. "OK, Angus, now that we seem to be at least temporarily out of harm's way, can you please explain what is going on?"

Turner took a long breath, apparently wondering where to begin. The leather from the steering wheel creaked as it slid through the old man's hands. "Let me answer your question with a question. What did Eva steal from the bank?"

Ying and Albert glanced at each other.

"A safe-deposit box."

"Ah yes, but what was in it?"

"Some guy's stuff?" asked Ying.

"Wrong. It wasn't just some guy's. It was mine. And it wasn't stuff; it was the very Tree of Knowledge that I've been telling you about. That book holds every thought I've ever had about the Tree. Every experiment. How it can be used. How it can be taught. Everything. In the wrong hands, the book holds nearly limitless power."

"Eva told me that it was a security code," said Albert incredulously.

Turner smiled. "Given that her family business is a security and defense company that makes everything from bombs to fighter jets, that's technically true. But the Tree of Knowledge is capable of much more than security."

"Poor Albert," teased Ying in her singsong voice. "The first girl that falls in love with him turns out to be a thief and murderer."

As Ying chortled at his misfortune, Albert fought to control his flush. He realized how naïve he'd been. In the logical recesses of his mind, he knew that Eva's story was unlikely, if not absurd, but her presence dulled his reasoning. He had *wanted* to believe her. He shuddered at the realization of how easily his critical faculties had succumbed.

"But isn't this something for the police?" asked Ying.

At the word "police", Albert perked up. "Yes, it is, but considering the fact that I'm probably their chief suspect for the murder of the security guard, I'm not sure contacting the police is the right answer at this moment."

"Touché," said Turner. "We have almost no evidence to show the police, and even if we did, they tend not to look kindly on conspiracy theories offered by suspected criminals. I think our best bet at this point is to hunker down on the Travis Farm and make a plan."

"Hunker down?" asked Albert. "Angus, I have to teach. I can't just hunker down."

"And I have classes to attend and teach . . . and a couple of dates to go on," added Ying.

Albert looked sideways toward Ying at this new piece of information.

Turner glanced into the rearview mirror, noting everything they were leaving behind.

"I'm afraid you are both going to have to put your lives on hold for a bit. I'll cover for you with the school, tell them you're working with me on something top secret for the Defense Department and need to take a sabbatical or something of that nature. What you tell your friends and family is your business. But tell them now, because I need those cell phones out the window in fifteen minutes."

Albert imagined what he would tell his friends and family. Truth was, he hadn't talked to his mom and dad for years. He had a few colleagues on the Princeton faculty, but were they his friends? Would they even notice he was gone?

"That was my next question, Angus," said Albert. "Who are these 'friends' of yours that you're taking us to? You're not getting us involved with criminals, are you?"

Turner laughed. "Heavens, no. This is a group I affectionately call the Book Club. They are the few people in the world that I have taken into my confidence in developing the Tree. With each of them, I have shared one aspect of the Tree, so together they represent the full potential of what it can do."

"Exactly what can the Tree do, Professor? I have to admit, I'm a little skeptical of this theory," said Ying.

"I understand," replied Turner calmly. "I was skeptical at first as well, and it was *my* theory. The most important thing for you to understand is that life is nothing but a series of goals and actions, and so if you can understand those goals and foresee the actions of individuals, then you can manipulate them. Unfortunately, with Eva, we've seen how she used this concept in hand-to-hand combat."

"What do you mean?" asked Albert.

"Well, if a person does not have a weapon, they have a finite set of viable options for harming you. Punching, kicking, headbutting, biting, grabbing, and tackling."

"Just like chess," exclaimed Ying, seeing where Turner was going with this.

"Yes, similar to chess, in which you are limited to twenty possible opening moves. Also, like chess, we can calculate the likelihood of each of these methods of attack. In chess, eighty-nine percent of the time, a competent player will use one of three moves to begin the game. So it is with hand-to-hand combat. Predicting human behavior in combat becomes even easier when we consider the demographics of the person and then adjust our strategy based on their body position. Eva knew the security guard was an overweight man over the age of sixty."

"So, she could assume with a high level of certainty that the man would not kick, headbutt, or bite," said Ying.

"Exactly. Because at that age and in that physical condition, he was unlikely to have the flexibility or the creativity to attempt any of those methods. And even if he did, he'd almost certainly injure himself. In combating the security guard, all Eva had to watch were the man's hands, and this drastically reduced the complexity of fighting him and enabled her to subdue him in probably less than a minute. No more difficult than beating a beginner in chess. Of course, the Tree gives you the power to subdue much fiercer foes than an overweight security guard."

Albert thought back to the comic books that he used to read and couldn't help daydreaming of himself as some type of masked superhero using the Tree of Knowledge to fight against ruthless enemies. The idea of using his brain to win against physically more powerful men excited him. For a moment, he forgot his fear.

"So, you're going to use the Tree to clear Albert's name and bring down Eva," said Ying incredulously.

"Yes," said the professor with a smirk. "But that's the easy part."

CHAPTER 3

Detective Weatherspoon's eyes opened. He let out a whimper. He strained through the fog to see what lay in front of him, but his pupils were not yet adjusted to the light. As the blur of sleep faded from his vision, he made out what looked to be the cheap square tile of a hospital ceiling. He rubbed his face and looked around. His mouth and throat ached. He rolled over on his left side to see if he could locate a glass of water, but before he could get any further, a voice from behind interrupted him.

"The sleeping bear comes out of hibernation," said a gravelly baritone.

Even in his dazed state, Weatherspoon knew the gruff voice of his captain, Pete Willard. While Willard had always been Weatherspoon's superior, the two had been good friends for over two decades.

"What happened?" asked Weatherspoon, struggling to find enough liquid in his mouth to make sound. The cool air trickled up the open back of his hospital gown.

The smile of relief that had first greeted Weatherspoon immediately faded from Willard's face. "You mean, you don't remember?"

Weatherspoon searched the files of his mind to remember how he had arrived at the hospital. "No, I don't," he said, surprised by his own words.

The captain bit his lip and assessed his confused patient. He broke the news slowly. "Mike, our police station was attacked."

The detective rubbed his face to make sure he wasn't still sleeping. "What?"

"I know. It's unbelievable. We're still piecing together what happened, but what we know is that a white male, tall, slim build, entered the station at five p.m. He then attacked multiple officers and jammed enough Rohypnol in you to take down an elephant. You've been out for seventy-two hours."

"What? Why?"

"We don't know that, yet. He took out Peggy, as well, so we think it has something to do with the property room."

Weatherspoon leaned back in his bed, exhausted.

The captain grabbed Weatherspoon's shoulder and gave it a friendly pat.

"One last question, and then I should let you get back to sleep." Willard pulled out a printout of a blurred black-and-white photo. "This is a still from the video recording of the perp who assaulted the station. Ever seen him before?"

The detective squinted at the picture. The man looked familiar, but as he searched his drugged memory from the last few days his mind returned only blackness. Through the pounding in his jaw and the cloud in his brain, he just couldn't make a connection.

"I've seen the face before, but I can't quite place it." He paused and closed his eyes. "Give me some time. It will come to me."

"Great. I'll let you rest. If you remember who it is, let me know. In the meantime, I snuck in a few of your files on the chair here next to your bed in case you get bored. Oh, and while you were out, we ran the hair and fiber sample evidence for the McCutcheon case. Info's in the file."

The captain gave Weatherspoon a kind pat on the back of the hand and strolled out the door of the hospital room.

After fifteen minutes of staring at the ceiling and failing to find sleep, Weatherspoon grabbed the McCutcheon file. He opened the manila folder to distract himself.

DNA Match: Albert Puddles.

CHAPTER 4

Turner, Puddles, and Ying crossed the Vermont state line around midnight. Albert had reclined his seat and was now listening to Professor Turner explain how to bring the Tree of Knowledge to life. The combination of darkness, motion, and the steady approach and departure of headlights had lulled Albert into a sort of automotive hypnosis, which he wished he could escape.

"You see, in order to master the Tree, you must abandon the assumptions and habits that we grow up with and embrace the rational laws that are the foundation of modern mathematics and logic," said Turner.

"But don't we do that in class every day?" asked Ying, keen to explore the powers of the Tree.

"Yes, but dedicating your mind to reason when faced with a math problem is one thing. Focusing it when faced with the emotions, assumptions, and distractions of the real world is an entirely different animal."

"Is this why you spent all that time on syllogisms in your logic class, Angus?" said Albert. He was beginning to see that there might be more to what the professor was saying.

Turner's smile broadened. "A magician never reveals his secrets."

"Syllogisms?" asked Ying. "I'm not exactly sure I see how logic puzzles are going to help me navigate the real world, Professor."

"Well, why don't we try a few right now, and we'll find out."

Turner glanced at Albert and chortled with a knowing grin. Ying looked around at the chuckling, older white men and suddenly felt distinctly outside of the club. It was a feeling she had felt before, and she dealt with it as she had in the past ... with bulldog-like persistence.

"Alright, bring it on, old man."

Turner's smile dropped at the slight, but he pressed on. "OK. Here are the rules, Ms. Koh. I am going to describe a situation that is not quite what it seems. The more logical you are in your approach to asking questions, the more expeditiously you will derive the answer. I will allow you to ask me—"

"Yes or no questions in order to find the answer," interrupted Ying. "Yes, I know how this works. Give me your best shot." She cracked her knuckles like a brawler before a fight.

"Perfect. Then let's commence. Here is your first puzzle. Seven people are found dead in a cabin in the woods. They all died at the same time, but there are no footprints in or out. How did they die?"

Ying looked out the window, attempting to picture this cabin. "Is this cabin a house?"

"I'll take the Q and A part, Angus," said Albert. "No."

Ying sat up in her chair. "Aha. So, this is not a typical cabin. Is it made of wood?"

"No."

"Is it made of metal?"

"Yes." Albert smiled, knowing the end was nigh.

"It's an airplane cabin. The people died in an airplane crash."

"Well done, Ms. Koh," exclaimed Turner.

"Thank you, thank you," said Ying, mock bowing from the back seat.

"But, tell me this . . . when I first told you about the cabin, what did you picture?"

Ying thought back to the horrifying scene she had visualized. "I pictured a log cabin full of dead bodies."

"Exactly. And that is the challenge of using the Tree of Knowledge in everyday life. Our brains are so filled with assumptions and images, emotions and fears, that it clouds our ability to focus on the pure information that we have been given. The second we picture that cabin as a log cabin and imagine those dead bodies, we have let emotion overwhelm the logical process. The pure logical process would tell us that the word 'cabin' is ambiguous and so our first step must be to clarify what the meaning of the word 'cabin' is."

"Aristotle's law of identity," added Ying.

"Precisely," said Turner.

"Let's do another. I'm on a roll, now."

Turner thought back to some of his favorite puzzles. "Ah, this is a doozy. A man pushes his car up to a hotel. The hotel owner says to him, 'You owe me four hundred and fifty dollars,' at which point the man announces that he is now bankrupt. Your charge, Ms. Koh, is to determine why."

Ying took a long look out the car window at the dark forest speeding by and gathered her thoughts.

"Did the man owe the hotel owner money for staying at the hotel?"

Turner smiled as he observed Ying's intellect grinding away.

"No, it's not money for staying at the hotel," replied Albert.

"Is it for some other past debt?" asked Ying.

"Nope."

"So, it's because he parked the car at the hotel?"

"Yes," said Albert with a smirk.

"This guy is paying four hundo for parking?"

"No."

"But you said it's because he parked the car at the hotel."

"Yes."

At this piece of information, Ying's brow furrowed, and she hummed. She often hummed when she was thinking, a habit that Albert thought quite odd.

After a few minutes of steady humming, Ying resumed her questioning. "OK, let me focus on the car. He's pushing it, right?"

"Correct."

"Is the car broken?"

"Nope," said Albert, as pleased with himself as though he had invented the riddle.

"Is this a large car? I mean, I'm not sure I could push a car even with these guns," said Ying, flexing her practically nonexistent muscles and chuckling.

"No."

"Is the car smaller than a Mini?"

"Yes."

"Is the car a real, functioning automobile?"

"No."

"So, it's a toy car. Aha," shouted Ying, shaking Albert's shoulders from the back seat.

As his shoulders shook, Albert looked at Turner, who seemed to enjoy Ying's progress.

"Yes, it is," said Albert.

"OK, let me get this straight. A man pushes a toy car up to a hotel, and the owner tells him he owes him four hundred fifty dollars?"

"Yes."

"Why would a guy push a toy car up to a hotel? Was there a convention, and he was selling the toy car?"

Albert laughed. "No."

"Aaaargh! What the heck? Why would a man push a toy car up to a hotel? It makes no sense."

After another pause and a quiet round of humming, Ying resumed her questioning.

"Was the man outside when he pushed the car?"

"No, and you've got two minutes."

"So, he was inside the hotel?"

"No."

"But I thought you said he pushed his car up to a hotel?"

"Yes," Albert said, fondly remembering his past efforts to solve this riddle.

"How can you push a car up to a hotel and not be inside or outside?" said Ying, visibly flushed.

"Yes or no questions, please," said Albert sarcastically.

"Professor Turner, this feels rigged. Is this a joke?"

Turner shook his head. "No, Ms. Koh. This isn't a joke. Keep going. You're on the right track, but remember ... to be successful, disregard assumption and pursue logic."

"I am a logical machine, right now."

"Regardless, you're going to have to put your riddle-solving on hold for a moment because we need to make a quick stop at this little pub." And with that, Turner pulled off the country road they'd been navigating down and onto the unpaved parking lot of a bar with a neon sign that read "Tim's Toolbox".

Tim's Toolbox was little more than a shed covered in neon beer signs of brands long since deceased. The parking lot consisted of a unique combination of pebbles and dirt that caused the rear end of Turner's Buick to slip and slide as it entered.

Turner pulled the car in between two large pickup trucks sitting on even larger wheels, and Ying popped up to the edge of the back middle seat and began nodding her head.

"Yes! This is amazing. We're going to a good old-fashioned country roadhouse, right now. Where's Patrick Swayze when you need him?"

Ying's enthusiasm was matched by Albert's apprehension. "Angus, why exactly are we stopping here?"

"Well, we need directions to get to my friend's farm, and since we can't use any electronic device, I thought we'd do it the old-fashioned way and simply ask someone."

Albert frowned. "OK, but isn't the creepy roadhouse on the side of the road the worst possible place to stop? How about a gas station or motel? It just doesn't seem like a very safe place to pull over."

Turner opened the car door and leaned back through the open window to talk to Albert.

"Albert, shame on you. These are just people. Yes, they may not be academics, but I'm sure they'll be more than happy to help y—"

Just as Turner was about to finish his sentence, Ying interrupted him, shouting, "Whoa!" and pointed out the windshield.

Turner rotated his head to find two large men stumbling from the bar amid what looked like a full-blown brawl. The bigger man, who sported a beard reminiscent of ZZ Top, quickly gained the advantage and pounced on the smaller man as a crowd spilled out of the bar to root for their favorites.

Albert let out a loud snort and sat back in the front seat, crossing his arms like a toddler refusing to eat his broccoli.

Turner leaned his head back in the window and with a sheepish grin continued, "OK, I may have soft-pedaled the demeanor of the esteemed patrons of Tim's Toolbox, but trust me, we'll be just fine. I assure you we won't be on the premises for more than five minutes. We'll walk in, I'll find someone who can give us directions, and we'll walk out. No harm done. Ms. Koh, wouldn't you like a little adventure in your life?"

Ying and Albert exchanged a long glance with each other and against their better judgment exited the car. As the group approached the entrance of the bar, the crowd around the two pugilists let out a loud cheer and clanked glasses in celebration of the bearded victor.

Turner, Ying, and Albert followed the elated mob into the establishment and sidled up to the bar. Upon entering Tim's Toolbox, Albert realized he had found the one place on earth that was everything he wasn't. Tim's Toolbox was loud, dirty, intimidating, smelly, disorganized, rugged, and chaotic. He sat at the bar and understood the meaning of the word "alienation". If there had been an operating jukebox in the establishment, it would have stopped upon Albert's arrival. Fortunately, Tim's jukebox had been out of order since late 1987.

Ying plopped down next to Albert at the bar, while Turner went to the other side to inquire for directions.

The bartender, a small, weaselly looking older gentleman, stared at the two new customers as though a pair of Martians had just sat down in his pub. His face held deep lines that told the story of a lifetime of smoking and scowling. Yet somehow with each moment that his gaze held Albert's and Ying's, those lines seemed to grow deeper.

As was her typical fashion, Ying remained unfazed by the bartender's hostile stare. She smiled and made the obligatory half wave of a person trying to get a server's attention without seeming overbearing. Albert had always found it amazing how Ying could operate in some type of parallel universe, oblivious of social signals and norms, yet always charming everyone in her path. She could visit a death row inmate and have him smiling and playing a game of checkers within an hour.

After a few minutes of concerted effort on Ying's part, the bartender made his way over to Ying and Albert and disdainfully spun two napkins at them.

"What can I get you folks?" he growled with a rasp that continued long after the words had left his throat.

Attempting to avoid further irritating the bartender, Albert demurred. "Nothing for me."

This was clearly a miscalculation. Puddles could see the bartender cursing these two outsiders who were taking up space in his establishment and weren't ordering anything, to boot.

Ying's order compounded the error. "Could I have a vodka cranberry?" she said, eagerly bouncing on the wobbling barstool.

"We don't have cranberry juice," barked the bartender.

"Oh, well, OK, whatever you have that's close to that. And he'll have a beer."

The old man snarled and walked away.

"We should get the hell out of here," said Albert, looking over his right shoulder and noticing three men eyeing Ying like hyenas at dusk. "Where is Turner?"

Ying just laughed. "Oh, Albert. Stop being so paranoid."

"Albert? What happened to Professor Puddles?"

"I think we're way past formalities now, don't you? Anyway, I think this bar has a certain gritty charm. Sure, the bartender's grumpy, but that's part of the whole vibe. You can't have a chipper bartender in a roadhouse bar. It just wouldn't fit. Have a beer, and try to enjoy yourself. We're on an adventure."

Once again, Albert felt the familiar pit in his stomach. Adventure. He had always craved it, but now he wanted absolutely nothing to do with it. As soon as his beer arrived, he grabbed it and drank it down, hoping that the cold liquid would extinguish his sense of dread.

"What do we have here?" asked Ying as the bartender brought her drink. "A vodka Sprite?"

"A vodka vodka. Enjoy."

Ying looked puzzled and then took a sip of her drink, coughing as the pure vodka went down her throat.

Just then, two of the three hyenas that had been staring at Ying approached. One of them leaned in over her right shoulder, while the other one stood in between Ying and Albert, pushing him out of the way. The smell of alcohol was overwhelming, and Albert could see the eyes of the one on the right swimming in booze.

"Well, hello, little lady, I'm Darrell," said the dark-haired man on Ying's right shoulder as he scratched his unshaven chin.

"Hello," said Ying, leaning back to create some space between the two.

Albert could see Ying was trying to be friendly but that she wanted nothing to do with this man. He slid his seat forward and to the right and put his elbow on the bar to edge back between Ying and the man who was blocking him.

Darrell continued to press. "I'd love to have a dance with you," he said.

Ying looked at Albert in confusion. There was no music playing in the bar. Albert shook his head at Ying as if to say, "Don't get into the details with this guy."

"No, thanks," said Ying politely and turned back to the bar, attempting to resume a conversation with Albert that they hadn't been having.

"Oh, c'mon now," slurred Darrell, grabbing Ying's arm.

Seeing Ying wince, and without thinking, Albert pushed aside Darrell's friend and put his hand on Darrell's shoulder.

"Sir, I don't think she wants to dance with you. I'd appreciate it if you'd leave the two of us alone."

The activity of the joint came to a sudden stop. All conversation ceased as if a string had been cut. Albert heard Darrell cackle and with the man's yellow, gap-toothed smile realized he had fallen into his trap. This was exactly what the three hyenas had wanted. Ying wasn't their prey; Albert was.

In an instant, Darrell had Albert by the collar and up against the wall, with his two friends holding back his arms. As he grabbed Albert by the throat, Darrell whispered into the side of his head. The whiskey-tinged breath burned in Albert's ear like acid.

"No, I'm not going to leave you alone, pretty boy. I'm gonna kick the living shit out of you, and then I'm gonna have my way with your little Chinese girlfriend. How's that sou—"

But before Darrell could finish his sentence, two arms and a wooden stick encircled his neck and ripped him backward. Albert looked on as Darrell took a blow to the knees and dropped to the floor, revealing Angus Turner behind him. He held his walking stick in both hands and rocked it up and down.

Albert knew he would never forget the look Turner gave him in the instant that Darrell dropped to the floor. It was a look of absolute calm and focus ... and then, to his amazement, the professor cracked a smile and winked. But as shocking as that expression was, what followed exceeded it tenfold.

After pausing to understand what they had seen—an old man disabling their best friend with a stick—Darrell's two friends immediately charged the aging professor. Turner dispatched them like two ants in the way of his boot. As the first man charged him, he slid out of his way and cracked him on the back of his neck with the metal handle of his stick, immediately dropping him to the floor dazed.

Next up was Darrell's bearded friend, the same man who had triumphantly thumped his opponent outside of the bar to much acclaim. Newly aware of the danger in charging Turner, the bearded man chose to throw a long, powerful punch. Turner dodged the punch with the slightest head movement and then hooked the man's leg. The giant tumbled down on his back like a pile of lumber, shaking the floor and walls of the bar.

Without the slightest acknowledgment of what had just transpired, Turner pivoted toward Albert and Ying.

"Friends, since we have our directions and seem to have made a bit of a mess, it is probably time for us to make our exit."

And with that, the old professor took a ten-dollar bill from his wallet, placed it on the bar, and exited while holding the door for his two colleagues.

As Ying and Albert scrambled to the car, Turner looked over to Ying, whose face stared directly at him, frozen in awe.

He chuckled as he readjusted his tweed coat. "Ms. Koh, I bet you're still wondering about that riddle we were working on in the car?"

"Wha—?"

"The logic puzzle. Well, I'll tell you the answer. The man pushing his car up to the hotel and the hotel owner ..."

"Yeah?" said Ying, still trying to recover from what had just transpired.

"They're two gentlemen playing a game of Monopoly."

CHAPTER 5

Cristina Culebra hung up the phone and barked at her assistant.

"Lexi! Who's next?"

Her assistant scurried into the office from the other room.

"Eric Crabtree is here to see you."

Cristina leaned her head against her white, high-back leather chair. She knew what this meeting was about. Another battle with an inferior opponent.

"Fine. Send him in."

She grabbed the pen on her desk and began clicking it, an old habit from her college days. She looked out her office's floor-to-ceiling windows. She watched the Pacific Ocean sway back and forth, and calculated her approach.

Crabtree was Cristina's speechwriter. He had joined the campaign right after working as an assistant speechwriter in the White House office of communications. In the president's second term, Crabtree had seen the writing on the wall and hitched his wagon to Cristina's campaign. His soaring speeches had helped catapult Cristina to stardom. Today, he was here to cash in on his success.

The speechwriter walked in the office and Cristina looked at her watch. 2:00 p.m. exactly. She had to give him credit. He knew her well. She abhorred tardiness because it revealed a disorganized mind. Yet she had equal disdain for those who arrived early, as it reflected inefficiency.

"What do you have for me, Eric?" asked Cristina, not looking up from her computer screen. Eric craved approval, so for this conversation Cristina would give him none of it.

"I've got the latest draft of the closing argument for you."

"Good. Let's have a look," said Cristina, finally glancing up from her computer.

"Before we do that, I'd like to discuss something else with you."

Cristina looked at Eric with a knowing smirk and positioned herself in her chair like a tiger settling in for a meal.

"Oh really? What is it you'd like to discuss?" she said, placing the pad of her long, thin pointer finger on her lips.

Cristina watched as Eric carefully absorbed the look on his candidate's face. She could see the instant that he knew he had grossly underestimated his opponent in this negotiation. But he had come too far to stop.

"I—I'd like to discuss the position that I'll have in your administration when you are elected."

Cristina made one simple movement—taking her index finger from the tip of her lips to the side of her cheek. She said nothing. She allowed the silence in the massive office to drive Eric forward, goading him into continuing like a palm pressing him in the back.

"I think I've more than proven myself as a speechwriter and that it's only appropriate for me to be awarded the position of head of communications in the new administration," said Eric, now barely able to stifle cracks in his voice. "And if you don't think that's fair, then—"

"Eric, let me stop you right there," interjected Cristina, rising from her desk and looking out the windows of her magnificent office.

She paused as if to decide what approach to take with the impudent challenger, but she had already made the decision. "Oh, Eriiiic. In the back of my mind, I always knew this day would come, but a part of me hoped you would contain your ambition just a bit longer."

The speechwriter looked around him as though a SWAT team were coming through the door. He interlocked his fingers, sliding them back and forth together.

"Let me guess," said Cristina, now turning to face her protégé. "You were planning on using our final campaign speech as your bargaining chip to secure the communications job. If I didn't give you the job, then you were going to withhold the speech. Is that about right?"

The speechwriter continued to wriggle in his chair but said nothing.

"I thought so. See, the problem, Eric, is that you don't understand one very simple truth about me. And that is that whatever you are plotting at any given moment, I've thought of, months and sometimes years in advance. You must remember, Eric . . . I grew up on a farm. And when you grow up on a farm, the seasons are everything. You plan for the winter, plan for the harvest, plan for the rain, and plan for the drought. Now, only God can create the weather, Eric . . . so if I can handle him, I can certainly handle you."

"No, no, I just wanted you to know I was interested in the job, ma'am. I had no intention of withholding the speech."

"You see, Eric, I knew you would try to weasel your way out of this. Just like I know you hit on Lexi multiple times, just like I know you lied on your resumé, and just like I know that in your weakest moments, you seek the companionship of older men because they flatter and spoil you."

Eric sat motionless. His body sat bolted to the chair in stark embarrassment and horror.

Cristina glared at him and then smiled, knowing that she had achieved her intended effect.

"Now, why don't you hand me the latest draft of the speech, and we'll forget about this whole incident." She held out her hand and summoned her politician's smile.

The speechwriter fumbled through his bag, stood, and with shaking hands, handed over the draft of the speech. Eyes locked on the floor, he then turned to leave the room; his shoulders carried a newfound weight.

"Oh ... and, Eric. If your ambition ever creeps up into your head again, just understand one thing ..."

"Yes?" said the defeated speechwriter.

"Politics is a team sport."

CHAPTER 6

What the hell was that?" shouted Albert as the car sliced through the rain-covered highway, spraying a steady mist around the tires.

"Yeah, Professor Turner. That was ridiculous. You were like a ninja in there," echoed Ying.

The corners of Turner's lips crept upward. "Ah, so now you admit that the old man may have a few tricks up his sleeve? I told you . . . the Tree of Knowledge is an incredibly powerful tool if you are willing to believe in its potential and learn how to use it."

"I see what you mean now, Professor," exclaimed Ying. "It looked like everything was moving in slow motion for you. Like you knew exactly what they were going to do."

"You mean to tell me you got those moves from the decision tree we've been talking about?" said Albert in disbelief.

"Well, yes and no. It is one thing to know what you have to do, but quite another to execute. That is where our friends here in lovely Vermont come in."

"I'm not following," said Albert.

Turner adjusted in the driver's seat and slid his hands across the leather steering wheel. The steady clatter of rain on the windshield sounded in the background. "As I mentioned, years ago, I realized I could use the Tree for self-defense. As was my habit I ventured to test my hypothesis. So, on one Saturday morning, I strolled down to that quaint little martial arts dojo on Carlton Street."

"You mean House of Jiujitsu," said Ying through a disbelieving smile.

"Yes, fortunately, the instructor was in the dojo, but was not holding any classes. I remember him vividly to this day. Kojuki Sensei. He was a small, compact man, no less than forty years old, with a kind face. I explained to him I was from the university, was conducting an experiment with a new self-defense technique, and was wondering if he would spar with me. Truthfully, he looked at me a little askance, but he eventually agreed to play along.

"Now, back then, I was not the doddering old man with a cane that I am today," Turner said with a self-deprecating grin. "I was probably fifty then, but I was fit as a fiddle and quite strong. Armed with the knowledge of the Tree, I eyed the tiny man in front of me, and I must admit I fell victim to that most irrational of feelings: overconfidence."

Albert nodded.

"I looked at Kojuki and guessed what I thought he was likely to do and the steps I would take to thwart him, and so we began. Of course, you can imagine how the battle between me, a man with no self-defense training, and a black belt in jiujitsu turned out. Kojuki soundly beat me in a matter of seconds. I tried again and again to defeat him, but his reflexes, balance, and technique were impeccable, and he dispatched me with ease. Out of respect, he maintained a serious demeanor, but I could tell he was laughing inside. It wasn't enough to understand what a man was likely to do in a fight and what the response should be; one must train the body to implement that knowledge in an instant.

"I reached out to my friend Sergeant Travis. I knew that if I were going to maximize the Tree's power in self-defense, I would need training from someone of the highest caliber, and a total commitment to secrecy. Fortunately, shortly before my beating at the hands of Kojuki Sensei, I had delivered a cryptography lecture at a cybersecurity conference and met Sergeant Travis. Travis is widely considered the father of modern hand-to-hand combat. He's a former sergeant first class Army ranger who literally wrote the manual on modern combatives. After several tours of duty, he tired of the rough and tumble and moved to a beautiful old farm in Washington, Vermont."

"So, you've been trained by a Special Forces guy," said Ying, propping herself up in the rear seat and leaning her head in between the two professors.

"I'm getting there, Ms. Koh," said Turner with slight impatience. He enjoyed spinning a yarn and didn't particularly appreciate interruptions.

"As I was saying, I called Sergeant Travis and explained to him I was doing some research on hand-to-hand combat and was wondering if he'd teach me a thing or two. He agreed, and over the next few years, we trained regularly. He would share his knowledge of combat and give me training programs to utilize in his absence, and I would occasionally give him my insights from the Tree. Not the whole Tree methodology, mind you, but I created various exercises that I thought might improve cadets' rational thinking and help in the field. We've been friends ever since."

Albert stared absently at the professor. During Turner's story, he had been absorbing what was being said, but in a state of dreamlike removal. His rational gray matter couldn't accept that this kind old professor, whom he'd known for years, could moonlight as a Special Forces–trained brawler—one who could physically defeat three bar thugs like children.

Albert couldn't stop himself from laughing. It all seemed so absurd.

"So, how good a fighter are you, Angus? I must admit that was a pretty impressive display in the bar, back there."

"I'm really quite good," said Turner. "In the vast majority of situations, I will be able to defeat my opponent and, normally, multiple opponents. Where I would have difficulty is against an enemy who was both younger than I am and well trained. For example, Sergeant Travis would defeat me easily. Luckily, we have the Book Club on our side, so I don't expect us having a problem."

"How long are we going to hide from the police?"

"We're not hiding from the *police*, Albert," Turner snapped.

He pulled the Buick over to the shoulder of the road, shifted the car into neutral, and looked out the driver's side window. His sudden change in demeanor shook Albert and Ying.

"I'm afraid I haven't been completely honest with both of you. I was trying to protect you, but . . . Albert . . . the people who hold my journal hold the key to absolute power. Do you understand? Absolute power. Fortunately, they haven't been able to decipher it yet. The only reason you and I are alive right now is because they decided they wanted us alive. But at some point, that will change, and when that day comes, I won't be able to stop them alone, and neither will the police. And if they are coming for me, then that means they are coming for you, and there will be no classroom, no place that will be safe from them. Our only hope is for you two to lay low out here with us while we figure out how to get that book back and clear your name.

"If you stay close and keep an open mind, you might learn something."

CHAPTER 7

I*t'll all be over soon*, thought Eva as she opened the door to the underground R&D lab. Eva loathed the "code lab", as they called it. Deep under the ground and completely devoid of natural light, the code lab reeked of confinement and isolation, two of Eva's least favorite words. The woman in the black pinstripe suit took shallow breaths through her mouth to prevent the dank, musty smell from seeping into her nostrils. As she walked along the cold, rugged cement floor and approached the two men in front of her, she attempted to mask her scowl.

Eva nodded at the gaunt military man and the corpulent scientist in front of her. "General . . . Dr. Belial . . . how are you?"

"I would be better if the burglary at Princeton weren't front-page news," said the scientist in his nasal lisp. Every movement the cryptographer made, from his heavy nose breathing to the sweat under his double chin, screamed of ill health. Eva found this repulsive and representative of a profound character flaw. That Belial levied criticism at everyone but himself heightened her disdain.

"You let me worry about the issue with the police, Doctor. You worry about cracking that code," snarled Eva.

"Yes, Doctor," growled Moloch. "Give us a summary of your progress."

Belial snorted as if reporting on progress were beneath him, but then continued in his sardonic manner. "Well, thanks to the fine work of Ms. Fix here, we now have the book that we need. Unfortunately, it is written in an extremely complex cipher. I might be able to solve it—*if* I don't get any more interruptions from detectives." He paused and threw a smug gaze at Eva and Moloch. "However, I have grave concerns about moving forward with this project due to all the public scrutiny."

"What did you just say?" countered Eva, her voice reaching a crescendo.

Once again, Moloch intervened. "What are you getting at, Doctor?"

"Well, the whole point of us stealing the book was so that nobody could trace it back to us, but now, because of Ms. Fix's bumbling, people know. In addition, it will be difficult to solve the cipher unless I have the entire book. You've given me a mere five pages."

"Doctor, I appreciate your concerns, but the only people that know of the theft of the Tree are the people in this room, an overmatched police officer in Princeton, and a couple of fugitives who will be behind bars or dead shortly. I assure you, everything is well in hand. As far as the book is concerned, five pages will have to do. The full text is far too sensitive to share and will remain in my safekeeping for now."

The large, lizard-like scientist with the patchy hair adjusted his tie. "I don't know, General," he said, rubbing his scaly hands in dramatic fashion. "Maybe if my compensation for this project weren't so limited, I could take the risk."

Eva crossed her arms to prevent them from reaching out and choking Belial.

Moloch smiled a shallow, yellow-toothed grin, and his eyes glittered. "Ah, so that's what this is about ... money ... You want more money?"

"It might help grease the wheels," said Belial, now slightly unnerved by the general's sneer.

"Well, you have completed most of the job, correct? I mean, you know what type of cipher it is, right?"

The scientist nodded his head and began rubbing his hands.

In an instant, Moloch's smile vanished, and he reached into his military jacket to produce a black service revolver. "Then what do we need you for?"

He held the revolver up to Belial's temple and discharged a single shot.

The crack echoed throughout the subterranean laboratory and was followed by the sickening sound of the scientist's body crashing against the cement.

Eva flinched from the specks of blood spattering her face, then stood motionless. No decision tree would produce this result. The Society would never approve of this. This was madness.

Moloch placed his pistol in its holster and moved his tall, steely frame toward the exit of the code lab. The staff watched his every move in horror. As he passed Eva, he put his arm around her shoulder, guiding her to walk with him. She could feel the weight of his bones around her neck. The general ate very little. He reminded Eva of a reanimated skeleton, like some sort of grim reaper.

He removed a handkerchief from his coat pocket and wiped the blood from her face. "You're probably wondering why I killed that poor excuse for a human being. It wasn't in today's decision tree, was it? Well, if there is one thing I know, it is people. And that was a person who would have been a problem for us. He believed we needed him. And when someone thinks you need him, that's when he starts walking all over you. One thing I can't have—I won't have—in my unit is people walking all over me. You understand?"

Eva nodded, not trusting herself to speak. She had disliked Belial intensely, but his death was hardly a comfort. She hadn't quite admitted to herself before this that Moloch was a psychopath. He was just logical, she had thought. But it was not logic that drove Moloch to shoot Belial. It was something far less predictable. *Would she be next?*

"Now, what's the status on your boy Puddles and that Professor Turner? Have the police got them yet?"

Eva shook her head and swallowed, attempting to regain her voice. "Um, no—no, they haven't. Apparently, they've gone missing."

Moloch pivoted and grabbed Eva by both shoulders. "I find that extremely disappointing, Fix. Until Puddles is in jail or dead, he's a threat to us. I want you to call one of your buddies down at the FBI and get this wrapped up." He released his grip and turned to walk away. "I don't want to kill that professor of yours, Fix, but if he remains a threat, I'll be forced to. Understood?"

Eva whispered, "Yes, sir."

CHAPTER 8

The Travis Farm rolled and tumbled across the Vermont countryside in bucolic splendor. The term "farm" was a bit of a misnomer since the land yielded no crops and was overgrown with woods. The white-and-gray farmhouse stood atop the hill like a watchtower.

As Turner's Buick pulled up the dirt road to the weathered wood gate, Albert immediately sensed the powerful loneliness of the countryside. It was now three o'clock in the morning and the rain had stopped, but the trees slowly, ominously dripped rainwater. Through his cracked window, he could hear the song of crickets and other unknown creatures in the woods. The gate's callbox stood alone under a single light in the darkness, a light that was steadily and constantly being devoured by the maples above.

Turner pushed the intercom button, setting off a loud buzz. Silence. He tried a second and third time.

"Who is it?" barked a voice over the intercom.

"Sergeant Travis, I'm so sorry to disturb you at this ungodly hour, but I'm in a bit of a pickle."

"Turner?"

"Yes, dear friend. Do you mind letting us in?"

"Ha, this is a first. Of course, sir. Come on in." The gravel voice paused and chuckled.

"But first, as punishment for waking me up so damn late, you have to pass a little test. The main house is down one of three roads, but you have to guess the right road. One road leads to the main house, and the other two lead to maintenance sheds."

"Ah, the shoe is on the other foot, now," said Turner with a grin.

Albert did nothing to disguise his irritation. "Angus, it's three in the morning. Are we seriously playing a guessing game, right now?"

Turner put a conspiratorial hand on Albert's shoulder. "Don't worry, my boy, it's merely payback for my teaching him about the Monty Hall game."

"What's the Monty Hall game?" asked Ying.

"It's a probability puzzle based on the game show *Let's Make a Deal*," said Albert.

"Oh, you mean the show with Wayne Brady? That's good television."

"Who's Wayne Brady?"

"I think we're getting off point here," interjected Turner. "The point is that there is a game show called *Let's Make a Deal* that was originally hosted by Monty Hall, and is now apparently hosted by Wayne Brady. In the show, contestants are given different opportunities to select prizes or trade those prizes for a potentially better prize. One particular version of the game is a wonderful veridical paradox."

Albert added, "That's a situation in which the result of a problem seems to go against common sense—"

"But is mathematically true. Yes, I'm aware," said Ying.

Turner resumed. "In this particular game, you as the contestant are asked to choose between one of three doors. Behind one door is a brand-new Mercedes; behind each of the other doors are goats. You first pick a door—say it's door number one—but the door is not opened, and the host, who knows what's behind the doors, opens another door, say door number three, which has a goat. He then says to you, 'Would you like to switch to door number two or keep your original choice?' Is it to your advantage to switch your choice?"

Ying thought back to her days in undergraduate statistics. She was a little rusty. "Ahhh, yes, I remember this one . . . it seems like it's a fifty-fifty choice, because there're two doors left. But it's not."

"Once again, Ms. Koh is at the head of the class," said Turner with a glint in his eye. He pivoted to the speaker box and said, "We'll take road number one."

"Road number three leads to the maintenance shed and shooting range. Would you like to stick with your original choice or choose road number two?" squawked the box.

Albert shook his head. He was tired, and the last thing he wanted to do at three in the morning was go through an old math puzzle that he barely remembered.

Ying plowed ahead unfazed. "I got this one, Professor. Let me talk this out. When you first pick door number one, there is a one-third chance that it is the door with the car, right? Well, then it logically follows that there is a two-thirds chance it is not behind door number one and that the car is behind doors two or three. Correct?"

"Correct."

"Then, continuing on that logical path, when the host shows you that door number three does not have a car behind it, but we know that there is a two-thirds chance the car is behind either door two or door three, then there is now a two-thirds chance it is behind door number two since we now know for a fact that it's not behind door number three. Consequently, we should choose to switch to road number two because there is a two-thirds chance road two is the correct road and only a one-third chance that road one is the correct road."

"Correct again," grunted the speaker, and the gates opened.

"You're welcome, Albert," said Ying.

Albert raised his hands in mock enthusiasm. "Thank you so much. Can we go now?"

"Yes, we can go, you big stick-in-the-mud," said Turner. "Well done, Ms. Koh."

Turner took road number two through the blinding darkness. Upon reaching the main house and exiting the car, he pulled Ying and Albert aside.

He whispered, "Just so you know, Sergeant Travis is a military man who's lived hard and does not put much stock in pleasantries and small talk, so if he seems somewhat gruff and rude, don't take it personally, and *don't* try to small talk him or soften him up. He won't appreciate your efforts."

The two nodded their consent, and as they entered the large wood building, both Ying and Albert knew exactly what Turner had meant.

Standing before them in the middle of a beautiful great room was a man who resembled a monument more than a human being. To his left crackled a blazing fire. The flames lit up his face and skin as though he had been created out of molten rock and the left side of his body was just now cooling off. His face was that of a man in his late forties, but a rugged strength belied those years. He wore brown boots, starched jeans, and a shirt that clung to him like a second skin. Underneath him was a rug made of an animal skin that Albert couldn't readily recognize, and he was flanked by leather couches from a time when men smoked cigars, drank brandy, and thought great thoughts.

"Hello, Sergeant. Thank you so much for taking us in," said Turner, offering a fake salute and scampering over to the man of rock.

"It's good to see you, Professor," said Sergeant Travis, though his face provided no hint of pleasure or welcome.

"Sergeant Brick Travis, I'd like to introduce you to two of my colleagues: Ying Koh and Dr. Albert Puddles."

Despite himself, as he approached the sergeant to shake his hand, Albert let out a small smirk.

"Is something funny, Doctor?" asked Travis, grabbing Albert's hand and bringing it toward him in a way that made Albert yearn for the crushing shake of Detective Weatherspoon.

"I'm sorry, is your name really Brick? It just sounds like something out of *G.I. Joe*," said Albert, looking around to Turner and Ying like a comedian searching for a laugh from his audience. The second the words dropped from his lips, Albert realized his mouth had disassociated from his brain. This occasionally happened when he was nervous, but until right now, he had thought he was overcoming it.

Brick stared at Albert without smiling and replied, "Real name's Jeremy, but you can call me Brick. Is your name really Puddles?" He still gripped Albert's hand like a vise.

Albert had to admit the sergeant had gotten the better of him, but the pressure in his hand—and his attempt not to yelp—made any response impossible. The silence between the two men was fortunately interrupted by a loud guffaw from Ying.

Brick gave Albert one more long look up and down as if he were sizing up a recruit that he knew would take some work and then turned to Ying.

Ying smiled and gave a dramatic mock curtsy.

Just as he had seen so many times before, Albert watched as a man made of power and stone turned into a teddy bear around

Ying Koh. Brick turned to Ying and said, "Welcome, ma'am," in a soft voice, and shook her hand gently.

"Brick, I'm sorry I had to be so brief with you on the intercom, but we are in a spot of trouble and I'm afraid I couldn't get into the details," said Turner.

"I figured," said Brick. "Why don't we have a seat and you can give me the lowdown."

"Albert, since you have been the hub around which the story spins, why don't you do the honors."

Albert laid his eyes upon Brick one more time and attempted to gather his thoughts. It was clear that Brick would not appreciate any artistic embellishments in storytelling.

He gulped and began his tale. "Yesterday morning, I received an unexpected visit from the police. A burglary, which turned into a murder, had been committed at the Bank of Princeton. In the struggle with the thief before he died, the security guard snatched a paper from the thief's pocket."

Albert briefed Travis on the details of the last few days until the military man raised his hand to interrupt.

"Did you say she took out the entire police station?"

"Correct."

This piece of information clearly piqued Brick's interest. Albert was slightly flattered that he had shared something interesting enough to capture the attention of a man who fought battles for a living.

"We knew that if the police found me, they would arrest me and potentially worse, and so Angus suggested we come here, collect ourselves, and make a plan to clear my name and expose the truth about Eva."

"Eva? You don't mean Eva Fix?" questioned Brick, his eyes narrowing and a rough emotion evident in his voice.

"Yeah, that's right," responded Albert. "Do you know her?"

Brick rose from the couch and bolted the door. He gazed into the darkness and turned to the rest of the group. "Have you all turned off the power on your cell phones, laptops, etcetera?"

Turner and the rest of the group nodded.

"Angus, have you called the Book Club?"

"Yes. Gabe, Raphael, and Ariel are on their way."

"Gentlemen and lady, I suggest you get some sleep, because you're in much deeper than you thought."

CHAPTER 9

When Albert finally collapsed into the immaculately made bed that Brick had provided to him, every part of his body cried out in happiness. The sensation of the mattress and soft pillow propping up his weary muscles and strained neck was so sublime that Albert hoped sleep would never come; he simply wanted to bathe in slumber. Still, his mind refused to rest. Ideas and images danced in and out of his head like flames in a fire. Eva, the Tree, Turner fighting, the fear in Ying's eyes, his own panic. He thought of his parents. How he wished he had called them. About his friends, about the school. Would they believe his story? He wondered if he would ever sleep, now that his life had changed.

But he did sleep. And when he slept, he dreamed. And when he dreamed, he saw one image: Eva.

She sat beside him swathed in white lace, looking up at him with those charcoal eyes and holding his hand with the rare blend of delicacy, devotion, and trust offered by a woman deeply in love. Albert returned her gaze with a pursed smile and a twinkle in his eyes, then stood and turned to his guests, who were anxiously clinking their forks on their wineglasses.

He wore a tuxedo, but unlike the cheap rentals that he rented for his friends' weddings, the coat and pants fit him as though they could never know another owner. The tailored fit made him a man. He ran his hands across the luxurious satin lapel and slid his left hand in the front pocket to reach for his glasses, but realized that he didn't have any—yet he could see perfectly.

Standing at the center of the crowded dais with his loving bride by his side, he looked at the aesthetic spectacle that was his wedding. The event was held outside on a flagstone patio under a full moon. The men wore tuxedos, and the beautifully coiffed women wore elegant gowns and sparkling jewels. In one direction, an emerald lawn sloped down to a white-sand beach, gently lapped by the waves of what he knew was a warm ocean; in the other, a mansion of honey-colored stone dominated the sky. The dinner tables and dance floor were flanked by gently gurgling fountains, the water flowing from the mouths of carved nymphs and fauns. Each table glittered with china, silver, and crystal beneath the light of the candelabra. Intricate flower arrangements adorned every spare surface. As Albert looked out at his friends and mentors, he was transformed. Suddenly, the staring eyes, which had so haunted him in the past, shone with admiration and envy. A holistic calm replaced the uncertainty and impatience he had previously felt around women and men of power. He realized that while he was present in this space, he somehow hovered beyond himself. He felt completely at ease in his own skin but also deeply understood how his guests perceived him.

And at this moment, standing in front of the microphone, about to make a grand toast at his even grander wedding, he was being perceived as a man of consequence. He imagined that this must have been how James Bond felt as he calmly smoked cigarettes, played baccarat, and traded witty repartee with the glamorous and dangerous. The tangible wave of admiration that surrounded him produced a crush of happiness that Albert had never experienced, and as he looked back at Eva, noticing how her crisp white gown contrasted brilliantly with her shimmering dark skin, he wished this night would never end.

On this night, the man of consequence spoke with passion and heart. He skillfully spun the story of how he and Eva had met in Professor Turner's class at Princeton. He carefully intertwined self-deprecating jokes with poetic admiration for his wife, until he knew that his guests truly understood that theirs was a love most people dream of.

And as he concluded his toast, Albert looked to his left and saw his parents. They were together, and they were happy. He traded a knowing glance with his father, who raised a champagne glass and winked.

The next thing he knew, Albert was in the hotel suite looking into the mirror and untying his tuxedo's bow tie. It had been a glorious evening. Speeches, congratulations, dancing, music, the perfumed air. The large room was immaculately appointed, and rose petals drifted on the floor and bed. He could hear Eva's humming from the bathroom as he calmly popped the bottle of champagne and smiled back at himself in unvarnished contentment.

The bathroom door opened, and Albert turned to give his new wife one of the champagne flutes. He immediately spilled half the glass in stunned disbelief when he saw what was in front of him.

Eva stood before Albert in an exquisite white satin corset and stockings brandishing a giant, glistening butcher's knife. Her blood-red lips parted in a smile, and she fondled the pearls of her necklace in an expression of visceral menace. As Albert looked at her, his shock fading, he felt no fear, only sadness. Earlier in the dream, while he danced and drank the night away with his new bride, Albert had known that it couldn't be truly real, that this feeling could not endure. He had hoped it would last longer, but he shrugged and accepted that his bliss had now come to an end.

The woman in white plunged the butcher's blade into his stomach, and as Albert cried out, she gently touched his lips to shush him. Sharp burning spread through Albert's chest as Eva calmly guided him to the ground. He looked down and could see the bright-red blood, so gloriously vivid, so alive against the white placket of his tuxedo shirt. Tears seeped down his cheeks, but Albert felt no physical pain. Looking at Eva one last time, he closed his eyes and lay still, as death crawled over him . . .

And then he awoke.

For a moment, Albert did not know where he was, how he got there, or what had happened to him. He only knew heartache. Acidic, unrelenting heartache. And as he stared up at the ceiling of the old farmhouse and slowly recognized his whereabouts—his immediate past, his future—he shook in silence.

CHAPTER 10

Albert crept out of his room to grab a glass of water, or something stronger, hoping to forget his dream. As he made his way down the carpeted hallway, he could hear hushed voices trading jabs in the night. The hallway leading from Albert's room opened into a mezzanine that looked over the great room. He pressed himself against the wall and stood on his tiptoes to avoid being seen by the guests below. He tilted forward to catch a glimpse.

Five people sat neatly arranged around the fire engaged in intense but quiet discussion. In the center sat Turner, and directly across from him sat Brick and a woman of such height that she looked like a picture that had been scaled up twenty-five percent.

On Turner's left was a bowling ball of a man in a cowboy hat. Jolliness bounced from every body part. His flannel-clad belly was jolly. His oversized mustache was jolly. Even the toothpick in his mouth bobbed around like it was in on the joke. Behind this jolliness lurked an unseen power. It was the eyes. Underneath the smile and the oversized hat, the eyes were always watching, assessing, waiting to spring.

The man on Turner's right carried no secrets. He vaguely resembled a rodent, but a kind rodent, more like a hamster than a rat. His receding hairline accentuated his narrow face and sloped jawline, and his keen eyes spoke of compassion. While he sat in a wheelchair, he was not weak. The T-shirt he wore beneath his unbuttoned button-down shirt revealed the toned physique of an athlete and a soldier. Albert wondered how the man had become imprisoned in his wheeled cell.

Brick spoke first. "Our top priority has to be getting back that book. We can worry about your two friends later. But we're going to need a bigger team than just the five of us if we're going to get into Fix Industries. Angus, who else can we bring in on this?"

Turner stood and paced the room. "No one. You four are the only ones who know about the Tree intimately, and we can't risk bringing anyone else in on it. Plus, we don't have time."

The man in the wheelchair spoke next. "I understand that, Professor, but can't we bring in some ex–Special Forces people to help us get into Fix headquarters? They don't need to know about the Tree. We can just tell them it's an important state secret. I'm sure Brick knows some mercenaries that won't ask a lot of questions."

Brick shook his head. "No, we need someone with no law enforcement or military affiliation. Fix has moles and contacts in every department. If we start recruiting a team, the cat is out of the bag, and we're toast."

Silence hovered over the room while the Book Club pondered the next move.

Finally, the blonde woman spoke. "Why don't we use them?" She pointed upstairs.

"Who, the nutty professor?" scoffed Brick.

"Yes. The nutty professor. And the girl. Think about it. Angus, haven't you always said that only a savant can harness the true power of the Tree? Well, we've got two mental calculators sitting upstairs, right? We're talking about bringing in outside people who we can't trust when we've got the two people we need right here."

"This is crazy," said Gabe, wheeling away from the circle. "I'm sure your two friends are wonderful, very smart people, but they've never been in any kind of combat operation in their lives."

The blonde woman leaned forward in her chair. "So, we teach them. Angus, you can teach them about the Tree. Brick, you can teach them hand-to-hand. Raphael, you can teach 'em to shoot; Gabe, you can show them a few of your toys; and I can give them a crash course on psyops."

The bowling ball with the toothpick leaned forward. "This is a little bit crazy . . . but I like it. We got a few weeks before they crack the code, right? I can do shooting and explosives in a week. We can make this happen. Whatchya think, Professor?"

"I can't believe I'm saying this, but it might be the best option we've got."

CHAPTER 11

"Ugh," grumbled Detective Weatherspoon as he slumped into his desk chair at the police station.

The digital clock on his cluttered desk showed ten a.m., but the burly detective already wanted to go home. He had approached the station this morning eager to get back to work after his brief stint in the hospital, but before he could get through the door, the local media mobbed him, hungry for the latest gossip on the "Princeton Station Massacre", as it was being called. Weatherspoon had attempted to explain that no one had died in the Princeton Station Massacre, but the reporters seemed to find that statement of fact irrelevant, if not downright annoying. He had tried to ignore the mob as he entered the station, but their ridiculous questions still seeped into his brain: "Did you see this coming? Did you identify the attacker's face? Was al-Qaeda involved?"

Weatherspoon had answered with a curt "No", "No", and "What are you, an idiot?"

Things got worse as he entered the station. A daunting barricade of balloons, flowers, and get-well cards surrounded his desk, and every person in the station felt the need to check in on his health and emotional well-being.

The men said things like "How you feelin', champ?" or "Man, if I ever get my hands on the guy who did this . . ." The women asked, "Are you alright, sweetheart? We were so worried about you." or offered encouragement: "I'm sure you'll track down the murderer in no time."

The one good thing about all these balloons is at least now I've got a place to hide out.

The detective's hope vanished when he saw a long, suit-clad arm reach through the sea of balloons. Weatherspoon glanced up to see what fool dared to break his balloon wall of peace.

In front of his desk stood a young, short, clean-cut blond man in a modern, overly tight blue suit. The man wore black Wayfarer sunglasses despite the dim lighting inside the station. A woman in an all-black pants suit with dark, luminescent eyes stood to his left.

"Detective Weatherspoon?"

"Yes."

"I'm Special Agent Scott Beel. FBI. Do you have a moment?"

"Do I have a choice?"

The agent smirked. "Not really." He pulled up a chair but spun it around backward so that he was straddling the front. The woman in black quietly sat down next to him and placed her fedora on his desk.

"Detective, we have reason to believe that the gentleman who attacked your police station the other day is the same man who robbed the Bank of Princeton, and whom we also suspect of other related crimes."

"Oh, really," said Weatherspoon, raising an eyebrow. "And who do you think this man is?"

The agent slid his chair closer to Weatherspoon's desk and leaned in. "I think you already know."

Weatherspoon leaned right back. "I might, but I'd like to hear you tell me."

Eva sighed and rolled her eyes, stretching out one Chanel-clad foot and flexing it. It was clear she had little patience for turf wars. "Detective, we believe that a Princeton professor named Albert Puddles has stolen several national treasures and committed the murder at the bank."

"I'm sorry, who are you?" asked Weatherspoon, growing increasingly uncomfortable with the exchange. The woman was neither intimidated by the setting nor appropriately businesslike. In fact, she wore an expression of faint amusement, as if the station were her playground.

"My name is Eva Fix. I'm the head of security for Fix Industries. We believe that Dr. Puddles has stolen our intellectual property. We have been working closely with the FBI on this case and have a major interest in determining his whereabouts."

"I'm sure you do," said Weatherspoon evenly, rising from his swivel chair, which spun and slid a half-dozen inches. "Would you two excuse me for a minute?"

The detective stormed into his captain's office and slammed the door.

"Pete, what the hell are they doing here?" he shouted, pointing at the two unwelcome visitors through the glass office.

Captain Willard glanced up from his paperwork and took off his glasses. He massaged the bridge of his nose with his bony forefinger. "Who's 'they'?"

"You know who I'm talking about. Sonny and Cher sitting at my desk."

The captain grumbled and returned his eyes to his paperwork. "Some big muckety-mucks in DC want this case resolved, so they sent an agent down. Just play nice and keep them in the loop."

"But don't you think it's a little odd that an FBI agent and a defense contractor are taking an interest in a murder-burglary here?"

The captain had known Michael Weatherspoon long enough to sense that the detective wasn't going to go away until he got his full attention, so once again, he took off his glasses, stood up, put both hands on the table, and leaned over with a full glare. His bright-blue eyes held Weatherspoon's.

"Look, of course I think it's odd. But apparently this guy Puddles has stolen defense secrets, so she and the FBI are very interested. I don't know the details, and I don't want to know. All they're asking right now is for us to keep them informed so that they can be helpful if necessary. And since the professor has probably crossed state lines, we're likely going to need them, anyway."

Weatherspoon knew when his friend was pulling rank. "OK, but I'm telling you, Pete, there's something going on here."

The captain just grunted and returned to his reports.

Weatherspoon stomped back to his desk, but continued standing so that his visitors knew that the conversation was over. Through gritted teeth, he stated, "I appreciate you two coming down. I will be sure to keep you in the loop." He handed out two business cards from the stack on his desk. "Here's my card. Please feel free to call me if you need anything." Then he made his face as blank and forbidding as he could to make sure they knew he didn't mean a word of it.

The detective watched Agent Beel open his mouth in protest and then shut it like a mousetrap with the simple touch of Eva Fix's hand on his shoulder.

She cracked a gentle smile. "Thank you so much for your time, Detective. We'll get out of your hair, now."

The former offensive tackle reclaimed his desk chair and watched the odd couple exit the station.

Something's not right there.

***

Outside the station, Agent Beel fumed. "Why did you let him run over us like that?"

Eva kept walking to the car without looking back. "Because that old cop wasn't going to let us in without a lot of effort and time that we don't have. Besides, we've got his cell phone number, which is all we need. Haven't you and the boys down at the FBI ever heard of a phone tap?"

CHAPTER 12

Albert rose from his bed and stretched his back, which felt like it had been beaten with sticks in the middle of the night. His coddled body was not used to the less than robust support provided by the Travis Farm's twin guest bed. Looking out the small cross-paned window of his room, Albert noticed that the macabre drip of the farm at night had given way to a lush morning light reminiscent of the horse farms outside of Northfield. He could smell the rich scent of goldenrod mixed with a faint aroma of eggs and bacon. He heard the bubbling of Ying's voice below blended with the hum of men's laughter and hurried downstairs to see what he was missing.

As he crossed the threshold of the Travis Farm's kitchen, he couldn't help feeling that he had stumbled into a sequel of *The Big Chill*. There, sitting and laughing over breakfast at a round cherry-wood kitchen table, was the odd assortment of people from the night before. And at the center of it all was Ying, enthusiastically recounting a story in the fully animated way that was her trademark, with the entire table doubled over in laughter.

Albert's eyes first met those of Brick, who converted his broad smile into a menacing frown. Witnessing the sharp change in

Sergeant Travis's face, Turner and the man in the wheelchair stopped laughing and pivoted to see their new guest.

"Maaan, you got some bad taste in ladies, amigo," shouted the man in the cowboy hat with a smile.

After holding their faces in ill-disguised seriousness, the entire table burst out laughing while looking at Albert.

Albert smiled the confused smile of a man who knew that a joke was in the offing but had no clue what the joke was. Slowly, he approached the table, socks slipping and sliding along the hardwood floor.

Mercifully, Ying shattered Albert's befuddlement. "I'm sorry, Albert. I was just telling the guys here about how the one girl with a crush on you framed you for murder."

More laughter.

"I'm glad you all get so much joy out of that story."

"Oh, don't be so sensitive, Puddles. So, you got your ass kicked by a girl. It's probably not the first time, and I'm sure it won't be the last," said Brick with an unsympathetic smirk.

"Why don't you join us for breakfast, Albert, and we'll introduce you to our new friends here," said Turner.

Albert reluctantly joined them at the table and dutifully shook hands while pulling out a backless chair.

Turner began, "This, Albert, is the Book Club. The man beside you is Gabe Abernathy."

Albert carefully sized up the man next to him.

"Gabe knows more about cyber-intelligence than anyone in the game. He and Sergeant Travis met in the Green Zone in Iraq and have been friends ever since. He will teach you how to use technology to maximize the Tree's impact during your training."

"I'm sorry, did you say training?"

"Of course. I've spoken more with Sergeant Travis and the rest of the club here about our situation, and it seems that things are even more dire than we expected. We may have to fend for ourselves for a while. So, we need to initiate the process of whipping you and Ms. Koh here into shape. The Book Club is here to make that happen."

Turner continued, "This powerful gentleman here is Captain Raphael Salazar, who is an expert marksman and possesses a deep knowledge of small munitions. He'll be teaching you how to shoot and use other weapons."

Salazar tipped his hat and twirled the toothpick that seemed permanently attached to the end of his mouth.

Albert fired a look at Ying. "We're shooting guns, now?"

Ying smiled and nodded furiously, her cheeks bright pink. "I know, isn't this great?"

Turner returned to his introductions. "This lovely lady next to me is Ariel Kelly. She specializes in psychological warfare." Even when she was sitting down, Albert could tell that Ariel was a tall woman, well over six feet. She sat with perfect posture, and she looked sidelong at Albert through squinted eyes.

"And, of course, you now know Sergeant Travis. He will train you in physical conditioning and hand-to-hand combat."

Albert and Ying nodded at their new colleagues.

Brick began. "Turner briefed the four of us on your situation last night, and since we don't have a lot of time, we're going to throw you into the deep end of the pool. Puddles, I understand you're a chess player."

"I was."

"Well, this is gonna be a lot like chess. There are some basic skills you need to learn, but at the end of the day, the best way to get better is to simply play the game. Each day will consist of basic physical training combined with competitions in each of the major fields that you will need to master. I will compete against you in hand-to-hand combat; Mr. Salazar will compete against you in small-arms fire and protection. Ariel will compete against you in psychological operations. Professor Turner will observe and assist you with each of these modules."

"You mean we're going to fight you all?" sputtered Ying.

"That's right. The professor here thinks his special sauce can make soldiers out of you. Frankly, I'm skeptical, but I've learned a lot from this gentleman, so I'm willing to give it a shot. We don't have a whole lot to work with here, but I've set up the old farm as best I could. We'll do hand-to-hand combat in the old farmhouse down the hill. We'll use the hay bales out back for shooting practice and strategy. And we'll go into town for the psyops stuff. Now go change, and we'll reconvene out back in fifteen minutes."

The Book Club simultaneously pushed their chairs out and rose from the table. Albert watched, eyes darting back and forth. Ying seemed to be genuinely enjoying the pace of military life.

"Puddles, since you were late, you won't get to eat this morning," said Brick.

"Oh, I wouldn't have anyway," replied Albert, oblivious of the slight.

"What, you don't eat?"

"Oh, I eat," replied Albert. "But I feel that traditional food is haphazard. So, I just eat nutrition bars that provide me with my daily values of calories and vitamins." Albert removed a bar from his pants and slowly unwrapped the wrapper.

Brick stared at the bookish fellow. "You mean to tell me that all you eat is nutrition bars?"

"Nutrition bars, power bars, fruit bars, vegetable bars. To be honest, I don't understand why everyone doesn't do it. You always know how many calories you've consumed, and you can regulate your vitamin and mineral intake."

Brick closed his eyes briefly and then looked at Turner. "It's going to be a long week."

CHAPTER 13

Fifteen minutes later, Albert and Ying were walking with Professor Turner along the back border of the Travis Farm. Tall green grass rolled along for miles, framed by an ocean of trees. Most were still green, but a few sported the flaming reds and bright golds of early fall in Vermont. Long rows of hay bales about twenty yards long and five feet tall punctuated the lawn. In the middle of the field stood individual hay bales in intermittent squares like the alternating boxes of a chessboard.

Ying and Albert stood in the middle of the shooting range in Brick's leftover military athletic wear. It made for an absurd scene. Albert's pale legs protruded from the slightly too-short shorts like sticks from a scarecrow. And Ying looked more like a child preparing for gym class than a soon-to-be combatant.

Looking at the expressions on the faces of Professor Turner and Sergeant Travis, Albert could see that they were thinking much the same thing. Turner scratched his chin, while Brick merely shook his head and sighed.

"We didn't give ourselves much to work with, did we, Professor?"

"Well, I'm not much to look at in a T-shirt and shorts either, but I turned out alright."

"True."

Turner walked the two of them to one side of the range, stopped next to one of the hay bales, turned to Ying and Albert, and began. "Puddles and Ms. Koh, this is the beginning of your training. From now on, I want you to stop thinking of me as your professor or friend. Think of me as your drill sergeant. As you both well know, we are in an extremely delicate situation, and the best chance we have to get out of it is if you two become fluent in the Tree and its power. As it stands, I am the only one who fully knows what the Tree can do, but I'm getting older, and I won't have it die with me. I also won't have it fall into the wrong hands."

Turner paused and looked around at the peaceful setting. "You know, I once estimated that it would take me a year to teach a student what I've come to know about the Tree. Unfortunately, I also estimate that it won't take more than two weeks for Eva and her team to find us, so for the next two weeks, I need you to be extraordinary. You will work sixteen-hour days, and we will plan every single moment. You will learn a set of skills and concepts about which you currently know absolutely nothing. This will be hard for both of you. You will feel pain that you've never felt, in parts of your body you've forgotten about. You will doubt yourself. You will want to quit. You will certainly decide to quit—more than once. But I want you to remember that what you are doing here will change your life and may end up changing the world. To succeed, you must stop *feeling* like a human being and start *thinking* like a logician. No emotions, no anxiety, no pity, no morality, no shame. Just pure tactical reasoning."

Turner paused again and took a deep breath. His words hung in the crisp country air.

"Before we begin, I need to ask you for one last thing. I need you to agree that you will commit yourself fully to this training and push yourself to the absolute limit of what you are capable of. I can't and won't babysit you through this process. I need you to be soldiers, not students. Any doubts you have, you must overcome by yourself and keep to yourself. When you decide to quit, I expect you to talk yourself out of it. And you must never, ever tell anyone what you know. Do I have your commitment?"

"Yes," said Ying and Albert in unison. Though Albert wasn't sure he believed it.

"Good," said Turner, clapping his hands together. "Let us commence. As Brick mentioned, the two of you are going to compete in a series of challenges over the next few weeks. The goal of these challenges is to teach you how to think logically and problem-solve not just mathematics problems but every situation you face. You will compete against the absolute best in the world in hand-to-hand combat, weapons and strategy, and psychological operations. Without a doubt, you will lose and lose badly at first. However, if you use your logical mind and trust the Tree, eventually, I assure you, you will prevail. Brick was right when he said this is just like chess. You have a goal, and so does your opponent. Your job is to manipulate your opponent so that you achieve your goal."

The two nodded their agreement, and Turner patted them supportively on the shoulders.

"Now, the first challenge will teach you tactics and strategy. Think of it as a real-life chess match. Behind the hay wall on the other side of the course are Captain Salazar and Sergeant Travis. Each of them has a paint gun. Their job is to do everything in their power to prevent you from crossing over their hay wall. Your job is to cross those walls."

Albert swallowed deeply and looked at Ying.

"What's in the bag?" asked Ying, pointing to the big canvas bag slung over Turner's shoulder.

Turner nodded. "These are your 'weapons'. Forgive the randomness of these items, but obviously, Sergeant Travis and I didn't have much time to prepare, and we had to work with the odds and ends from his personal collection."

Turner poured out the contents of the bag. On the ground were one small paint pistol, a paint shotgun, a bulletproof vest, and a clear, polycarbonate riot shield.

"What's the story on the bulletproof vest? If a paint pellet hits me there, does that not count?" asked Albert. He thought he saw a twinkle in Turner's eyes.

"That's correct. Also, if you are able to hit Salazar or Travis with the paint pellets, then they are out of the game and can no longer fire at you or prevent you from climbing their wall."

"And what's that thing?" asked Ying, pointing to the shield.

Turner grabbed the shield. "This is a bulletproof shield that you can use to protect yourself from the paint pellets. It's similar to what police use in riots."

"I like this; it's like an episode of *American Gladiators*," said Ying as she grabbed the paint shotgun.

"It always comes back to television with you, doesn't it?" replied Albert, trying to disguise his nervousness. He could see that Ying had goose bumps, as well.

Ying pumped the shotgun. "Yes, yes, it does. You ready to do this?"

"That's what you're going with? The paint shotgun? Shouldn't we think this through a little?"

"I have thought it through. Quite logically, I might add. I am not a very good shot ... yet ... and so I took the weapon that requires the least accuracy. This sucker will hit anything."

Albert looked wholly unconvinced by Ying's logic but decided not to argue. "OK, I'm going to go with the shield because all I need to do is get over that hay wall without being shot, and the shield will provide me with the best chance of doing that."

"Whatever. That's what the hay bales on the field are for. You'll be thanking me when I'm covering your ass with shotgun fire." Ying fired paint in the air like an honorary member of the A-Team.

Albert simply shrugged.

"It appears that the two of you have made your choices," said Turner, walking out into the middle of the range. "Let the games begin," he shouted and blew on his whistle.

Albert's voice cracked. "Wait, we're starting now?"

At the sound of the whistle, Ying hurled herself over the hay barrier and into the shooting range all the while unleashing a tribal yell and indiscriminately firing her paintball shotgun at Sergeant Travis and Captain Salazar, who were carefully crouched behind their barrier, showing little more than rifles and well-trained eyes.

Before Albert could even move his body over the barrier, paint pellets rained down on Ying's chest, legs, and body.

"Nooooooooo," she cried out as yellow and blue pellets exploded over her person, creating a seamless collage of color.

While Ying fell to the ground looking like a Jackson Pollock painting, Albert rolled over the hay bale. Holding his shield in front of him, he crept toward a couple of stacked hay bales and crouched low. Paint pellets popped and crackled on his shield and around the hay bales, but Albert looked down at his clothes and noticed that he was clean. He smiled.

These bozos won't be so hard to handle, thought Albert. *All I have to do is stay low, keep my shield in front of me, and I'll be set.* He peered out from behind the hay bale, expecting that the thunder of paint pellets against his shield would resume, but instead Brick Travis simply walked toward him.

What is he doing? thought Albert. *Giving up already?* He covered himself with the shield and crouched behind the hay bale to collect his thoughts. But before he realized what was happening, Sergeant Travis walked up behind the hay bale and shot Albert three times in the shin.

"You're not much of a threat when you don't have a gun," said Brick and jogged back to his side of the range.

Albert and Ying returned to their end of the course to find Turner scowling with his arms crossed. He shook his head, handed them a paper and pencil, and uttered two sentences. "Think like a logician. Use the Tree."

Albert took the paper and pulled Ying over to a hay bale. He began sketching a game tree and walked Ying through his logical process.

"OK, that wasn't our best work. Let's think this through ... we have one objective: to cross over their hay wall. Our obstacles to achieving that objective are Brick and Raphael. To overcome these obstacles, we must do one of two things: one, fully protect ourselves so that we can't be hit by pellets, or two, prevent them from being able to fire pellets."

"Roger that, but neither of us is a good enough shot to do that, and they hit me about ten times before I hit the ground. Other than that, I love the plan," interjected Ying.

Turner broke up the conversation. "Time's up. Go again."

"What? We're not done. Can we have a few more minutes?" begged Albert.

"No. Using the Tree effectively is just as much about speed as accuracy. In the real world, you won't be able to sit around and draw decision trees. You must be able to envision the Tree instantly. This is speed chess, not traditional chess. Go again."

Turner raised a hand, and paintballs rained on Albert and Ying's hay bales.

"Grab your shotgun, Ying, I've got an idea." He dropped the paper and pencil, grabbed his shield and whispered his plan into Ying's ear as paint pellets rained down on them.

Albert was the first over the wall with shield in hand. As Brick and Salazar looked on and tried to find a gap in the shield, they gradually noticed that Puddles was not alone. Walking in lockstep behind him was Ying. The shield and Albert's tall frame easily shielded her shorter body, and by walking backward, she protected their rear flank.

Brick and Salazar gave each other knowing glances and sprinted out from their walled defense in separate directions. Brick ran along Albert's left side, and Salazar jogged along to his right. Ying pivoted to her left and fired a round at Sergeant Travis, but he dove behind a hay bale, avoiding her errant shots.

As Albert looked to his right and left, he knew Brick had checkmated them. "This isn't going to go well."

Brick raised his gun and aimed at Ying. Albert turned to protect her. He saw the pellets from Brick's gun spraying against the glass shield but could hear Ying's squeals as Salazar peppered her with fire from the opposite side of the range. Seconds later, the pellets began splattering against his back.

Again, the two stumbled back to their hay wall. And again, Turner greeted them with a disappointed look.

"Two minutes and then we do it again."

This time, Albert and Ying ran over to the hay bale by which they had begun the logic tree. In silence, they diagrammed together, calculating each move and each reaction.

While the two partners scribbled on the paper, Turner looked at his watch. He watched the secondhand tick away and wondered if he had made a mistake. *Should we have just gone to the police? Maybe Fix won't be able to crack the book's code. Can these two truly understand the Tree? Albert is a genius but cannot understand people. Ying is equally smart and understands people, but does she have the experience to handle the hundreds of logical calculations needed? Can they deal with the responsibility?* He turned to tell Ying and Albert that their time was up but found the area empty.

"Ready, Professor," shouted Ying. The two teammates crouched behind the hay bale like sprinters waiting to explode from the blocks.

Turner raised his eyebrows, curled his lips, and walked toward the middle of the shooting range. "Let the games begin."

In training soldiers in this game with Brick and his team, Turner had seen several interesting and brilliant tactical maneuvers, but nothing could have prepared him for what he saw next.

Instead of climbing over the hay wall, Ying and Albert tipped it over, each of them rolling a hay bale out in front of their bodies. Ying carried the shield while Albert carried the shotgun. Albert displayed a surprising comfort with the paintball gun. He calmly strafed Brick and Salazar's hay wall with paint pellets.

Before, Ying and Albert had crept in a straight line. This time, they sprinted in an unpredictable diagonal pattern, all the while rolling hay bales in front of them. The combination of Ying's small size, the shield, the unpredictable pattern, the steady roll of hay bales, and Albert's shotgun fire made it nearly impossible for Brick or Salazar to find a target. Their hesitation gave both Albert and Ying enough time to run three-quarters of the way across the field untouched.

Sensing they had outmaneuvered him, Brick took over. "Raphael, you stay here. Puddles doesn't have a shield other than that hay bale, so I'll take him out first. You stall Ying, and then after I get Puddles, we'll gang up on her."

As Brick emerged from the hay bale to come after the supposedly shieldless Puddles, Albert and Ying began running again and calmly threw each other their weapons. Ying caught the shotgun and quickly fired at the now totally exposed Salazar while Albert grabbed the shield and sprinted toward the goal line. The stunned Sergeant Travis fired at his feet, hoping to slip under the shield, but it was too late. Albert gleefully leapt over the hay wall and screamed, "Wooooohoooooo!"

All Travis and Salazar could do was stand and watch, hands on hips and guns at their sides, while Ying Koh jumped over the wall, and the two of them danced in celebration.

Turner sidled up to the two vanquished combatants. "I don't think anyone's ever beaten you two that fast. Are you a believer yet?"

Brick bristled. "That was beginner's luck, Professor. We'll see how they do in hand-to-hand combat."

"Yes, we will," said Turner with a wry smile and a twirl of his walking stick as he strolled toward the victors. "We will, indeed."

CHAPTER 14

Cristina Culebra stood quietly behind the curtain of Stanford's Memorial Auditorium. Neither she nor any prominent surrogates from her campaign had intended on visiting Stanford during the tail end of her swing through the state, but over ten thousand students—almost two-thirds of the student body—had signed a petition requesting a visit from the future governor of California. Standing in the wings of the auditorium stage with Eric Crabtree, her newly rededicated speechwriter, Cristina Culebra could see that she had made the right choice. She licked her lips like a vampire at the sight of blood. The multilevel auditorium shimmered with red T-shirts and flags. Every one of the appropriately colored red seats held the body of an enthusiastic Culebra supporter. As the head of Stanford University's RED Party concluded of his introduction, the crowd's energy crashed against the walls of the circular room.

Cristina's security personnel had warned her not to attend the event. While most of the student body clearly supported the candidate, the campaign had received death threats from certain campus radicals who had called her "tyrant" and "Queen Cristina". But in typical fashion, Cristina saw this rabid opposition as an opportunity rather than a threat, for she knew what events would transpire on this day.

I know you're here . . . and I can't wait, she thought.

The candidate entered the stage and waved to the crowd, which rose in near-unanimous approbation. As she walked toward the lectern, Cristina's eyes carefully ran across the crowd in search of the needle that hoped to disrupt her campaign. *The tree would guide her.*

Cristina's crowd held seventeen hundred people. Seventeen hundred potential assassins. She had seconds to determine who that assassin would be. An eternity.

She assessed the crowd, highlighting and discarding people in her mind.

Eight hundred men.

American political assassins were always men. The women faded into the background.

Approximately two hundred over twenty-two years old.

Most of these kids were college kids, and college kids don't assassinate. They need a few more years to realize that the world isn't what they were promised. She grayed out the chanting college students.

Fifty between twenty-two years and thirty years old.

Once you hit thirty, your delusions of grandeur fade.

Now, to the logistics. How many could get a shot off? Her mind pushed everyone over thirty into the backdrop until fifteen young men glowed like Technicolor actors in a black-and-white film.

Fifteen young men were within sufficient range that they could hit her.

Fifteen faces. Which one of these differs from the others?

It took her one moment. The waifish boy stood out to Cristina like a red crab on a white beach. He hovered on the balcony to the immediate left of the stage, wearing a red shirt, but it wasn't a campaign shirt, it was a stiff, unironed red T-shirt, something you'd buy in a pack of ten. It was a minor inconsistency, but to Cristina Culebra, it was everything. Identifying these minor inconsistencies in every situation she faced had enabled Cristina to always stay several steps ahead of the rest of the world. She read his face. Fear, anxiety, anger. All the other men in the crowd were cheering, while this man stood stiff and still, arms suctioned to his sides, fists clenched as though any wrong move might blow his cover. This was not a true believer. This was the enemy.

Cristina continued to walk toward the lectern and wave to the crowd, all the while keeping one eye on this disgraceful ode to Booth, Oswald, Hinckley, and the others that followed. *The question is . . . does he have the guts to do it? Or will he panic? How will he do it?*

It must be a gun. No way this twig thinks he can get me with a knife. And he couldn't get a bomb through security. He could get a 3D printed gun through the metal detectors, though. She calculated the distance and angle for his shot. The balcony was about twenty feet above the stage. The lectern was another twenty feet from the edge. The shot would be about twenty-eight feet. *Very possible, but tough with a homemade pistol, someone next to him bumping him, and the building shaking with the crowd. He'd have to get closer. He'd have to jump onto the stage.* Cristina directed her eyes at the cold, angry gaze of the young man and knew. *He'll try. But he will fail.*

At that moment, the boy leapt from the balcony wielding a gun and landed on the stage screaming, "Sic semper tyraaaaaann—" Before he could finish his cry, the lioness had taken three catlike steps toward him, grabbed his right arm, dislodged the gun from his hand, and shoved him to the ground. The maneuver took less than five seconds. Cristina Culebra paused a moment to absorb the look of sheer shock on his face while her security team sprang on top of him. As she turned, she gave him a wink and a silent wag of the finger.

The crowd stood motionless as Cristina Culebra calmly straightened her formfitting gray suit and approached the lectern. Her footsteps echoed like the knock on a door. Even her security team just crouched and held the boy, waiting for what would happen next. She grabbed the lectern with absolute poise, looked down at the dark wood grain, and knew that this was her moment. She raised her eyes to the audience and delivered the line that she had written over a week ago.

"If only President Lincoln had taken self-defense classes."

A roar that exploded from Stanford's Memorial Auditorium. The crowd was hers.

CHAPTER 15

"A job well done, the two of you," said Turner after Ying and Albert had ceased celebrating.

"Thanks, Professor," replied Albert, wiping the sweat from his face and putting his arm around Ying. "You know, I never played sports when I was a kid, but that was really fun. I kind of wish I had."

"Well, there's going to be plenty more where that came from. I believe Mr. Salazar is ready to give you some weapons training over in the east barn, which, based on Ms. Koh's shooting performance, at least one of you badly needs."

The two of them continued to talk as they walked into the barn, where Raphael sat perched on a hay bale.

"Yeah, where did you learn to shoot like that?"

Albert blushed. "Oh, my dad and I used to go hunting all the time in Minnesota. I used to like the shooting, but I always felt bad for the animals. I probably haven't shot a gun for about twenty years."

"And you're not going to shoot a gun today, either, my friend," said Raphael, eavesdropping on their conversation. He wore an impish smile as he waved the two over.

Albert and Ying sat down on each side of Salazar and looked on as he stared off into the distance, twirling his toothpick in his mouth. His neck was short and thick, which gave his head the appearance that it was sprouting directly out of his shoulders, with nothing in between, a snowman in a cowboy hat.

"So, you liking the Tree, so far?" he asked in his heavy accent.

Albert and Ying nodded, wondering what exactly they were doing.

Salazar continued, "Yeah, I guess it's pretty cool. I don't really get it, but I think we're on the right team."

Ying glanced at Albert as if to say, "Are you going to tackle this one, or am I?"

"What do you mean, you don't get it?" she asked.

"Did you two ever read *El Paraíso Perdido* ... in English, *Paradise Lost*?"

They both shook their head.

"Ohhhh, that book's one of the great ones. You got to read it. The story of the real Tree of Knowledge, from the Bible. The devil, who's originally an angel called Lucifer, starts a revolution in heaven to try to overthrow God because he's jealous that God is focusing all his attention on people. So, God kicks the devil's butt and sends him down to hell with all the other rebellious angels. That's when the devil says, 'It's better to rule in hell than serve in heaven.'"

"Uh-huh," said Albert, creasing his forehead.

"So, while he's down in hell, the devil cooks up the idea that to get back at God, he'll screw up human beings. So, he flies up through the gates of hell where he convinces Sin—his daughter—and Death, who's his son by his daughter ..."

Salazar paused when he saw the look on Albert's and Ying's faces. "Yeah, I know it's pretty messed up, but stick with me.

"Anyway, he convinces his two incest kids to let him out of hell and up to earth. When he gets to earth, he finds Adam and Eve roaming around naked in the Garden of Eden as happy as can be, totally innocent and clueless. So, he realizes he's going to corrupt them. And the way he's going to do it is by getting them to eat an apple from the Tree of Knowledge, so they'll be aware that they're naked and also curious and horny and all that other stuff."

Ying and Albert looked on, engrossed by Salazar's odd recounting of this ancient tale.

"So, as we all know, he changes into a serpent and convinces Eve to eat the apple, and then she convinces Adam, and that's when the shit hits the fan. But here's the thing ... all the while God's watching all this. He knows what the devil is doing, and he still lets it happen. So, here's what I'm thinking. God wanted us to have the knowledge. He wanted guys like Turner and you to come up with crazy shit that can change the world. So, when Turner claims he invented the Tree of Knowledge and all that blah, blah, blah, I just laugh, and say, amigo, God came up with that shit in the beginning; it just took us all this time to figure out how to use it. It's like rubbing two sticks together and saying you invented fire. Lucky for us, our boy Turner wants to use it for good and wants us to help. But now we got some other people that want to use it for bad. So, the way I see it, we and Turner are on the side of God, and your girl Eva's on the side of the other guy. The rest of this shit is just details."

Salazar plopped his round body off the hay bale and turned to face them. "Now, let's talk weapons."

Albert and Ying shook their heads as though they'd just awakened from a trance.

"Yay! I want to shoot some guuuuns," exclaimed Ying.

Salazar shook his head. "Lady, you're not shooting guns for a while. You know why."

"Why?"

"First off, I saw you out there by the hay bales. That shit was terrifying, second, cuz when you're in a fight, guns don't do shit for you compared to some other stuff."

"Like what other stuff?" said Albert skeptically.

Raphael looked past the two and shouted to Ariel, who was walking by the barn entrance. She wore designer jeans, rain boots, and a heather sweater, her pale hair pinned up with a silver barrette. She looked deep in thought. "*Chiquitita,* come over here."

Ariel frowned and walked over.

"How are you doing, beautiful lady?" said Salazar as he grabbed Ariel's unadorned hands.

"Why, I'm doing fine. Thank y—" Before she could finish her sentence, she collapsed to the ground.

"Like that," said Salazar with a smile.

Albert and Ying ran to Ariel in horror. "What did you do?" shouted Albert.

Salazar howled with laughter. "Oh, don't worry. I just put one of these on her hand." He held a small green disk that looked like a pull-and-peel sticker. "Just peel it off and she'll be up in no time."

"Is this poison?" snapped Ying.

"Yep. It's a poison patch. You simply put it on someone's pulse point, and they go right to sleep. Not bad, huh?"

Ariel awakened, blinking her eyes. Her chiseled face was the picture of confusion as she lifted herself off the chilly grass.

"You see, my friends, the point of this exercise was to show you that guns are a very messy business when you have so many other excellent options like this." He pulled out a jug of lemonade and a couple of cups from beside the hay bale. "Would you two like a cup of lemonade?"

"Sure," said Ying and Albert, thirsty from the day's exercises. They grabbed a couple of cups and raised them to their mouths.

"Wrong," shouted Raphael, slapping the cups out of their hands. "Never accept a drink from someone. I just put enough Rohypnol in this lemonade to kill a donkey."

Albert and Ying shrugged, wondering what would come next from this human tornado.

Salazar pulled out a gun from behind his oversized belt buckle. The two of them stepped back, and Ariel, who had just gotten to her feet, scrambled against the wall.

"Here's another reason guns aren't very useful." Salazar grabbed the police shield they had used earlier. He raised the shield and handed the gun to Albert. "Shoot me."

Albert shook his head. "I'm not going to shoot you."

Ariel, now fully alert, grabbed the gun from Albert, pointed it at Salazar, and snapped, "*I'll* shoot you." Her voice seethed with fury at Salazar's little stunt.

"OK, lady. Do it."

Ying and Albert trundled behind a hay bale, plugged their fingers in their ears, and looked on as the giant woman dusted off her sweater and took aim. She fired three shots. The bullets hit the shield with a clang and dropped to the ground.

"You see," shouted Salazar. "That gun didn't do her a lot of good, did it, compared with my shield and stickers?"

Everyone nodded.

"OK, you got to go train with Brick now, but I got three lessons for you. Lesson one: The best weapon is protection, whether it is a shield or body armor or a hay bale. Like Turner says, the Tree of Knowledge is about achieving goals, and you can't achieve your goal if you're dead. Lesson two: The next best weapon is surprise. I'd take a beautiful woman and some poison over a bunch of soldiers any day. Lesson three: Always be unpredictable. Class dismissed."

And with that, Salazar threw something to the ground, and a gigantic cloud of smoke filled the barn. Ying, Albert, and Ariel began coughing and stumbled their way out of the barn, attempting to catch their breath.

They looked around for Raphael, but he was long gone.

CHAPTER 16

The next day, Albert and Ying were subjected to a set of highly regimented meals that had been selected for them. Brick had decided that their diet and physical conditioning were completely inadequate and that he would take charge of their caloric intake and strength training for the rest of their stay. Albert hated to give up his nutrition bars but found Brick's regulated food intake infinitely more logical than the world's current smorgasbord.

After wolfing down their food rations, Ying and Albert hustled to the barn for their next class, hand-to-hand combat training. The barn was barely suitable for animals, let alone human beings. The dilapidated wood structure stood on a floor of dirt. In one corner was a medieval-looking weight set and in the other the remains of a boxing ring. A single ray of sunshine streaming in through a hole in the roof provided the solitary light. Despite the previous night's rest, Albert's body ached with exhaustion.

Brick began the session. His voice had a high pitch given his colossal frame. "OK, you two. The professor tells me I've got two weeks to whip you into fighting shape. Under normal circumstances, I'd need at least ten weeks to make real men out of you, so we're going to have to crank it up a notch. From here on out, we're going to treat your body like it's a machine in serious need of maintenance. This means that everything you do needs to be programmed. Your diet, your sleep, and your workout regimen. You're going to sleep when I tell you to sleep, eat what I tell you to eat, lift what I tell you to lift, and fight how I tell you to fight."

Albert and Ying nodded their heads like new recruits receiving a reprimand.

"Let's start with the bench. Show me what you can do."

"I thought we were going to learn how to fight today," complained Ying.

Brick tilted his head and stared at Ying for a long moment. She fidgeted under his glare, her lower lip pushing out in the closest she ever came to a pout. "Before you can fight, you need to get in shape. The way you two look, you'd probably hurt yourselves taking a swing at someone. I'm surprised you can climb stairs, drive cars, take baths." Ying's chin shot up and she fixed him with a glare. She was remembering when she couldn't do those things—not without help. Brick seemed confused by the intensity of her reaction, and his voice softened slightly. "First, we lift, then we fight. Now get to the bench."

Ying and Albert tiptoed toward the dumbbells.

"Puddles, what are you doing?" interrogated Brick, his voice dropping into the obligatory Southern drawl of a drill instructor.

Albert stifled the impulse to ask to be called *Dr.* Puddles. "Brick, I've got to be honest with you. I've never lifted a weight in my life. In fact, I don't think I've ever been in a gym. Is this really necessary?" His fatigue was showing.

Brick hung his head, and Albert didn't know whether the sergeant was going to hit him or break down and cry. "Yes, it's necessary. You think Eva Fix is going to take it easy on you because you dress nice?"

He pointed to the bench twenty feet away from the dumbbells. "Puddles, you see that bench over there? Lie down on it. Koh, you go grab some dumbbells and come back here."

Albert obediently lay down on the bench and grabbed the weightless bar sitting overhead.

"Don't we want to put some weights on the end of this thing?"

"Puddles, the bar weighs forty-five pounds, and given that you've never lifted a weight in your life, I'm not sure you can get it up eight times."

Albert scoffed, gritted his teeth, picked up the bar, and with his spindly white arms brought it down to his chest and back up again. "See, no problem."

Brick closed his eyes. "Now show me seven more."

Albert repeated the exercise, counting out loud, "Four, five," but as he continued, he could feel the exhaustion seeping into his muscles. By the sixth repetition, he knew he was in trouble. "Seven." Summoning all his strength, with arms shaking and face as red as an apple, he pressed upward. "Eight. I told you it would be no problem," he gasped.

Brick smiled. "Good, Puddles. Now give me two more sets."

***

For the next hour, Brick taught Ying and Albert the weight-lifting program they would use throughout their training. Ying took to the weight-lifting far better than Albert, regularly punctuating the silence with strained grunts and shouts of "Aaaaarrrrrrgggghhhhhh!"

Albert grunted out as he raised the two fifteen-pound dumbbells above his head and dropped them to the floor.

"Alright, we're done for the day," said Brick with a satisfied grin. "Now you fight."

Albert closed his eyes, pulled a towel over his head, and let the cool peace envelop him. He had always prided himself on his work ethic, but he realized that until this moment, he had never truly known work. His aching body simultaneously cried out for every basic need to be met. He wanted water, sleep, rest, food, air, and help, all at the same time and with such ferocity that he could do nothing but lie on the floor of the gym in an exercise-induced fog. What had the potential to be an exciting adventure had morphed into a humiliating monotony.

Brick took the next two hours to train his weary students on the fundamentals of hand-to-hand combat. Proper stance, basic defensive moves, basic offensive moves, grips, and clutches. Albert found himself surprised at how systematic fighting could be. Since he was a child, he had abhorred and feared physical conflict. The emotion, chaotic movement, and violence had always offended his senses, but now as Sergeant Travis explained the tools and objectives of combat, Albert realized that fighting—just like math and chess—could be reduced to ones and zeroes.

After Travis finished his training session, both Ying and Albert could perform a reasonable impression of fighters, if not yet able to execute in real life.

"Alright, you two, I think we've accomplished all we can for the day," said Brick, showing some pride in what he'd been able to accomplish over the last few hours.

"You mean we're done?" asked Ying, dropping to her knees and raising her hands in the air in exhausted celebration. Albert was too tired to even do that. He simply stood hunched over with his hands on his knees.

"Well, not quite yet," said Turner, entering with Gabe in tow as Brick exited. "Gabe and I have a little surprise for you."

Ying and Albert didn't even attempt to match Turner's excitement.

"Gabe, will you do the honors?"

With that, the man in the wheelchair opened a box and removed a small pair of glasses made entirely of glass with a long plastic strip along the side and over the ear. Several buttons lined the strip.

Gabe twirled the glasses in his hands with a certain pride and gusto.

"What is it?" asked Ying.

"It's the world's first virtual hand-to-hand combat-training device," replied Gabe.

"How does it work?" questioned Albert with suspicion.

Turner interjected. "It works by instantaneously computing the probabilities in actual combat situations. For example, when Eva fought that security guard, if she had been wearing this wonderful gadget, she would have been able to see in real time the probabilities that the security guard would punch, kick, etcetera."

"How is that possible?"

"That's the best part of it," said Gabe. "When Professor Turner explained how logic and probability could be used in hand-to-hand combat in much the same way it was used in chess, I thought to myself, 'If you could analyze data on past hand-to-hand combat situations in the same way that chess programmers analyze data from past chess matches, then you might predict future events.' Just like they do when they create a chess program where you play against the computer. So, being the nerd that I am, I downloaded every available UFC video I could find and had a group of interns note each time a fighter made an offensive move, what the move was, what position the person was in before they made it, and what its effect was."

"Oh God, that must have been tedious," said Ying.

Gabe smiled. "You don't know the half of it. But what was interesting was as the interns watched for longer periods of time and made notes, they started to predict what punch was going to be thrown. Once I noticed them doing this, I knew we had something. From that point on, all we had to do was load the data into the computer and develop a program around it. Then I just bought a few pairs of Google glasses, made some modifications, and voilà."

"OK, but how do the glasses operationalize that data?" asked Albert. Normally, he would have been fascinated by this newfangled device, but now he simply wanted the day to end.

"Using the data we obtained, we knew that, for example, if a man is in a crouched stance with his left foot forward, then there is an eighty-five percent chance that his next offensive move will be a punch with his right hand. This type of predictability resembles what we see in chess. For example, if a player moves a pawn first, followed by a knight, there is a seventy-five percent chance that his next move will be another pawn. Our next step was to integrate this video knowledge into the process. That's where the glasses come in."

"That's cool. It's like *Pokémon Go* for fighting. Does it record your opponent?" asked Ying.

"Exactly. I equipped the glasses with a small camera that records the person you are fighting. The glasses then send a video recording to our software program, which determines what stance your opponent is in and then sends back the data regarding what their next offensive move is most likely to be, as well as what areas of the opponent are most vulnerable at any given moment in time."

"Isn't that a lot to look at while you're fighting someone?" asked Ying. "I mean, I feel like I would be looking at what I was supposed to be doing and then get slapped in the face."

Gabe laughed. "Yes, that is a problem. Keep in mind that Professor Turner has been my lone test subject up to this point, but what we've found is that, at first, it is a distraction, but over time, your brain adapts, and you absorb the probabilities on an almost subconscious level. Your body just reacts almost as though you were playing a video game. In addition, we've color-coded the probabilities such that so-called safe areas are coded in blue and danger areas are coded in red. Pretty quickly, your brain will learn that if a man's fist is red in the glasses, then you should watch out for it. The fundamental challenge is that the action of fighting is so quick that it takes incredibly quick reflexes."

"Shall we give it a try?" posed Turner, clearly getting bored with the question-and-answer session. "Ms. Koh, why don't you put on the glasses and grab a helmet and some gloves. Albert, you can be her sparring partner."

After some light protest from Albert about the ethical issues associated with punching a woman, the two of them donned their protective gear and stepped onto the mat. Albert couldn't help but laugh at Ying. Her gloves were about two sizes too big, and the small girl looked like a Rock 'Em Sock 'Em Robot.

"OK, Albert, I want you to assume a fighting position just like Sergeant Travis instructed you."

Albert raised his arms, pivoted his legs, and assumed the position.

Immediately, the screen over Ying's eyes lit up. It was transparent so that Ying could see Albert and her surroundings clearly. Standing in front of her was Albert, knees bent, with his left foot and left hand forward. Just as Gabe had predicted, his right glove glowed red with "85%" pulsing on top of it. A soft blue shade surrounded his left fist and both feet.

Just as Ying glanced at Albert's feet to assess the likelihood of a kick, his bright-red right fist snapped at her head, knocking her to the ground.

"Oh my God! Ying, I'm so sorry," cried Albert, dropping to his knees to aid her. "I thought the glasses would tell you what to do. Gabe, what the hell—"

"No, no," Ying interrupted Albert as she jumped to her feet. "The glasses worked fine. I was just looking at your glowing blue feet when you swung at me. Lesson learned. Let's go again."

"Are you sure?"

"Yeah, you hit like a girl," said Ying, resuming her stance.

Albert grimaced and took the same stance as earlier. Once again, Ying could see his right fist glowing red, but the number had changed: "86%."

Ying bobbed her head back and forth, preparing for Albert's first punch. "Hey, Gabe, how come it says '86%' this time?"

Gabe turned from his computer monitor. "The computer updates the probabilities in real time based on the past actions of your competitor. Because every fighter has a distinct style, it's critical to—"

Albert's glowing right hand snapped forward at Ying again, but this time, she easily bobbed her head to avoid the punch. As she did, she noticed that Albert's stomach glowed green as he was throwing the blow.

Ying goaded Albert, "Is that all you got, Albert? I knew you were getting old, but I didn't think you were *that* old."

Albert's patience evaporated, and he took the bait, taking a full windup and throwing a roundhouse hook with his glowing red fist. But before his fist could even reach its intended target, Ying had ducked and sprung to the left. She then gathered her weight just as Brick had taught her and delivered a hook to Albert's exposed stomach.

Albert felt the air pop out of his lungs for the second time in two days and immediately crumpled to the ground. Ying danced around with gloves in the air mimicking Muhammad Ali. "I am the *greatest*."

He pulled himself to his feet. He could see Gabe and Turner congratulating Ying with a loud round of applause. The small woman was beaming, her round cheeks cherubic red.

Albert ripped his headgear off, tossed his gloves to the ground, and stormed out of the room.

CHAPTER 17

Albert jogged and then ran out into the broad green expanse of the farm. He wanted to keep running, past the hay bales and out into the forest where he could hide from Turner, Brick, and Ying, from his embarrassment, from his vulnerability. But he couldn't. His body had nothing left. Travis and Turner had taken every ounce of energy from him.

After a minute of running, Albert collapsed onto the trunk of a fallen tree. He was alone, and the only sound was the steady chirp of birds that occasionally swooped across the range. He looked back at the hay bales standing like soldiers under the fading fall sun. The crisp, fresh air ran through his clothing, riffled his hair, and blew into his ears. The sun glared against his warm, salty face.

In this open yet stifling expanse, Albert cried.

As the tears streamed down his face, he intellectually understood the absurdity of his weeping. He knew that crying served little functional purpose and would do even less to solve his problems.

He disdained his weakness.

Ever since the days of being teased by the neighborhood boys, Albert had worked with single-minded purpose to build a fortress of rationality. He enjoyed the security that scoffing at the emotions of others provided. While regular people battled heartbreak, disappointment, fear, and insecurity, Albert hovered above, comforted by the knowledge that he was nothing more than a machine, a collection of cells intermingling together to form a mind. One that could resist bursts of random feeling and conquer deep-seated emotions.

Yet now, within a few days, that edifice had crumbled under a near-constant assault from a mentor, a sergeant, a friend, and even a woman he had cared for. Exhaustion had certainly played a part. He hadn't taken into consideration what it meant to have no free time, no retreat, no career, no friends, no family.

Albert sat on the dead tree, and as the poisonous concoction of humiliation, vulnerability, and embarrassment filled his heart, he understood how people came to hate.

"The great man walks alone," exclaimed Turner, approaching Albert from behind.

"I'd like to be alone," said Albert with all the strength he could muster.

"I know," said Turner. He sat down next to Albert and joined him in staring at the sun sinking into the horizon. The streaky blue sky between the trees was turning violet, and the shadows lengthened.

The two sat in silence and watched the sparrows fly overhead for several minutes. Finally, Turner interrupted the silence.

"Look, Albert. I know that was hard for you. And in normal circumstances, I would apologize. But whether you like it or not, it was necessary. It was necessary because I needed Ying to understand that she can accomplish anything, even in that tiny frame. By the same token, I needed you to understand that you can't overlook anyone, no matter how benign or helpless they may seem."

He touched Albert on the shoulder to get him to turn.

"And if I waited for you to learn that lesson from Eva, then it would have been too late."

Albert saw Turner's eyes glistening and resumed looking out into the forest.

Turner tapped his stick on the ground and dug up the grass, exposing the soft dirt. He picked up the blades of grass and tossed them into the wind.

"You know, I've never told you this, but I believe that you have the potential to be a truly great thinker. I've watched your career since you came to Princeton and waited for you to make a seminal contribution to mathematical thinking. But you haven't. At first, I wondered why that was, but then I realized ... No one has challenged you. You've been content to while away your time teaching undergraduates and making incremental contributions to obscure mathematics journals, and nothing and no one has come along and pushed you to do something truly great. You could have been a brilliant chess player, but you quit, and everyone let you. You could have been a groundbreaking mathematician, but you avoided the big issues, and everyone let you. Well, I will not let you."

Albert looked at Turner but didn't have the strength to argue.

"You know, Albert, I believe it was Shakespeare who once said, 'Some are born great, some achieve greatness, and some have greatness thrust upon them.'"

Albert nodded, bit his lip, and closed his eyes.

Turner clutched Albert's shoulder, and his voice dropped to a whisper. "Think. Maybe everything you have been through in the last few days is just greatness being thrust upon you."

He rose from the bench.

"Professor, I don't want to be great. I don't want any of this."

Turner cocked his head and raised an eyebrow. "Yes, you do."

CHAPTER 18

For the next two weeks at the Travis Farm, Albert Puddles was the model student and soldier. He rededicated himself to mastering the Tree. He ate what he was told to eat, lifted what he was told to lift, and dedicated every ounce of brainpower he had to understanding how to use the Tree in every situation he faced. The results surprised even himself. Physically, he improved markedly. When he took his shirt off, he no longer looked emaciated, just skinny.

But the physical progress was nothing compared to the explosion of mental activity he was experiencing. Due to Albert's relentless scientific analysis, he and Ying were now beating Travis, Salazar, and all other comers handily in "hay bale chess", as they jokingly called it. Each day, Turner would stack the odds further against the two by giving Travis and Salazar additional support or removing hay bales. The old professor had even started taking away weapons from the two of them. Yet despite Turner's best efforts, Albert was always a step ahead. He covered the walls of his room with gigantic decision trees depicting potential moves by his opponents and his and Ying's corresponding reactions. What would he do if they had ten soldiers? What if he had no weapons? What if Ying got hit? He envisioned and mapped every plausible scenario. Albert had become so proficient at the game that he no longer required a paper and pen to map his trees; it was all in his mind.

The same was true for hand-to-hand combat. Albert had received his own set of "fighting glasses", and after several sound beatings, he could now give Turner a workout. Brick continued to beat him through a combination of experience and sheer strength, but Albert was good enough now that when they fought, Brick's formerly mocking smile was replaced by a look of measured concentration. When he arrived at the farm, the idea that Albert could ever beat the world's leading expert in hand-to-hand combat was unthinkable, but now with his knowledge of the Tree and Gabe's wonderful glasses, it seemed possible.

Ying's progress had been equally astounding. She had mastered hay bale chess and had become an incredibly adept fighter for someone of her stature. Because of her size, she could not defeat trained fighters like Salazar and Brick, but she regularly dominated the close friends that Travis brought to the farm. This was a source of endless confusion and humiliation among the townsmen. In addition to her considerable fighting skills, Ying truly excelled in the one area that Albert couldn't seem to master: psychological warfare.

As with everything else, Albert and Ying learned psychological warfare through games. In these games, Turner and Ariel would challenge Albert and Ying to convince someone to do something they would not otherwise do. Ying mastered each concept immediately. Ariel would explain various concepts like how to build trust with a stranger, how to intimidate someone, or how to manipulate group behavior. Ying would quietly listen, absorb the information, and then put it into practice. In the same manner that Albert could visualize ten moves ahead when playing chess, Ying could put herself in a person's mind and see what they were thinking simply by observing external indicators.

On this evening, Ariel and Professor Turner's lesson focused on the timeless art of seduction.

"Seduction is the single most valuable use for the Tree of Knowledge," said Turner, raising his voice above the din of the singles bar they had visited for their lesson. "If you can consistently generate attraction, you have real and lasting power over at least fifty percent of the population."

Albert was trying to listen to Turner, but he couldn't seem to focus. Everything about his surroundings made him nervous. Each person in the bar looked to Albert like they had fallen out of a celebrity magazine. It seemed like every man was tall, well built, tan, and bursting with lotion, cologne, hair product, and tailored clothing. And the women. Each one was gorgeous in her own way—some slim and elegant with sleek haircuts; some clean and blonde as sunlight; some buxom and knowing, like Shakespearean barmaids—and all wearing skintight jeans or dresses no bigger than Albert's washcloth. The lighting was absurdly dim, and the music was exceptionally loud. The entire experience made Albert feel small.

Where do these people come from?

"Albert," shouted Ariel. "Are you listening?"

"Oh, sorry. But are you sure we should be out in public like this? I mean, aren't the police looking for us?"

Turner sighed. "I find it highly unlikely that the patrons of these premises have been reading the local *Princeton Examiner* and noting the absence of a rogue professor on the off chance that they might assist in the investigation."

Ariel piled on. "Yeah, stop being so inwardly focused, Albert. And stop looking at my boobs."

Ariel was wearing a low-cut, electric blue dress to fit in with the crowd, and Albert couldn't seem to peel his eyes from her bosom, especially since the stilettos she wore meant her chest was at eye level.

"Sorry," he said, lifting his gaze.

"Lesson number one ... don't say 'sorry'. It makes you look weak. OK, now let's get to work."

Ariel handed out a sheet of paper to Albert and Ying titled "Seduction: Key Points". Point one simply said, "Peacocking".

Ying, dressed in a high-necked ruby red dress, giggled. "What is peacocking?"

Ariel smiled, carefully reached into her handbag, and pulled out two items: a pink feather boa and a tiara. "This is peacocking."

"I'm not following," said Albert.

"I figured you wouldn't," said Ariel. "The first thing you two need to know about seduction is that human beings are just like animals, and they respond to a lot of the same cues that animals do. In the wild, the male peacock's big, bright feathers serve a very basic function: to attract females. The concept is no different for human beings. Allow me to demonstrate."

The psychiatrist rose from the table and stood next to Albert. "Take our friend Dr. Puddles here. Right now, he might as well be a decoration on the wall. He is a lanky guy wearing nice khaki pants and a checkered shirt and is completely unremarkable."

Albert opened his mouth to protest, but one look at Ariel made it clear that it would not be advisable.

She continued, "However, if I wrap this pink feather boa around his neck, he becomes extremely remarkable. Now, it would be nearly impossible for someone to walk into this bar and not notice the gentleman with a feather boa around his neck. Am I right?"

"You've got to be kidding me," said Albert.

"Yeah, he looks ridiculous," said Ying, smiling, her eyes bright with mischief.

"Exactly. But that's the point. If you didn't know Albert and you saw him sitting here with a pink boa, wouldn't part of you want to go up to him and ask, 'Why are you wearing a boa?'"

Ying thought for a moment and then nodded. "I suppose so."

"Well, that's a huge deal. For a man to be so interesting looking that a random woman just can't help but go talk to him is a big first step. In addition, for someone like Albert, who isn't the most outgoing guy in the world, it really helps grease the gears." Again, Albert opened his mouth to protest, and again he thought better of it.

"So, do I get to be the princess? Or should I say a queen?"

"Yes, you do, Your Highness," said Turner, bowing his head and placing the plastic crown on her head. She beamed, gave a mock queen wave, and practiced moving so the tiara wouldn't slide off. Albert thought she looked like something from a Disney cartoon— not that this was a bad thing, necessarily.

"If my friends could see me now," said Ying with a whisper of longing.

For the next thirty minutes, Ariel painstakingly briefed the two on seduction. She explained to Albert that he should never buy a woman a drink, because it gave the impression that he was of lower worth than her and needed to buy her things just to have the honor of her attention. "Women should buy *you* drinks." Ariel told Ying about the importance of assessing and giving off "indicators of interest". This could be anything from a smile to a playful touch on the shoulder to a flip of the hair. Turner explained how this knowledge could be used with the Tree to manipulate anyone. Ying absolutely gobbled up the information, asking what it meant when a man did this or that. Albert just watched and listened in detached observation.

After Ariel and Professor Turner's lesson was complete, Albert stood up, put on his windbreaker, and said, "That was interesting. Weird, but interesting."

Ariel frowned. "Where do you think you're going?"

"To pull the car around. I assumed we were done."

"Oh no," said the psychiatrist with a twisted smile. "Not until you pass the test."

"What test?"

"You're going to get a phone number from one of these lovely young ladies," said Turner.

"Ha, I can't wait to see this," said Ying.

"I wouldn't laugh too hard, Ms. Koh. You're going to do the same thing."

"This is ridiculous. I'm not doing this. It won't work," Albert blustered, turning toward the door.

Ariel jumped up from her seat and put a long arm around Albert's shoulders. "Albert, let's grab a drink."

She guided him to the bar, leaning her head toward his, and gently pulled out a barstool for him to sit on. She pulled up a stool for herself and slid her legs in a deep cross while placing a hand on Albert's knee.

"Bartender, can we have a couple of Miller Lites?"

She turned to Albert and ran her fingers through her long blonde hair. He could smell the soft, sweet aroma of her perfume floating through the air. His face flushed, and he wriggled on his barstool.

Ariel put her hand on his other knee and leaned in toward him. "Albert, I understand that you're hesitant about this. You don't think it will work, right?"

Albert continued to adjust himself in his chair. "No, I don't."

She laughed and put her hand on his shoulder. "That's what I like about you. You're so logical and skeptical."

Albert smiled. He had never realized how understanding Ariel could be. "Thanks," he said, looking at his shoes.

The bartender brought the beers over.

Ariel kept her warm gaze on Albert and slowly blinked. "Would you mind paying for these? I left my purse over at the table."

Albert grabbed for his wallet and dropped a twenty-dollar bill on the bar, eager to return to his conversation with Ariel.

"I'm sorry, what were you saying?" said Albert, looking deep into her eyes.

Ariel's smile dropped to a frown as she cracked him across the face with her open hand.

"What was that?" cried Albert incredulously, placing his palm on his steaming-hot cheek.

Ariel rose from her chair and poked him in the chest with her pointed finger. "First, I told you to never buy someone a drink. And second, I think I've just showed that this stuff works. Now, here's a napkin and a pen. Draw yourself a tree and figure out how you're going to get some digits."

Stunned, Albert looked back at their table. Ying had already risen—tiara perched atop her head—and was making her way to a group of men at another high table. As he watched Ariel return to the table, Albert noticed Turner was just sitting there observing him with a look of fatherly hope in his eyes.

Taking a long swig of his beer and carefully placing the large pink boa on his shoulders, Albert diagrammed a tree on his napkin and pivoted to the scene in front of him. *Am I really going to do this?* He looked around the square-shaped bar and immediately could feel his body freezing up. *Every one of these women is way out of my league. They're not going to buy any of this crap.* His eyes scanned the bar and finally landed on one woman. She was a petite girl with milky skin, green eyes, and strawberry-blonde hair. Two friends stood by her side, and she seemed to be laughing at one of them. She had an impish, warm, inviting smile, and the freckles on her cheeks seemed to dance when she grinned. She reminded him of Ying.

But try as he might, Albert couldn't move from his stool. He just sat there, hunched over the bar like a stone statue. He sipped on his Pilsner and attempted to look cool, which made him look depressed. He could feel Turner's and Ariel's eyes burning into the back of his skull, urging him to act. Even so, he couldn't. Ariel had warned him about this. She called it "approach anxiety" and explained that the way to avoid it was to follow the three-second rule, which meant that once he saw an interesting woman, he should approach her within three seconds or he would freeze up. Albert realized that probably a full minute had gone by since he had set eyes on the strawberry blonde, and his body now seized up like it had been hanging in a meat locker for the last two hours.

To make matters worse, as he looked around the room, unable to move, he saw Ying having the time of her life. Albert watched as the table of three men hung on Ying's every word, oblivious to the rest of the room. And Ying was doing everything Ariel had told her. Playfully touching their arms. Laughing. Tossing her hair. *And it was working.* Each man seemed to be subtly and not so subtly vying for her attention, elbowing each other to talk to her.

Ying's success heightened Albert's sense of impotence. He realized he was playing a game he could not win. But just as he pushed out his barstool to turn tail back to Turner and Ariel in humiliation, he felt a playful tug on his feather boa.

"Well, isn't this the most ridiculous thing I ever saw," said the strawberry-blonde woman with a gentle Southern drawl.

"Yeah, I know," said Albert sheepishly.

"I was headed to the ladies' room, and I saw you sittin' here with that boa on, and I just had to see what that was all about."

Albert debated simply telling the woman the truth, but remembered the next step he wrote in his tree. Haltingly, he delivered his canned response, "Well, it's my birthday, so my friends gave me this feather boa to wear."

Right on cue, the strawberry blonde smiled, put her hand on his shoulder, and said, "Happy birthday!"

Albert couldn't believe it. She had touched his shoulder. *An indicator of interest. Could this stuff really work?*

"Would you like to buy me a drink? My name's Sarah," said the woman.

Albert could still feel the red in his cheek. "Well, it's my birthday, Sarah, so how 'bout you buy me a drink?" he said, trying to mimic her Southern accent. Ariel had told him that people tend to respond more to those who adopt their mannerisms, and they always love hearing the sound of their own name.

"Well, I suppose I could do that for you, sweetheart."

Albert attempted to stifle his smile. *Is this beautiful woman buying me a drink?* "Thank you, Sarah. My name is Joe."

"Pleased to meet you, Joe."

As the bartender brought them their drinks, Albert's new friend crossed her legs and rubbed her foot. "Oh, my feet are killin' me."

Albert noticed Sarah wore heels of at least five inches in height. He had always found this ritual by which women punished their feet absurd and couldn't help but comment.

He smirked. "See, I'll never understand that. Why do you women wear such uncomfortable shoes?"

Sarah leaned back with a perplexed look on her face. "Um, because they look good."

Albert pressed on. "Well, the reason you think they look good is that's what society tells you looks good. There's nothing inherently better looking about high heels than flats."

The second the words came out of his mouth, Albert knew he had lost her.

CHAPTER 19

Whatta we got?" said Eva as she entered the hotel room of the Princeton Hyatt Regency that had become her official war room. She hated this hotel room. Every time she walked through the door, cheap cologne and the stench of men insisted on making their presence known. Her face was showing the strain. Over the past several days, she had interviewed countless acquaintances of Puddles, Turner, and Ying and had come up with absolutely nothing. The illegal wiretap she had been running on Detective Weatherspoon had been equally worthless, and Moloch's impatience was showing more by the day.

"We've got something," shouted Agent Beel, waving a piece of paper in the air in triumph. Eva could measure Beel's excitement by the rate at which his jaws gnawed on his oversized wad of gum.

Eva gave a skeptical stare. Up to this point, the blond surfer-cum-FBI agent had done little to advance her investigation. Days ago, she had asked for data on Puddles's and Turner's cell phones, and Beel still hadn't produced anything.

The agent smiled. "You know, that cell phone data you wanted."

"Yeah."

"Well, I got it. It looks like Puddles and the gang are in Vermont."

"Now?"

"Well, as of a couple weeks ago. They shut off their cell phones."

Eva bit her lip. "That information would have been valuable then, but they could be anywhere, now."

"Don't be so pessimistic," chided the young agent. He leaned back in the undersized maroon hotel desk chair and ran his fingers through his overly gelled hair. "Let me talk to a few contacts and see what I can come up . . . Hey, where you going?"

Eva opened the door of the hotel room. "Vermont, and you're coming with me."

CHAPTER 20

After Albert's new friend Sarah politely explained that she needed to go to the bathroom and then never returned, the Book Club gave up on the night's lesson and headed back to the farm for their briefing on Eva Fix. Gabe and Ariel had spent the last couple of days gathering information on Fix and were eager to share it with the rest of the team. Albert's brain was clouded with exhaustion, and just keeping his eyes open was a herculean task. While he couldn't wait to learn more about Eva, he wanted nothing more than to collapse into his bed and sleep until he couldn't sleep anymore.

Albert and Ying flopped onto the living room couches, and Gabe passed out detailed portfolios to the group. The cover page, coated in plastic, said, "Eva Fix: Personal Profile". Albert found the minimalist order of Gabe's presentation to be quite pleasing and flipped through the binder.

Gabe began, tapping the computer keys to change slides as he went along. He adjusted his wheelchair toward the television screen. "Eva Veronica Portilla Fix was born twenty-eight years ago to Cristina Culebra and Calvin Fix."

Both Albert's and Ying's heads snapped around to look at each other and then back at Turner to make sure they had heard correctly. But Turner just sat stone-faced, absorbing Gabe's presentation.

Albert couldn't restrain himself. "Waaaiiit. You're telling me that Eva Fix is Cristina Culebra's daughter?"

"Yes. Why?" said Gabe, somewhat confused at why this first bit of information was having such an impact on the professor.

"So, Professor Turner, Cristina Culebra is the woman you fell in love with?"

Turner sighed. "I'm afraid so."

"Don't you think that was information that you should have shared with us?" asked Albert, doing his very best to contain his apoplexy.

"Cristina Culebra is not our problem. Eva Fix is our problem. I didn't feel that it was relevant."

"Didn't feel it was relevant? I . . ." Albert threw his hands in the air and looked at Ying, who appeared equally flummoxed.

Seeking to massage the tension, Gabe continued, "Eva's father, Calvin, owned Fix Industries, a defense company, but died of a heart attack when Eva was a baby. Cristina never remarried. She raised Eva while assuming leadership of Fix Industries. From an early age, Eva displayed exceptional abilities in mathematics and chess. At the age of twelve, she became a chess grandmaster, and at fourteen, she was admitted into Princeton University's mathematics program.

"While at Princeton, Eva became involved with the Society for Reason, Enlightenment, and Democracy or RED, a quasi-political, charitable movement founded by her mother. By the age of seventeen, she was a major force in the movement, leading the development and mass adoption of the 'Red Army'. Under her leadership, the organization built schools in every major state in the country and raised an annual budget of nearly five billion dollars—exceeding that of the United Way and Salvation Army.

The organization is particularly prominent in California, with over one hundred schools."

"Ahhhh, your girlfriend is a philanthropist," said Ying, elbowing Albert in the ribs.

Albert simply shook his head and maintained his focus on Gabe.

"Her success in RED led her to leave Princeton prior to finishing her doctoral program to begin an apprenticeship with her mother at Fix Industries. Under Cristina Culebra's leadership, growth at Fix Industries has exploded. At the time of Calvin's death, the company was a sleepy defense contractor, but now Fix Industries makes everything from advanced weapons systems to artificial intelligence, and is worth over one hundred billion dollars, making Culebra the richest woman in the world."

Gabe changed the slide to a picture of Cristina Culebra smiling and shaking hands in a rope line overflowing with fans.

"With her wealth and position atop the business elite secured, Ms. Culebra has now turned her attention to politics. Under the newly created RED Party, she has successfully launched a campaign for governor of California and currently leads in all polls by over twenty points. I've included a list of links to her speeches on page five of your packet. She's really quite impressive."

"I told you that Cristina Culebra was good," said Ying, pointing at Professor Turner.

"I never said she wasn't impressive, Ms. Koh, I said she was dangerous."

Ignoring the interruption, Gabe continued, showing clippings of headlines concerning Eva. "During this period, Eva has continued to work at the company and lead the Red Army. She has held several roles within Fix Industries over the last ten years. Currently, she is the company's chief security officer, handling all security issues, ranging from industrial espionage to proprietary government contracting. However, it is widely assumed that this is merely a holding position for her while she prepares to take over from Ms. Culebra."

Gabe paused and pointed. "Ariel, I think you would be best suited to go over her psychological profile."

The wiry blonde woman rose from her chair and calmly took command of the presentation, flipping the slides to a close-up shot of Eva in a full suit wearing her trademark fedora.

God, she's stunning, thought Albert.

"Eva's psychological profile indicates that she is of a very specific personality type commonly known as 'generals'. Generals like Ms. Fix consistently focus on the most efficient and organized means of performing a task in everything they do. She is a superior leader who is both realistic and visionary in implementing a long-term plan. She is fiercely independent in her decision-making, which has often created clashes with her mother, who is also a general. Eva analyzes and always structures the world around her in a rational way, which makes it difficult for her to consider subjective or emotional influences. This can cause questionable moral judgments and actions."

"Like framing her friends?" said Albert.

Ariel smiled. "Exactly. To that point, Eva Fix is widely thought of as an extremely dynamic problem solver with an abnormally high confidence in her own abilities. This is both a strength and a weakness. Throughout her career, she has consistently shown an arrogant impatience that has led to mistakes. Her errors in robbing the bank were a classic example. The force of her personality exacerbates this problem because she can so easily cow others into doing what she wants, whether or not it is the right course of action.

"In both her business and charitable activities, Eva has been hugely successful and receives unquestioning devotion and respect from her employees and volunteers. However, her staff universally see her as unsympathetic and intolerant of failure. She leads through a combination of fear and devotion, but not intimacy. As a result, her personal life is essentially nonexistent. She has no real friends and has had no discernible romantic relationship since . . . well . . . her high school crush on you, Puddles."

Albert felt a flush in his face.

Gabe resumed the presentation. "Now, we get to the scary stuff. In her post as chief security officer, Eva has used her not-trivial talents to develop a deep network of leaders in the defense, law enforcement, and security sectors."

"This is why I said you guys were in trouble," said Brick, rising from his chair and tapping the screen.

Gabe continued, "Indeed. Eva Fix commands the fealty of nearly every major military and law enforcement official in California and the US. She is on a first-name basis with the head of the FBI, the chairman of the Joint Chiefs, commander of the National Guard, the head of the California Department of Corrections and Rehabilitation, the LA County sheriff, and on down. These relationships are so voluminous and cover such a range of influence that multiple independent watchdog groups have investigated her for evidence of corruption. To date, no hard evidence has been found, but in talking with folks in the industry, we've discovered a widely held belief that there is a steady money stream coming from her office."

"Jesus," said Albert. "What does this all mean for us?"

"Big trouble," said Ying.

"Indeed. In my opinion, in not weeks but days, we will have the full weight of law enforcement bearing down on us."

CHAPTER 21

Ying's heavy eyes scanned the screen of the ancient computer in Albert's room while she worked her way through one of the Ring Pops that had been part of her peacocking arsenal from earlier that evening. Video after video on YouTube showed friends playing pranks on one another, families celebrating birthdays, lovers kissing. The moments that make life. In one day, those moments had been snatched from her and put on hold. Under construction until further notice. She knew there was no choice. She knew they had to leave. But the penetrating isolation of the Travis Farm, of being away from everything she had worked so hard to build at Princeton, crushed her. At Princeton, she was finally somebody. The person who might understand was Albert, but did he? Could he?

At that moment, Albert entered the room, not even noticing she was there. Ying quietly observed as he sized himself up in the full-length mirror to the right of the entrance. She stifled a laugh but couldn't help but notice Albert's wiry physique.

"Really checking yourself out there, aren't you?" said Ying.

Albert jumped against the wall and banged into his dresser with both his arms, all the while scrambling to keep his towel from dropping.

"Jesus, Ying! You scared me to death. What are you doing here?"

"Sorry about that. I wanted to watch those clips of Cristina Culebra, and I don't have a computer in my room."

Albert rubbed his eyes. "Can't this wait for tomorrow?"

"As my mom used to say, 'Tomorrow is promised to no one,'" replied Ying. The thought of her parents gripped her. She hadn't spoken to them since her last text telling them she was working on a 'top-secret project' with Professor Turner and would be out of contact for a few weeks. She worried how long a few weeks would really be.

"Ying? Hello?"

She cleared her mind and smiled at the skinny, wet man in front of her. He was a lot less intimidating in a towel.

"Come sit with me. We'll just watch one, and then I swear I'm out of here."

"Fine. Do you mind if I put some clothes on first?"

"Sure, no problem," said Ying, continuing to sit at his desk chair smiling. "Let's see the show."

Albert was too tired to argue, so he reluctantly slid his boxers and shorts on underneath his towel, grabbed a T-shirt, and sat down next to his graduate assistant.

"Boooooo!"

Disappointed, Ying turned and typed in the first link from Gabe's presentation.

The YouTube clip titled "Cristina Culebra on 60 Minutes" began rolling.

Anchor Scott Pelley sat on a chair in front of the iconic black 60 Minutes background.

"In just a few weeks, California will elect a new governor. Less than a year ago, political prognosticators predicted that this would be one of the closest races in the country, pitting two legendary

Democratic and Republican state politicians against each other in one of the most consequential elections that California has ever seen. But then along came Cristina Culebra, a legendary businesswoman and political neophyte. Despite her extraordinary wealth and success, experts gave her and her newly formed RED Party little chance of success.

"But now, with two weeks remaining, the entire state of California has taken notice. Backed by her Red Army of fervent political supporters, the candidate has developed an almost rock-star-like following and now leads most polls by over twenty percentage points. Recently, we sat down with the candidate-turned-political phenomenon to find out what all the fuss is about."

The video cut to a close-up shot of Cristina Culebra sitting poised and confident in a softly lit room. Albert marveled at how much she reminded him of her daughter.

The interviewer began, "You have supported a ballot initiative that would eliminate the state legislature and replace it with an advisory council. Your opponents have accused you of, quote, 'subverting democracy and attempting to establish tyranny in California'. What do you say to that?"

Cristina Culebra calmly flashed her paper-white smile and tilted her head. "I'm glad you asked that, Scott. Before I answer your question, let me correct you on a couple of points. First, the initiative is not my initiative. It is the initiative of the people of California. And the people of California are tired of a government that has failed them, and they are looking to reform a broken system. Over five million people have signed on to this initiative. I have joined these Californians in signing the initiative because I think it will enable me to do the people's business more effectively, but at the end of the day, it is the people's choice, not mine. Second, you mentioned that the initiative would replace the legislature, when, in fact, it would merely suspend the legislature temporarily so that the urgent business of the people can be done. After four years, if our reforms fail, we can always return to the old system.

"Now, to answer your question, you mentioned that my opponents refer to this as tyranny. I would argue that it is quite the opposite: that my opponents are tyrants. They are the ones who have ignored the will of the very people who voted them into office by racking up massive debt, starving schools, and neglecting roads and basic infrastructure, all the while providing payouts to their cronies. To me, this is the essence of tyranny. We built my campaign on overcoming this tyranny with reasoned, pragmatic problem-solving. At the end of the day, people ask for very little. They want safe neighborhoods, good-paying jobs, strong schools, a clean environment, and good transportation. And they want it done with as little waste of their tax money as possible. With the right system and the right leadership, those goals shouldn't be extraordinary; they should be commonplace."

Albert looked at Ying and nodded with a surprised look on his face.

"See, I told you she was good," said Ying.

The narration resumed. "Ms. Culebra's day job is the chairwoman and CEO of Fix Industries, one of the nation's largest companies, which makes everything from fighter planes to cutting-edge software. She toured us around a factory."

The camera cut to shots of Cristina and Pelley walking next to a bomber jet as Cristina shook hands with the mechanics. Cristina pointed to the nose of the plane. "You see this slanted nose here? It's a little design feature, but it can cut wind resistance by five percent."

The camera cut to the two of them walking through the lobby of Fix Industries.

"One of the things I'm most proud of, Scott, is our security here at Fix Industries. As our nation's leading security contractor, we are keenly aware of the trust that our citizens put in us. They trust us to build the defense systems that will protect them, but also to ensure that we keep the information about those systems classified. In the current environment, where hackers from all over the world are breaking into supposedly impenetrable systems, I want to make sure that we use not only standard methods, like encrypted computer systems, twenty-four-hour surveillance, etcetera, but also certain nontraditional methods that can only be overcome by the high-caliber individuals that currently work with Fix Industries."

"Nontraditional methods? Could you enlighten us?" Pelley questioned.

"I knew you weren't going to let me get away with that one. Let's put it this way: I'd tell you, but I'd have to kill you."

The two shared an awkward laugh, and Ying laughed along with them.

The door to Cristina Culebra's office opened, and the pair continued walking as Pelley narrated. "Culebra has used the enormous wealth generated by her company to run a highly unorthodox and successful campaign. She's bypassed traditional media outlets and used her funds to connect directly with voters, often presenting nontraditional and—some say—radical ideas."

The camera cut back to the interview. "You have said that on your first day in office you will sign an executive order that permits California residents not to pay federal taxes and will eliminate California's income tax. The federal government has said that you do not have the authority to do that."

Again, Cristina smiled, this time touching the interviewer on the arm. "These are great questions, Scott. Frankly, I just disagree with the federal government's interpretation. Currently, for every dollar that Californians pay to the federal government in taxes, they receive seventy-eight cents in federal spending. Now, imagine if I went to the bank and asked them to hold ten dollars for a year, and when I went back a year later, they returned seven dollars and eighty cents. The authorities would prosecute the bank for fraud or embezzlement. That is what the federal government is currently doing to the citizens of California, except they are doing it to the tune of two hundred and fifty billion dollars every year. To me, this is a scandal, when our state is on the verge of bankruptcy."

Albert practically popped out of his seat. "She's so right on this. I read that we in New Jersey only get sixty-one cents back for every dollar."

The interviewer continued as though he could hear what Albert was saying. "Yes, but folks in the federal government would say that the government provides for a lot of things that benefit everyone, like defense."

Cristina leaned back in her chair with a confident smirk. "That's true, Scott, but currently our federal government spends more on defense than all of our enemies combined. That is just wasteful. No offense to the folks in the federal government, but my company alone has enough firepower to handle any of our enemies, especially when you consider the two hundred thousand Californians serving in the military and our own Red Army, which at last count was at one million soldiers. I and the citizens of my state want to send a message to the federal government: we'll keep the two hundred and fifty billion and defend ourselves."

"But isn't what you're saying treasonous, Ms. Culebra? Isn't that what the folks in the South said before they seceded from the Union before the Civil War?"

"Scott, that's just silly. I and the people of California love the United States. We intend to follow the laws of the United States. We just want our money spent more wisely. If the federal government disagrees, we'll let the courts decide that. But until then, I'm going to make sure we get to work solving problems. One more thing I'd add is that politicians always say that our problems are hard and it will take a long time to solve them. I disagree with them. I think our problems are pretty easy to solve; it's just that the system we have in place makes it impossible. In my time as CEO of Fix Industries, I've seen problems ten times more complicated than what the state of California faces, but I solved them in a matter of months because I didn't have to deal with a corrupt legislature. All I'm asking is for the chance to do the same for the people of California."

With that, the clip ended.

Albert sat back in his chair, nodding. "I must admit, she's incredible. I would vote for her tomorrow if I could."

"I know, that's what I've been telling you all along," said Ying, pulling her chair up to Albert and grabbing him by the hands. "I've never been interested in politics, but every time I see her speak, I want to drop what I'm doing and go be a part of it. It's so exciting!"

Albert smiled at Ying. As she jostled up and down in her chair, some of her shiny black hair had escaped her ponytail and fallen in her face. He carefully put his hand on her face and brushed the hair away, but then quickly pulled it back down to his lap.

Ying smiled and then broke the awkward silence. "You don't think there's any way she knows about what Eva's doing, do you?"

Albert paused and took a long look into Ying's hopeful eyes. "My head says, 'no', but my heart says, 'yes'."

CHAPTER 22

The following day, three hundred miles away, Detective Weatherspoon's cell phone was ringing. The bullish detective had just returned to the station from another disappointing interview with one of Puddles's clueless colleagues and was getting ready to dive into his meatball sub lunch when the shrill ringing began. Groaning and licking the sauce from his hands, he pulled the small phone from its holster.

"This is Weatherspoon," he grumbled.

"Hello, Mike. It's Rich from Surveillance."

The detective leaned forward in his seat. "Yeah, Rich. Tell me you've got something."

"Yeah, well, you know how you told me to monitor the email accounts of Puddles and his accomplices?"

"Yeah?"

"Well, one of the accounts, the Google YouTube account for a Ms. Ying Koh, was just used in Washington, Vermont."

Weatherspoon leapt from his seat and quickly lumbered over to the captain's office, hanging up the phone as he entered. "Great. Thanks, Rich."

As the detective burst into the office, the captain distractedly looked up from his papers and removed his glasses. In all the years he'd been with Weatherspoon, he'd never seen the great bear of a man so excited. "What do you got ... besides meatball sauce all over your face?"

"Puddles and his associates are in Washington, Vermont," said Weatherspoon, wiping the sauce from his face.

"Great. Let's go get 'em. Call the Vermont FBI. They probably won't be there long."

"Got it." Weatherspoon turned to exit the captain's office.

"Oh, Spoon? Before you do that, make sure to call Agent Beel. I want to be certain we don't step on any toes."

Weatherspoon rolled his eyes at the thought of having to talk to that bleached-blond moron and his mysterious partner, but an order was an order.

"Got it."

The detective snatched Beel's card from his tattered wallet and dialed from his desk phone.

"Agent Beel?"

"Yeah, this is Beel. How are you, Detective Weatherspoon?"

Weatherspoon paused. *How did he know it was me? Our station's number is blocked on caller ID. This guy must really know voices.* "Um, good. I'm calling because we just got a lead on Puddles. He's in Vermont."

"Great work, Detective," said Beel. "I'll get a team down to Washington, immediately."

Weatherspoon resisted. "Oh, that's alright, Agent Beel. This is my case. I can follow up with the feds."

"Thank you for the offer, Detective, but that will just make it more complicated. I can take it from here. I will inform Captain Willard that I assumed command and that your work should be commended."

Beel hung up.

Weatherspoon stood at his desk with the receiver in his hand. He had just broken the case open, and now it was being ripped out of his hands. Dazed, he slumped into his chair.

How did he know they were in Washington? I just told him they were in Vermont.

CHAPTER 23

Albert's hands trembled.

Today was the day. Over the past few weeks, with the help of Gabe's combat-training glasses, he had mastered the Tree and could defeat any of Brick's friends. Albert was dispatching Salazar with ease, patiently anticipating every punch and countering with coldhearted efficiency. He'd even forced the stubborn man to take his toothpick out of his mouth before the fight. He could see his fights unravel in advance just as he could once see moves and countermoves played out on a chessboard. First a telegraphed punch, then an off-balance grab, then a swift kick, all revealing themselves like a dance. At times, he felt as though the fight were nothing more than a reenactment of an exchange that had already taken place.

The words of the Chinese military philosopher Sun Tzu now resonated with Albert: "Every battle is won before it is ever fought." Before his fights with Raphael or even Turner, Albert knew what they would do and what would happen. Winning was just a matter of reacting and acting.

But with Brick Travis, things were different.

Despite his best efforts, Albert still could not defeat Brick in hand-to-hand combat. The range of attack moves at Brick's disposal made the glasses' calculations unreliable. He would stand in positions where the glasses predicted an 80 percent chance of a right jab, but then Brick would issue a kick to the groin, debilitating Albert and ending the fight. Even when Albert did anticipate the correct move, he would often react too late. The rules of the game changed every time they played.

Earlier that week, frustrated with the consistent beatings, Albert had allowed his ego to get the better of him and had pledged that by the end of the week he would defeat Brick Travis. Brick gleefully accepted.

Now, this evening as the sun faded and starlight peeked through the barn, Albert stood in one corner of the ring, legs quivering, hot sweat pouring from his face, staring at the man he had promised to conquer. On the other side of the ring, Brick's eyes glowed and his mouth curved in the snarl of a predator confident of victory. The smell of straw and sweat tickled the edge of Albert's nose. He looked down at his oversized red boxing gloves, which looked like two overripe tomatoes ready to burst.

"Ignore him," said Turner, who had taken on the role of Albert's trainer for this fight. Turner grabbed both of Albert's wiry arms and pivoted the scared student toward him. "Look, I know you're afraid of Sergeant Travis, but you have to find a way to put that aside. You cannot win if there are emotions inside of you. If you feel fear or anxiety, he will beat you. But if you can calm your mind and clear those emotions away, then you can use your reasoning to beat him."

Albert nodded, breathing heavily, jogging in place as if to shake away the fear. "I know, but he's just so good. So fast."

Turner frowned. "Have I taught you nothing? It doesn't matter how strong or fast he is. You can see the future."

Albert snorted. "Yeah, right."

"No, I'm serious. How many times have you fought this man?"

"I don't know, probably eight times."

"Exactly. You know how he fights. You know what he's going to do. Think if you played a man for two weeks in chess. Do you think there is any way he would beat you after you had played him eight times?"

"Probably not."

"Not probably—from what I hear of how you used to play as a child, never. Now I want you to forget that this is hand-to-hand combat and pretend you are playing Brick Travis in chess. Would he intimidate you, then?"

"No."

"Good. Now go play Brick Travis in chess."

And with that, Turner walked into the middle of the tattered blue ring and announced the start of the fight.

Albert took a deep breath and closed his eyes. He pictured himself in the middle of the ring with the sergeant. Brick knew that Albert would expect him to begin with a right jab because of his standard stance, so he would probably attempt a kick. He envisioned himself grabbing Brick's leg and sweeping him to the floor. This would rattle the sergeant, who would then attempt to grab Albert as he pinned him . . .

The bell rang, and Brick strode confidently to the center of the ring, navy-blue trunks and red shirt like a rippling American flag. Albert took one look out at the small audience. He saw Ying, literally on the edge of the wooden bench, with both hands over her mouth, her bright eyes emitting both hope and fear. Ariel stood lookout at the barn's front entrance, arms crossed, her eyes darting back and forth between watching for unwanted visitors and evaluating the skirmish that was about to take place. Salazar stood, adjusted his cowboy hat, and smiled, toothpick twirling in his mouth, excited for Albert to get what was coming to him.

His gaze returned to Brick. But to his surprise, Albert was no longer afraid or anxious. He was calm. He could see what Brick was about to do, and he knew he would win.

Within seconds, the fight was over. It took Albert three moves. First, Brick fired a kick at Albert's stomach, which he unflinchingly caught in his hand. Then, using the giant man's foot as leverage, he sharply spun Brick to the mat. Finally, flopping onto the mat behind the sergeant, Albert swiftly curled his arms around Brick's neck and began choking him of oxygen. Eventually, the sergeant turned the same color as his shirt and tapped him on the forearm to prevent passing out.

Astonished by what they had just seen, Albert's audience first sat in awed silence, then began clapping slowly, and then erupted in a standing ovation. Though the "crowd" comprised just four people and a handful of crickets on a quiet evening, Albert felt as though a stadium-full were cheering his triumph.

"Bravo!" shouted Turner, waving his walking stick up and down.

Albert's heart pounded with joy, and his cheeks burned against the crisp air with the happiness of victory. Without thinking, Albert raised his hands to the sky as he had once seen Mike Tyson do, and he danced around the ring in total glee.

But as he passed Brick, crouched on all fours on the canvas in abject humiliation, he knew that his victory would be short-lived. Brick's face held the impatient rage of the superior man who through a twist of fate has been defeated; like Goliath, if David's stone had merely stunned him.

"Again" was all the sergeant said as he rose to his feet. The power of his voice silenced the gathered observers. The veins along his arms and forehead raged against his skin, his navy-blue trunks covered in sweat and dust.

Albert wished he could simply leave the ring and enjoy his victory, but he knew Brick would fight forever before he quit.

"OK, let's do it," said Albert, attempting to regain his composure as he returned to his corner for round two. He closed his eyes and envisioned Brick's moves in this next fight ... but try as he might, he couldn't. The pure adrenaline rush of defeating Brick had infected his thoughts, and as he approached his opponent, his mind dwelled on the image of his past victory.

Seeing Albert's hesitation, the fuming sergeant charged him and, in one swift move of his hand, spanked the combat glasses off the fledgling fighter's face. Albert looked up, but without his glasses, Brick was now a different man. His fists and feet no longer glowed blue or red. There were no percentages to show him what would happen next. He had been driving cross-country with a GPS that had now gone blank in the middle of an Iowa cornfield.

Brick smiled smugly as he sized up his helpless opponent. He paused for a second to consider how he would disable Albert and then sent a thunderous punch into Albert's nose and then jaw, dropping him to the mat.

Albert rolled on the ground in dazed confusion, blood pouring from his nose onto the filthy mat. His blurred eyes searched for orientation and fell on his opponent's enraged mug. Brick leaned in inches from his face. "You're nothing without those glasses. Never forget—"

Before the sergeant could finish, Ariel leapt from her seat and pointed.

"They're here! They're raiding the farm!"

Brick rose from his vanquished foe. "Who?"

"The FBI!" She waved her arm, pointing to Albert, Turner, and Ying. "They know you're here!"

PART III
RECKONING

*Therefore the Lord God sent him out from the garden of Eden,
to cultivate the ground from which he was taken.*

—Genesis 3:23

CHAPTER 1

Brick hoisted Albert off the canvas and shouted to Albert, Ying, and Turner. His voice echoed through the barn's worn wood panels. "You three, go out the back door and meet me at the shed at the bottom of the hill."

The trio remained motionless. The crickets had gone silent, knowing something was afoot. Albert heard the rumble of footsteps and shouted orders echoing outside. Dust trembled in the moonlight filtering through the cracks in the ceiling. Just then, Ariel screamed.

Albert looked back and saw her collapsed on the ground in the fetal position, shaking, two metal Taser strings rippling from her body. Salazar lofted two smoke bombs at the entrance to slow whoever was coming around the doorway. With inhuman strength, he threw the tall blonde woman over his shoulder and ran out the side door. The barn went black. Albert coughed as the smoke filled his lungs. *They've cut the power.*

"Now," shouted Brick.

Turner, Ying, and Albert hurled themselves through the back door. The field in back carried a vacant, haunting silence; a contrast to the cluttered chaos inside. It took a moment for his eyes to adjust, but peering through the darkness, Albert could see the fence surrounding the backyard with a small gate at its center and, beyond, silhouettes of hay bales. The stars and moon shone bright across the lawn. Albert wished they'd taken the night off to give them cover. The group tiptoed through the straw grass toward the gate, each crunch of earth under their feet louder than the one before.

As Ying opened the latch on the gate door, the old wood and stiff hinges screeched through the crisp night air.

"Freeze," shouted a deep male voice.

Before Albert could freeze, Turner shoved him through the swinging gate and down to the ground.

"Albert, listen to me," Turner whispered as they lay, faces buried into the ground. "Take Ying out to the range and hide behind the hay bales. Brick, Gabe, and I will grab the van from the maintenance shed and pick you up there in a minute."

"What about Salazar and Ariel?"

"Trust me. They can take care of themselves."

Albert couldn't believe what he was hearing. "Angus, I'm not leaving y—"

"Puddles, now is not the time for debate."

Albert lifted his face off the damp grass, grabbed Ying, and the two of them sprinted down toward the hay bales. He shuffled behind her but then looked back and stopped. He could smell a faint whiff of tear gas as it billowed from the farmhouse. It was dark, but Albert could make out Turner backed up against the fence, both hands clutching his walking stick parallel to the ground.

The nose of an FBI agent's gun poked out through the gate door. Albert braced himself to shout a warning to Turner, but before the words could leave his mouth, Turner snapped his stick against the butt of the gun, launching both the gun and FBI agent attached to it forward toward the ground. *The one opening that Turner needed.*

He grabbed the gun from the agent's hand and used it to hurl him against the fence. The agent's black-uniform-clad body sent wood planks scattering to the ground.

"Freeze," said another agent from behind Turner. "Put your hands—"

In one seamless motion, Turner jammed the butt of the assault weapon into the agent's helmet and then swiveled back to the other man he had just tossed against the fence.

The aging academic then looked up and noticed Albert staring at him from the field.

Turner took a deep breath, adjusted his button-down shirt, and brushed his hair back into position. With the same leisurely composure that he adopted to offer lemonade to guests at his home, he said through clenched teeth, "Dr. Puddles, I would greatly appreciate it if you would adjourn to the firing range. I will meet you out there after I speak with our friend from the FBI."

CHAPTER 2

W hat the hell is taking so long?" snapped Eva to Agent Beel. The two of them were stashed inside a black Suburban while the rest of the FBI team assaulted the farmhouse. Eva was not used to being a bystander, but the Bureau had demanded that she be excluded from any tactical operations as a condition of her involvement. A condition that she was rapidly regretting. The stale air in the SUV stifled Eva, and Beel and his aura of Axe body spray only made it worse.

"Would you relax?" said Beel, loudly slurping on a Diet Coke, his fifth of the day. "It's a big farm, so it's going to take them a little while to track everybody down. Trust me, within five minutes, they're going to be coming out either the door on the left or the door on the right in handcuffs." He pointed to the east and west side of the main house, each of which was guarded by an agent.

At that moment, two agents exited the east side of the house with a short, stocky man in a cowboy hat and a tall blonde woman in tow. Eva couldn't help but notice that the man in the cowboy hat possessed a knowing grin.

"See, I told you they'd be fine." Beel ran his palm against his over-gelled hair in self-satisfaction.

Eva suspected Beel was right, but she couldn't ignore the nausea that had crept over her since they arrived at the Travis Farm. She folded her arms across her stomach and stiffened in the black leather seat. *It's too easy. Turner's too smart to go out this way.*

"I don't like it. It feels like the riddle of the two guards," she mumbled to herself.

"What?"

"Oh, nothing. I was just talking to myself." The last thing Eva wanted was more conversation with Beel.

"What's the riddle of the two guards?" Beel asked, taking another slurp from his can.

"Nothing. It's just a logic puzzle I liked when I was a kid." Eva looked out the tinted passenger window into the darkness, attempting to signal that the conversation was over.

"Let's hear it."

"Can we focus on the operation?"

"Oh, c'mon. We're just sitting here with our thumbs up our asses. We might as well entertain ourselves." Beel crushed the pop can, tossed it on the floor in the back seat, and pivoted toward Eva. He wasn't going away.

Eva sighed and spat out the riddle. "You are trapped in a room with two doors—not unlike how I'm trapped in this car with you, right now—each being protected by a guard."

"OK."

"One door leads to certain death, the other to freedom. You don't know which door, but the guards do. Here's the catch . . . one of the guards always tells the truth, and the other guard always lies, but you don't know who is who. So, the riddle is, how do you figure out which door to choose?"

The agent leaned back in his seat and ran his palm across his slick hair in silence.

If I had known that all I had to do to shut him up was tell him a riddle, I could've saved myself a lot of pain, thought Eva.

"I got it," exclaimed Beel. "I would ask the guard if he was telling the truth."

Eva frowned while keeping her eyes trained on the east and west exits. Agents scrambled around the yard, but there was no sign of Turner's army. "No. That's not even close. If you ask the liar if he is telling the truth, he will say yes. If you ask the truth teller if he is telling the truth, he will say yes as well, so you're screwed."

For the next five minutes, Beel alternated between offering incorrect suggestions and sitting in silence. Eva continued to stare straight ahead, waiting for a sign of Turner and his gang. Finally, after the windows in the Suburban had almost fogged completely, Beel cracked.

"Alright, just tell me," said the exasperated agent.

Eva smirked, continuing to stare ahead. "That's it? That's the best you've got? I hope you FBI guys put more effort into chasing criminals than you do solving riddles." She steadied herself, trying to recover her patience. "The answer is you ask one guard, 'What door would the other guard tell me leads to freedom?' and then go out the opposite door."

"I don't get it," said Beel.

I'm not surprised, thought Eva. In her most condescending tone, she continued, "OK, let's say door A is the door that leads to freedom. If you ask the truth teller what door the liar would tell you to go out, the truth teller will tell you door B. Likewise, if you ask the liar what door the truth teller would tell you to go out, the liar will tell you door B as well. Therefore, regardless of who you're talking to, you get the same incorrect answer, so you do the opposite and go out door A."

As Beel pondered the riddle, his walkie-talkie crackled. A panicked voice reverberated through the speaker.

"Agent down. I repeat, agent down. Suspects have exited the rear of the west barn."

"Shit," yelled Beel, slamming the walkie-talkie into the cup holder and jamming the accelerator of the black SUV. Eva said nothing, clenching her jaw in an iron vise.

The SUV roared over the curb and onto the soggy green landscape, spraying mud and grass in its wake. Beel and Eva sped across the farm toward the back of the building. As they reached the rear firing range, the two pursuers peered through the moonlight to see what looked like a giant chessboard made of hay bales.

Immediately, Eva's mind jumped back to the marathon chess sessions at Turner's house in Princeton. *Turner. He's been training them.* Through the darkness, Eva could see the crouched figures of Puddles, clad in T-shirt and shorts, and his assistant scrambling along the hay bales. Seeing Puddles with his tiny partner forced unpleasant memories back into Eva's mind. A current of anger danced up through her core. The fibers of her turtleneck sweater constricted around her throat.

"Stop here," said Eva. "I'm in charge, now. Follow my lead."

Eva emerged from the vehicle. She calmly cocked her stainless-steel pistol and trained her eyes on Puddles and his partner.

Training is over.

CHAPTER 3

Albert and Ying peered over the hay wall at the far side of the field. The pair could see the dilapidated maintenance shed in the distance. Just to the right of it was a large black SUV. The lights of the vehicle poured over the field of hay bales like fog on a pond. At first, Albert and Ying had thought that the cavalry had arrived, a hope extinguished as Eva Fix and her partner exited the car.

"Oh my God, she's got a gun," screeched Ying breathlessly, sliding back behind the safety of the hay wall.

Albert continued to look on as Eva and her partner cocked their respective pistols and surveyed the empty landscape like hunters. The glint of moonlight on one of the pistols pierced the night air.

This is it. She's really going to kill us, thought Albert.

He glanced over at Ying and saw that she was shaking. Looking at the terror in her eyes, Albert felt a burst of emotion. It was as if some ancient evolutionary reaction had just catalyzed in his body and was telling him just one thing: "Protect her".

"Ying, listen to me," said Albert without thinking. He slid over to her and gently took her hands in his. His eyes locked with hers. Her palms were soaked in sweat, and she clutched him like she was never letting go. "We can do this." He pointed to the maintenance shed on the other side of the firing range. "See that shed?"

Ying nodded and wiped her eyes, smearing the tears across her cheeks.

"There's a van in there that's going to get us out of here. All we need to do is get across this field, and we're home free." He hoped Ying couldn't see his finger trembling.

"But they've got guns."

"I know, but we've been training for this. Brick had a gun, and he hasn't hit us for over a week," said Albert, offering his best reassuring smile.

"They're not shooting paintballs!"

"I know that, but you have to trust me. I've envisioned this scenario a thousand times. You've seen my room. That decision tree is so big it's starting to look like wallpaper. I've seen every scenario in my mind. There's nothing that Eva's going to think of that Turner hasn't prepared us for . . . Now, do you trust me?"

Ying searched Albert's eyes. "I trust you."

"Good. Now here's the plan . . ."

***

Across the firing range, Eva was quietly stalking her prey with Beel trailing. Her black boots gouged the soft ground with every step. She observed Albert and his assistant, and envisioned a decision tree in her mind. *What's the goal of the game? To stop Puddles and his assistant. My first move? To approach him with weapon visible. His response? To run? To attack?* She shook her head. *Lack of information. This is just like that security guard. I don't have enough information. Does he have a weapon? What are his exit options?*

Before Eva could finish her thought, Albert hurdled over the hay bale and sprinted directly at her. *What is he doing? This is suicide.* She raised her pistol and put him in her sight. He looked stronger and broader than the last time she saw him. As she prepared to take a shot, she observed that Puddles seemed to be jogging with an awkward stride. *Was he hurt? Had the FBI already hit him?*

A shot cracked throughout the firing range, followed by a metallic clang and the spice of gunpowder. Eva ducked and spun to see smoke billowing from Beel's gun.

"What the hell are you doing?" she screamed.

"What? I had the shot."

Eva's eyes darted back to the firing range, expecting to see the prostrate body of Albert on the field. To her shock, he kept coming. *How is that possible? Did Beel miss? Something isn't right.*

As Puddles crossed the field, moonlight struck his outline, and she knew what was wrong.

"He's carrying a police shield," shouted Eva.

She looked at Beel to make sure he'd heard, and another shot boomed through the night silence. The agent screamed as his neck burst, spraying dark liquid. "I'm hit," moaned Beel, falling to the ground.

Eva pivoted back to Albert, who was three-quarters of the way across the field but now sprinting at a diagonal toward an abandoned shed. *He doesn't have a gun? Where did that shot come from?* She couldn't believe what she saw next. Hanging upside down from the academic's shoulders by her legs was Ying Koh. She had a gun in hand and a mischievous smile on her face. Ying raised her pistol with furious determination and aimed directly at her.

Eva dove behind a hay bale as projectiles slammed the hay bale. Beel groaned, and Eva moved to examine him. A dark, thick liquid covered his face and neck. Eva placed her hand on his neck to find the wound, hoping to stanch the bleeding. As her fingers touched the blood, Eva noticed it felt wrong. It was cool, and the consistency was off. There didn't seem to be an entry wound. Then the familiar smell hit her.

"This isn't blood. This is paint. Get up, you moron."

Eight cylinders roared in the distance, and Eva looked up to see Puddles's assistant diving into a minivan. Albert had not yet entered the van, and she raised her gun for one last shot, bringing his moppy brown hair into her view. As if he could feel her, Albert turned and looked back, face fully in the pistol's sight . . .

And then, he was gone.

Eva stared, frozen, as Albert dove into the van with Ying, while a square-jawed associate of his leaned out the window, pistol in hand. With four distinct shots he crippled every tire on her SUV.

"What the fuck? Why didn't you take the shot?" yelled Beel, now recovered from his imaginary injury.

Eva simply stood and stared, mouth agape, speechless.

CHAPTER 4

The eyes of General Isaac Moloch squinted before the bright lights of the Pentagon press room. The general flashed an eerie smile and surveyed the abnormally full room of underslept reporters through snakelike eyes. Deep lines sprang out across his face like river tributaries. A patchwork wall of medals dangled from his deep-green uniform. Normally, he loathed his interactions with the media, the way they typed on their keyboards, the way they smelled, like their bodies had never known fresh air.

But today was different. Today, he was officially resigning as the general in charge of the United States Central Command, the military unit with responsibility for the wars in Iraq and Afghanistan and all of Central Asia, and all the press had come out to watch him ride off into the sunset.

Typical of the media. Host a press briefing on progress on the war or casualties, and you get a half-empty room, but a four-star general retires, and everyone's here, thought Moloch.

A mousy-looking reporter raised his hand. With one look, Moloch sensed that he could intimidate this man. He had seen men like this in war. They were usually the first to die.

"Yes, you," said Moloch in his trademark dry rasp.

The reporter rose from his seat and faced the general.

"General, earlier this week, to the great dismay of many of the powers that be in Washington, you announced your retirement as head of the United States Central Command, ending a career of over thirty-five years in the military. My first question is: When you look back over your career, who were the men or women that inspired you the most?"

Good. A softball.

Moloch's tongue slithered across his thread-thin lips as he considered the question. "The first man that comes to mind would be General Douglas MacArthur. The thing that has been completely overlooked in our history is what General MacArthur did in Japan after the war. When the US defeated Japan, the country was in chaos. No one knew who was in charge, and nothing could get done. Fortunately, President Truman had the foresight to understand that the only way that something was going to get done was for us to put our democratic instincts on hold and let General MacArthur take charge. As you may recall, Truman gave MacArthur total authority over Japan in 1945, and by 1951, the Japanese had a new constitution and a democratic government. And land that had been previously held by the emperor and his cronies was distributed to the folks who farmed it. The army had been completely disbanded, and the constitution committed the country to peace. In addition, a whole industrial machinery was created that paved the way for Japan to become an economic power. None of that could have been done without MacArthur having full control over the Japanese government."

When Moloch spoke, he emanated a polished authority that gave the listener the sense that what they were hearing was an indisputable fact. His colleagues used to whisper behind his back that the general could say that the sky was purple while you were staring at it, and you'd start to question yourself.

Seeing a potential opening, a reporter from the *Times* followed up. "That's interesting. And how has MacArthur's experience affected your career?"

"It's quite simple," said Moloch with quiet condescension. "In every military mission I've commanded, whether it was reconstruction in Haiti or the war in Iraq, I've made sure that we had full control over all the machinery of power, not just the military. Because if you're an occupying force, it's not enough to just scare people with guns; you've got to show them you can make a real difference in their lives. You've got to build schools, pave roads, give people clean drinking water, keep them safe. That's what MacArthur did in Japan, and that's what I've done in Iraq and Afghanistan."

The reporter scoffed. "Of course, MacArthur was derisively called 'Gaijin Shogun' or 'foreign military ruler' by the Japanese, and you have been called 'King Isaac' by the Iraqis, haven't you?"

Moloch's face reddened, and a vein crept out of his large, weathered forehead. He leaned forward over the lectern, and his body appeared to gain several inches in height. He extended his long, bony, pale pointer finger.-

"I agree with you that they have used those names. But I disagree that it was derisive." His voice dropped to a raspy whisper. "I think if you spoke with any Japanese person or Iraqi from those particular eras, they would be thankful for the work that General MacArthur and I did."

Silence permeated the room, and the enterprising reporter quietly returned to his seat.

Over the next half hour, the assembled media continued to venture inane backward-looking questions. "What was your most memorable moment? What was your most difficult campaign?"

When Moloch thought he could stand it no more, he turned to his left and pointed to a newsman who had written favorably about him in the past and snarled, "Last question," hoping to close on a positive note.

The reporter obliged. "General Moloch, your career has been a seemingly endless string of awards and honors. Upon graduating from West Point Military Academy, you became an army ranger, the army's most elite unit, and were a distinguished honor graduate. After graduating with a PhD, you commanded missions in Bosnia, Iraq, and Afghanistan, along the way earning the Bronze Star, the Defense Distinguished Service Medal, and the NATO Meritorious Service Medal, not to mention becoming a four-star general. Your 'surge' in Iraq is widely credited with winning the war—"

"Do you have a question or are you just reading my resumé?" interrupted Moloch with a wry smile.

"My question to you is this . . . what's next? There are rumors you may be a candidate for president."

Moloch paused and grinned, his yellow teeth flashing coyly.

"No, I'm afraid that I wouldn't be much of a politician. But, I'll tell you what . . . there's a lady running for governor out there in California whom I'm awfully excited about. I might just join her team."

And with that, the press conference was adjourned.

CHAPTER 5

As the hollow desert sun dropped beneath the taupe horizon line, Albert's mind began to clear. The spare minimalism and dry air of the desert gave him peace. He listened to the quiet crunch of sand and rock beneath his feet as he sipped a burned motel coffee, nibbled on his Clif Bar, and meditated on the past few days.

Turner's army had driven nonstop for forty-eight hours after their run-in with the feds and had finally taken refuge at the aptly named Desert Motel outside of Barstow, California. During that time, Turner and Brick had come to the unpleasant conclusion that training time was over and that the team had no other choice but to go on the offensive. They needed to see what exactly Eva was planning, and they hoped to clear their names.

Albert doubted that this was the right choice. He wasn't naïve about the danger inherent in his situation. He could still visualize the cold end of the FBI agent's pistol pointed at his head and the shrill pangs of bullets glancing off the shield as he and Ying escaped. Rather, it was the absence of reason in it all that shook him.

I know Eva. There must be a way to reason with her.

Albert watched flustered families packing up their station wagons and SUVs for the next leg of their road trips and thought back to his encounter with her in the parking lot back home. It seemed so long ago. He remembered looking into those gunmetal eyes. They weren't the eyes of a madwoman. They were the eyes of a woman of logic, a woman with whom one could reason.

If I could talk to her ... one more time.

"Mmmmm ... that coffee smells goooood. Whatchya doin'?" said Ying as she shuffled up next to Albert. Her oversized glasses were sliding down her nose, and her floral tank top fluttered in the wind. The long road trip had produced a fierce sunburn on one of her arms.

"Oh, nothing. I was just thinking about Eva."

"Oh, boy." She rolled her eyes. "What is it with you and that girl?"

"No, it's not that. It's just ... well ... I just can't accept that she'd be involved in something like this. There has to be a reason." As he said this, Albert paced back and forth, kicking pebbles from the Desert Motel's landscaping.

Ying paced right with him. "Yeah, there is a reason. You heard Ariel. She's caught up in this 'Society' and wants power."

Albert shook his head and continued to kick the pebbles at his feet. "I know what Ariel said, but that just doesn't fit. I know Eva. She's not like that. She's more rational, more thoughtful than that. There has to be something more to it." Albert paused and once again looked out at the horizon bathed in dull orange light. "I don't know ... maybe it has something to do with her mother?"

Ying slapped Albert's chest with the back of her sunburnt hand, nearly spilling his coffee all over him. "Albert, I don't understand why you keep defending her. I mean, wake up. In less than a month, she's framed you and shot at you. What more do you need? Her mother may be a good woman, but Eva isn't."

Albert snorted and stopped his pacing. "Oh really? What about you? You seem to think that Cristina Culebra is some type of saint, when everything else points to her involvement with whatever it is Eva's doing."

"What are you talking about?" said Ying, now reversing course and pacing away from Albert.

Albert stammered, his face reddening. "You really believe that Eva is engaged in a manhunt across the country, and her very smart, very powerful mother knows absolutely nothing about it? C'mon."

Ying wagged her head back and forth in defiance and started to argue but stopped herself. She pursed her lips and walked toward him. She stared into Albert's eyes.

"You're right. Maybe I'm wrong about Cristina Culebra. But you have to understand, when my parents were growing up in Singapore, they had nothing. My grandparents were killed in the Japanese occupation, and my parents had no family. They weren't educated and didn't have any money. The country was poor, and there were no opportunities for people like them. Then a man named Lee Kuan Yew came to power, and everything changed for them. His government provided free housing and adult education programs. My dad got a scholarship. And my mom got a loan to start her own clothing business. Lee cleaned up the government, so they didn't have to pay bribes. None of that would have been possible without him. It was because of Lee Kuan Yew that I was able to come to America."

Ying kicked her own patch of dirt. The light was fading, and Albert could barely see her face, but her voice was clear. "When I look at Cristina Culebra, I think I see the same thing that my parents saw in Lee Kuan Yew. Or that you see in Abraham Lincoln or George Washington. Someone who can really make the world better. When I see how rich this country is, and then I walk around the city and see all of the homeless people, or drive on roads that feel like they're going to break at the seams, I'm embarrassed."

Albert was struck by the intensity of her feeling. He opened his mouth to speak, but his voice was drowned out by Brick's harsh bark.

"Puddles! Stop wandering around kicking pebbles with your girlfriend and get in here. We need to go over the game plan," he shouted from inside room eight.

Albert turned red and said, "She's not my girlf—" but Brick had already slammed the door and headed inside.

CHAPTER 6

Eva stood at attention next to her mother and marveled at the army she had built. Over seventy-five thousand people gathered at the Rose Bowl to watch the latest graduating class of the Red Army march in perfect order along the sun-soaked field. Row after row of straight-backed men and women goose-stepped onto the field, snaking their way to the podium where their leader would finally address them as full members in the Red Army. The silver buttons and bayonets shimmered in the sunlight, and the thud of soldiers' boots shook the surrounding ground. Eva recalled the first class of the Red Army that she had trained. Just ten men graduated that year as she struggled to teach the most basic principles of the Tree of Knowledge. In many ways, today was her graduation day as well, for her mother's army was now complete. Over fifty thousand men and women stood ready to serve the woman they simply called "Cristina".

The master of ceremonies took the podium. Clad head to toe in a uniform that brilliantly covered the extra pounds that crept along his beltline in old age, he addressed the breathless crowd and stoic cadets. His eyes shone with pride as he spoke of the virtues of their leader, while Cristina and Eva looked on from behind.

"You've done well, Evalita, my girl," said Cristina as she watched the troops file in front of her. She wore a rich-charcoal suit with a simple red scarf around her neck. It was Cristina's tradition to wear red at her biggest events. It reminded Eva of how sharks perked up when blood was in the water.

"Thank you, Mother, but we still haven't located Turner's army."

Cristina smiled smugly and placed her delicate yet powerful hand on Eva's shoulder. "Ahhhh, but we have. We have flushed those mice from their holes, and now all we have to do is set the cheese in the trap." As she said this, her other hand closed into a crushing fist.

Eva scowled and pulled the hair off her forehead. "Wait, if we're setting a trap, why did you send me across the country to find them?"

Cristina shook her head and fussed over Eva's outfit, a mother's old habit. She picked lint off the shoulder of Eva's jacket, straightened her daughter's hair. "Oh, Evalita, please. Sometimes you think like a child. The only people on the planet that can stop us now are Angus Turner and his associates." She paused to let her anger dissipate. "As long as he is free, we are in danger. He has associates that know of the Tree of Knowledge, so as long as *they* are free, we are in danger. But now that you've sent them on the run, the enemy is in broad daylight. We know who his associates are and can neutralize the entire threat."

Eva dropped the stiff pose that she had adopted for the crowd and turned to her mother. Despite her best efforts, her voice took on the tone of a child's plea rather than an impassioned argument. "But some of those people aren't even involved in this. They're just acquaintances of Turner. They don't know anything about the bigger picture."

Again, Cristina turned away from the crowd and looked her daughter in the eyes. The spark in her irises had grown to fire, and her lips turned deep red as she spoke. "Eva, you don't understand. Anyone who has even a glimpse of the Tree is a threat to us. It was not Jesus who spread the gospel; it was his disciples. Until we have Turner *and* his disciples, our success cannot be certain."

Eva opened her mouth to speak but was drowned out by the explosion of crowd noise as the master of ceremonies announced the candidate's name.

CHAPTER 7

The inside of Ying's motel room, which had been turned into the headquarters of Turner's army, looked more like the playroom of a schizophrenic than a well-coordinated war room. Every inch of the laminate-paneled wall was covered with an elaborate game tree that mapped out all the potential avenues for retrieving the book. Over the past day, Turner, Albert, and Ying had methodically developed the tree with one aim: find the book. *Should the journal be recovered openly or surreptitiously? Through force or persuasion? With each move, how would the opponent react?* The team even briefly considered having Albert meet with Eva and use Ariel's seduction skills to get the information from her. However, after considering his performance with Sarah at the singles bar, the group jettisoned that idea in favor of a more auspicious approach.

Brick was stewing. "I don't like it. In fact, I hate it." The flat-topped military man clad in a green **ARMY** T-shirt and jeans stood staring at the game tree laid out on the wall while the rest of the gang perched on Ying's bed munching on vending machine candy and soda. The motel's vending machine failed to offer nutrition bars, so Albert was reluctantly feasting on something called "Mike and Ike".

"What are your issues, Sergeant?" replied Turner from the one armchair that the Desert Motel provided.

Brick clenched his fists and puffed his chest out as if he could overpower the group's will through sheer physical strength. "What are my issues? Where do I begin? First, your plan delivers the three of you right into the hands of the enemy. Of course, I don't mind giving Puddles up, but you two are a different story. Second, you've got a seventy-year-old man and a hundred-pound woman breaking into a secured R&D division, while the guy in the unit that has actual combat experience is on the sidelines."

Gabe grabbed a slice of day-old pizza and chimed in with half a slice in his mouth and the rest of it on his T-shirt. "He does have a point."

Turner grabbed his walking stick and approached the far wall of their hotel room. A series of eight-and-a-half-by-eleven papers combined to form a game tree from floor to ceiling. He sighed, pointed, and tapped a section of the tree with his stick.

"I don't know if I'm more disappointed in Sergeant Travis's lack of faith in me or that Gabe is endeavoring to eat that day-old pizza. Good Lord, man, have some self-respect."

Gabe's face flushed as he quietly gulped down the crust and finally noticed the pizza stain on his T-shirt.

"Sergeant, let me tell you a brief story. When I was a young man, I was quite good at chess. Most of the time I played, I disposed of my opponents with ease. However, like any young man, I was impulsive and prone to mistakes. It happened rarely, but when I made a mistake and found myself in a lost position, I would become furious and quickly concede the game in frustration." Turner smiled. "A time or two, chess pieces may have been sent flying as a result."

Ying and Albert smiled at each other. Turner's stories calmed them.

"One day, I played a younger chess player named William Wessel. He was a mousy-looking British boy, but he was a tremendous player, and eventually, I found myself once again in a lost position. Knowing that he had me at a profound disadvantage, I forfeited the game. After the game, Wessel took me aside. And in his peculiarly quiet voice, he said to me, 'Why did you forfeit?' I laughed and said, 'Because I was in a lost position. You had me beat.' He just smiled, shook his head, and said something I'll never forget."

Turner paused for effect and then crouched forward and spoke just above a whisper as though he were divulging a secret. "He said, 'Lost position is the best position to be in,' and then walked away."

He paced the room and continued, "I went home that night and tossed and turned, trying to understand what he meant. The next day I saw him at the tournament and asked, 'William, what did you mean when you said lost position is the best position to be in?' He said, 'If you know you are in a losing position, then the pressure is gone. All that remains is the game in its purest form. You're expected to lose. You should lose, so you never have to play with the fear of losing. You play to win. You have nothing to protect, so you can play your best chess, whereas your opponent has everything to protect. That is what makes a swindle—the art of winning from a losing position—possible.'"

Gabe and Brick leaned forward in their chairs and stared at Turner, searching to find his meaning.

"Sergeant, we are in a 'losing position' right now. The police are after us. We are short on friends, resources, and time, and our enemy knows we are coming. If we attempt to infiltrate the compound by force, they will be ready, and they will capture us or kill us. In life as in chess, the way to win is a 'swindle'."

"Hmmmph." Brick growled his assent and made his way to the diagram, signaling Turner to return to his seat. Turner, knowing Brick's distaste for losing, obliged.

"Thank you for those inspirational words, Professor. OK, let's review our 'swindle' one more time. Both the book and everything we want to know about Cristina Culebra are at Fix headquarters. Our friend Gabe here has been kind enough to duplicate a top-clearance employee key card, which will give us access to the building at night."

Gabe sarcastically bowed from his wheelchair.

"All you have to do is swipe, and you're in the building. Puddles, even you can't screw this up. Now that I think about it, do I need to go over swiping with you?"

Albert rocked his head back in mock laughter. "Har, har, har."

Brick pinned a blown-up image of the building and a rudimentary layout of Fix headquarters to the wall on top of the game tree. Albert marveled at the sheer footprint of the building. The entrance, made of polished steel, formed a trapezoid from which sprang massive glass corridors divided into three sections, like the body of a moth or other winged insect. The building's design was sleep and beautiful, but Albert couldn't help but sense a certain isolation and emptiness to the complex. As though a giant alien spaceship had set down years ago, undisturbed.

Brick pointed to the layout. "Angus believes the book will either be here, in their R&D department where General Moloch and his team are probably frantically attempting to decode it, if they haven't already, or in Cristina Culebra's office. Gabe?"

He gestured to Gabe to take over the presentation. Gabe took the last bite of his cardboard pepperoni slice, rolled his chair up to the chart, and wiped the remaining pizza grease onto his pants. He pointed to a large space in the top-floor corner of the building plan.

"Cristina's office is here. As Brick mentioned, we will get into the building using the employee key card. Unfortunately, that is just one of the security protocols. According to our sources, Fix has installed some type of two-factor authentication once you get inside the building that controls access to the various sectors. The issue is that we don't know what the information required to enter these sectors is, and apparently it varies by what sector you're trying to access. It could be questions about the company like when it was founded, its mission, etcetera, or it could be personal information about an employee like birth date, first car, or pet's name. Rumor has it that in certain sectors there are logic questions that only people with experience in the field can solve. I've prepared binders for you with information on Fix Industries, employee profiles, as well as answers to common logic puzzles in case you come up against any of these."

Albert and Turner simultaneously scoffed at the mention of answers to logic puzzles. The notion that either of them would need help in that area struck them as absurd.

Brick ignored the haughty professors and took over the presentation. "Angus and Ying, you will take Moloch. His department is in the East Wing over here. Albert, you will access Cristina's office. Gabe and I will monitor the security systems to make sure you're in clean and head off any trouble if it comes."

"Where are you going to be while we're doing all the dirty work?" joked Ying, sitting cross-legged on the bed like a guest at a slumber party.

Brick smiled and patted her on the shoulder. "I'll be driving the getaway car. We'll rendezvous on the north side of campus at five a.m."

The group nodded.

Brick clapped his hands in one thunderous clap. "OK, now that we've got that done, I suggest we all hit the sack so that we're well rested for tomorrow."

Brick, Gabe, and Turner rose from Ying's bed in unison and exited the room. Albert trailed slightly behind, tidying up the loose wrappers, pizza boxes, and cans as he left.

After tossing the last piece of trash in the bin, Albert turned to see Ying sitting on the mauve floral blanket at the edge of her bed, her head hung and her fingertips running across her mouth.

"You OK?"

Ying looked up slowly, biting her nails as she turned. "Yeah, I'm just . . ."

Albert hesitated and then reentered the room and sat down on the bed next to her, his hands folded in his lap and legs shaking. He never knew what to do in these situations. *Do I hug her? Do I pat her on the back?*

"You're going to do great tomorrow," he said, barely lifting his eyes.

Ying's lips curled upward in a half smile, and she softly bumped Albert's shoulder with her shoulder, tilting her head toward him slightly. "Yeah, thanks."

Albert turned toward her. "Just think about it. Whatever security system they've got is based on logic. You'll have the world's greatest logician right by your side, and you're no slouch, yourself."

"I guess." She moved her hands to her legs as if to keep them from jumping back into her mouth. She bit her lip and looked up at him. He watched as she mustered the strength to say something.

"Would you mind just holding me for a while?"

Albert leaned back, surprised. "Oh . . . yeah . . . of—of course."

He awkwardly rotated his body and wrapped his arms around her. As he leaned in close, he could smell the soft citrus scent of her hair.

She sank her head into his shoulder, and their cheeks rubbed together. Her skin was warm and soft, and as Albert's lips grazed her cheek, he felt at peace. She slowly turned her head, and their mouths touched. The plush heat of Ying's lips was pure exhilaration. Without thinking, Albert ran his hands through her hair. He felt the delicate strands tumble over the back of his hand and forearm. It was bliss. Dangerous, intimate, heart-palpitating bliss. His mind floated away, and his senses surged ... but he simply couldn't let go.

I can't do this, he thought. *I work with her. This is wrong. I'm taking advantage of her anxiety.*

With a snap, Albert yanked the connection and stumbled off the bed. He adjusted his suit and glasses.

"I should really go."

Ying looked up in abandoned confusion. "What?"

"I—I just think I should go. You should get your rest."

"No, I want you to stay. Stay with me," she pleaded.

Albert could see the fear and need in her eyes.

"I can't. I just can't." He reached for the door. "Good night, Ying."

CHAPTER 8

"Uh-huh, yeah, um-hmm, yes. Yep. No, I understand," said Michael Weatherspoon into the receiver of his office telephone.

Slumped in his seat, the detective was doing his utmost to sound interested, but Mrs. Carruthers on Glenview Road had been droning on for the past fifteen minutes about the "suspicious" characters roaming the neighborhood. Over the last ten years, Weatherspoon had grown to accept the monthly ritual of early-morning phone calls from Mrs. Carruthers. In her mind, everyone from the mailman to the pizza delivery boy was a suspicious character and "something must be done".

"I know, Mrs. Carruthers," said Weatherspoon, trying to sound interested. He spun around in his vinyl desk chair, attempting to get it to stop at a perfect one hundred and eighty degrees from its starting point. As he spun, he noticed that his other phone line was blinking. *The perfect excuse.* "Yes, it is outrageous. Well, I will get my men out there right away. Mrs. Carruthers, I'm sorry, but I have another call coming in." He switched lines, not even waiting for her to finish. "Detective Weatherspoon speaking."

"Detective Weatherspoon? I don't know if you remember me, but this is Albert Puddles."

Weatherspoon leapt forward in his rolling chair, crashing his knee into his desk and nearly toppling the cup of coffee he had placed on the edge. Wincing in pain, the detective attempted to stifle his alarm. He snapped his fingers at the other officers in the precinct to be quiet.

"Oh, of course, I remember you, Dr. Puddles. What can I do for you?" The detective's thoughts bubbled. *Didn't the FBI go after him a few days ago? Shouldn't he be in jail by now? Is he calling me from jail?* He plopped himself on top of his desk to relax his voice for the call.

"Well, sir . . . I'm calling you because I know who murdered the security guard at the bank."

Oh great. Another whack job calling me from jail to protest his innocence. Weatherspoon had seen it a hundred times.

"Oh really," said the detective sarcastically. "Because I was under the impression that you were the one who killed the security guard."

"No," snapped the voice on the other end. "I know that's what it looks like, but you have to hear me out. Before the attack on your police station, you came to me with a decision tree that had a code on it. That tree linked back to the actual murderer. So, she attacked the police station, drugged you so you wouldn't remember, and then framed me."

"I'm sorry, did you say 'she'?"

"Yes! Eva Fix—that's the murderer."

"Eva Fix? You mean the daughter of Cristina Culebra? You mean the woman who has been aiding our investigation of the crime? Apparently, you've had some time to fantasize in your cell, Dr. Puddles."

"I'm not in a cell. Why do you think she was so involved in the investigation? She was making sure you didn't find out the truth."

The detective rubbed his head and scratched the beginnings of his five-o'clock shadow. He remembered thinking it was odd how involved she was in the investigation. His eyes surveyed the crown molding of the station, searching for a memory of that day. *Maybe he is telling the truth.*

"Dr. Puddles, we have you on video with a needle in your hand."

"That's because she handed it to me after she took you out. Didn't you think it was odd that I happened to be in the most conspicuous pose possible right as the cameras came on? Do you really think I would be that stupid? She was setting me up."

That was *strange.* Weatherspoon slowly stroked the maroon sweater that his daughter had given him and considered Puddles's story. He dropped the phone down to his waist as he thought and then returned it to his cheek. "OK, I'll bite. Why would Eva Fix want to kill a security guard at a local bank?"

"She didn't intend to kill the security guard. That was an accident. She was really after a book. A . . . um . . . rare book."

The detective squeezed the receiver in his hand so tightly that the plastic casing moaned. He was rapidly tiring of this cat-and-mouse game. "Where are you now? I'm coming to meet you."

"I can't tell you where I am. But I can tell you where to meet me. I'm going to be at Fix Industries headquarters in Los Angeles tomorrow morning. We believe that there will be evidence implicating Ms. Fix in the burglary as well as broader crimes potentially involving Cristina Culebra."

"Puddles, I can't do that. It's out of my jurisdiction. This would be a matter for the FBI."

"The FBI? They're the ones who nearly shot my head off the other day. Detective, you're the only person we can trust. You've got to figure out a way to get out here."

The detective paused and stared up at the cracked plaster ceiling, shaking his head. *This is none of my business.* But he knew that there was something behind what Puddles was saying. He picked up the phone's base and walked over to the wall so as not to be heard.

"Alright, I'll see what I can do."

CHAPTER 9

While Albert spoke with Detective Weatherspoon, Ying Koh steadied herself to make the most important phone call of her life. She picked up the faded yellow receiver of the motel phone, twirled the ancient cord around her finger, and dialed. As the ringtones purred in her ear, Ying looked into the desk mirror and thought of how far she'd come from the scared little girl she'd once been.

"*Wei,*" answered her mother's voice at the other end of the line. Ying's family often spoke Chinese at home.

"Hi, Mama."

"Ah, Mao Mao! Let me get your father."

Ying's chest ached at the sound of her family's nickname for her. Since she was a child, Ying had been called Mao Mao, which literally meant "fuzz fuzz," because of the way her hair stuck up on her head. That simple phrase transported her back to her family's kitchen, where she and her mother would prepare dumplings while her father and the boys talked politics around the dining table. She heard her father pick up the receiver.

"Hey, Mao Mao," exclaimed her father. His voice sounded weaker than she remembered it.

"Hey, Baba," said Ying, holding back tears. "Are you OK? You sound sick."

"Ah, just a little cold. Nothing to worry about. How are you, my little girl? How are things at Princeton? Do you need me to send you some money?"

Ying laughed. Her dad would always try to send her money for books. It made him somehow feel useful now that his daughter was gone and the boys were grown up.

"No, Dad. I'm fine. School is good. I'm on a special project right now with two of the best professors in the Math Department, Professor Puddles and Professor Turner."

"Oh, wow," said her mother. "That's great, Mao Mao."

"Pay attention to those men, Mao Mao. They can teach you a lot," said her father.

"Are you studying hard?" asked her mother.

Hearing her parents' familiar nagging crushed Ying's resolve. Suddenly, everything she'd been caught up in—the Tree, running from the FBI, her affection for Puddles—seemed so foreign and cold, as though she'd lived it in a dream. She was tired and weak, and wanted to run home to her mother's embrace and her dad's protection. But that time had passed. She was a part of it, now. A part of the Tree. A part of the Book Club. A part of the resistance— to Eva, to Cristina Culebra, to the serpent.

Silently, she began to sob. She covered her mouth to keep the sound from her parents.

"Mao Mao? Is everything alright?" said her mother.

Ying breathed deeply to choke down the tears. "Yeah, Mom. I just—I just wanted you both to know that I love you very much and that I hope you're proud of me."

"Of course, we're proud of you. Why would you say such silly things?" questioned her dad. His voice soothed her like the roll of ocean waves.

But her mother sensed something more. "Mao Mao, if there is anything you need to tell us, you know you can."

"I know, Mom. I know. Like I said, I just wanted to tell you I love you both and that I might be on this project for a while, so you might not hear from me too often." Her voice quaked with every word.

"OK," her mom said. "Well, we love you very much, Mao Mao, and your father and your brothers and I are here whenever you need us, OK?"

"OK, Mom. Good night. Good night, Dad."

"Good night, my girl."

Ying placed the receiver back on the hook. She wiped the tears from her face, put on her coat, and left the musty, old motel room, closing the door on everything she had ever loved.

CHAPTER 10

The four a.m. wind whipped across the dark, empty parking lot of Fix Industries, carrying a faint smell of ocean life and asphalt. Angus Turner and Ying Koh stood outside the R&D wing steeling themselves for a fraught entry. Brick and Gabe kept watch in the car from a distance. The building jutted out violently from the Long Beach coastline, all steel and glass, making no attempt to welcome guests or visitors. Turner shivered as he slid the key card Gabe had given him through the secure door's card swipe. Relief overtook him as he heard a soft click and saw the card reader light turn green. He pulled the door open and gestured for Ying to enter, following closely behind. The security entrance anteroom hallway was dark save the faint red glow of an exit light. The sterile smell of floor cleaner wafted through the cold corridor. A guard desk and metal detector stood empty. At the end of the room stood another doorway with a sign that read:

R&D
AUTHORIZED PERSONNEL
ONLY

Turner turned to his partner in crime and sagged. Standing before him was a young woman who didn't deserve this. Ying was twenty-three years old, but she looked no more than sixteen. She wrinkled her nose, pushed her glasses up, and looked at him with large oval eyes. Silence hovered over them.

What have I done? This young lady has nothing to do with this. And now I'm asking her to help me break into a building to cover for my mistakes.
Noticing the look on Turner's face, Ying whispered, "What?"

"I can't ask you to do this," whispered Turner, patting Ying's arm like a grandfather.

Ying sighed and shook her head. She had seen that look before. "Professor, it's alright. You're not *asking* me to do anything. All my life, people have been protecting me or pitying me or underestimating me. I want to do this. I need to do this."

Turner took one long look at the foreboding door ahead of them, one long look back at Ying, and buttoned his jacket.

She put her small hand on his shoulder and clenched, all the while nodding.

He straightened his back and exhaled. "Alright, Ms. Koh, then let's have at it. Once more unto the breach, dear friends."

Ying stepped forward and swiped the key card again.

The door opened to a room of glowing white, magnified by the purest artificial light. To the left stood a bright-red door. To the right stood another red door. Straight ahead of them, seven white steps extended to a second floor with a third red door. The room was silent absent the hum of fluorescent lights and air pumping through the vents. They had reached purgatory. All that remained was a choice.

Over a loudspeaker, a calm woman's voice purred. "Welcome to Fix Research and Development. You have five minutes to pass through security."

"Where is this?" said Ying, scanning the blank room for something familiar.

Turner rubbed his salt-and-pepper beard, thinking. "A better question, my dear, would be 'What is this?' And it appears that we have stumbled upon some type of three-dimensional maze."

"A maze? Well, how are we supposed to get through this in five minutes?"

"We will have to hurry. Do you have a pen?"

Ying began digging through her backpack. "A pen? Umm ... yeah, I've got a pen."

"Good. The thicker, the better." Turner held out his hand. Ying noticed it was shaking.

Ying handed Turner a thick blue Sharpie.

"Do you have some gum as well?"

Ying squinted her eyes and then handed Turner a stick of gum.

"A few more pieces, please."

She looked on as the old professor shoved five pieces of Bubble Yum into his mouth and chewed. He gnawed on the wad of gum until it molded into a well-formed mass. Then he extracted the gum and used it to secure the marker to his walking stick.

Ying wondered if Turner had finally gone mad. "May I ask how a big blue pen and some gum is going to get us through this, Professor?"

Turner smiled, drew a long arrow upward on the shiny white wall, and tapped the steps with his walking stick. "Ever doubtful, eh, Ms. Koh? Trust me. I'll enlighten you as we move. Up we go."

"You have four minutes," chirped the automated female voice.

Ying and Turner marched up the steps and opened the red door. A long corridor of bright-white paneled walls sprawled out in front of them. Turner continued walking, dragging his walking stick behind him. A bright-blue line ran along the floor wherever they went.

"To understand what we're doing, it's helpful to understand a bit about mazes."

"Ohhhkaayy," said Ying.

"The first mazes were called labyrinths and stemmed from Greek mythology. In the myth, a legendary artisan named Daedalus built the first maze for the great King Minos."

Ying remembered the myths her dad would tell her. "Yes, Daedalus designed the labyrinth to hold the Minotaur, which could kill the king and his subjects. The labyrinth was so difficult to escape that Daedalus himself dragged a string behind him to ensure he could find his way out."

"Precisely. This pen is our string, Ms. Koh."

"You have three minutes."

Turner paused. They had reached the end of the corridor, and the maze turned both to the left and right. A red door stood at the end of both hallways. The light reflecting off them generated an ominous red glow.

"What do you think, Ms. Koh? You're a woman of good instincts."

"I say, right," said Ying with conviction.

"Then, right it is."

Turner pushed open the door to reveal another set of stairs heading down.

As Ying came through the passage, Turner whipped around and shouted, "Don't let the door sh—"

But it was too late. The door slammed behind Ying. Frantically, she tried to open the door behind her, but it was locked.

"I'm so sorry, Professor." Her face was flushed and her eyes frantic.

Turner wagged a finger. "No worries. I should have spoken sooner. As always, from our mistakes, we learn."

"Is this a 'loops and traps' maze?"

"Yes, these mazes are uniquely tricky because they have one-sided doors. Let's press on. How much time do we have?"

"You have two minutes."

Turner's face wrinkled with concern, and Ying noticed sweat simmering along his hairline. "OK, we're going to have to run, Ms. Koh."

The pair began jogging down the hallway, Turner dragging a line of blue ink behind them.

"Can't we just hold one wall of the maze with our hands as we walk, Professor? That would ensure we never repeat the same route. Eventually, we'd stumble upon the correct path."

"Normally, it would, but years ago, someone very clever, much like the designer of this maze, realized that if you break the maze up using levels and trick doors, then the one-hand-wall method becomes obsolete."

"You have one minute."

Turner and Ying reached a dead end and doubled back, running, now sprinting down a hallway to the right with Turner dragging his stick behind him. Again, the pair hit a wall. They continued sprinting in the opposite direction but were stopped again by a third wall.

"You have thirty seconds."

Ying wheezed, out of breath. "What are we going to do, Professor? We've got to get out of here!" Her hands scrambled up and down the white walls looking for an exit, or a trapdoor, a button, anything.

Turner chuckled while struggling to catch his breath. "I wouldn't worry, Ms. Koh; thanks to our good friend Charles Pierre Tremaux, we've now reached the point in the maze that must lead to the exit."

Ying paused in the middle of a junction of four intersecting hallways. At her feet, three lines of blue marker on the floor spanned every direction except one.

She squinted and eyed Turner. "Who's Charles Pierre Tremaux?"

Turner detached the pen from his walking stick, deposited the gum into his handkerchief, and began strolling down the hallway. He mopped his face with the outside of his handkerchief as he strode. "He's the man who came up with the ingenious idea that if we trace the floor of a maze and make double markings at the entrances to paths we've already taken, then it will inevitably lead us to the path out."

"Ten ... nine ... eight ... seven ..."

The two burst through the door as the robotic voice over the loudspeaker crowed, "Five seconds. Alarm deactivated. Welcome to Fix Industries. Have a nice day."

Ying looked back and watched as the walls of the maze slid together like the pieces of a jigsaw and re-formed into what looked like a standard office hallway with a long corridor and office doors on each side. All traces of the maze, except for the red doors, were gone. Ying wiped her glasses on her blouse to make sure it wasn't a dream. Sweat covered her body. She turned to Turner to verify he had seen what just happened, but he had already moved forward.

Ahead of them lay a glass-walled pedestrian bridge with the right side open, overlooking a large room that resembled a futuristic factory. Platoons of soldiers clad in red stood on the light-gray epoxy floor in rows like bookshelves. Sections of soldiers took turns performing various military drills and marches. Shouted orders from the men below bounced off the walls.

Turner turned to Ying. "My God, they're building an army."

At the head of the force stood General Isaac Moloch, cradling a weathered journal under his right arm.

The Tree.

Turner and Ying watched and waited as the lithe Moloch surveyed his burgeoning army. The general walked between the men with total command, prodding here and pushing there. As they performed their maneuvers, the recruits' eyes kept darting back to Moloch as though they had received a visit from God himself.

Finally, Moloch dismissed the cadets and exited the production floor. Alone, he headed up the stairs directly toward where Ying and Turner were standing.

Turner steadied himself. Moloch would not be easy. This was no drunk at a bar. This was one of the most decorated soldiers in American history, a man schooled in the Tree of Knowledge, if not fully comprehending it.

Turner's eyes shifted toward Ying. He shielded her with his body as he crept forward along the bridge. He widened his stance and spoke up as Moloch reached the top step.

"Are you enjoying my book, General?"

Turner was attempting to project confidence, but Ying could hear the quake in his voice.

Moloch froze and raised his head from the floor. His lips slid open across his teeth to reveal a frigid sneer.

"Ahhh, Angus Turner. Just the man I'm looking for. Deciphering this code will be so much easier once I choke the key from your throat." Moloch removed the pistol from his holster, measuring the professor.

Turner swiveled toward Ying. "I'll handle him from here. Remember the plan . . . you know what to do."

Ying opened her mouth to speak, but one look from Turner silenced her.

She ran.

CHAPTER 11

Handle me?" scoffed Moloch.

A vein snaked its way up the general's forehead as he paced toward Turner.

"You think you can just 'handle' me?"

Turner pulled his blazer tighter to bolster his resolve. He observed his opponent. He had anticipated this moment ever since he discovered the Tree. He knew the Tree's power. He had tried to bury it. Bury it deep. But a force of this magnitude could not lay dormant forever. Like an ocean of oil under the ground, Man would hunt for it, would seek to exploit it, would dominate others with it. He had tried to build himself into the bulwark, the keeper of this power, protecting it from those who would seek to corrupt it. He had visualized every outcome, trained his body and mind to be instruments of the Tree's power. He had tried to stifle emotion, to push ego, lust, anxiety, pride, and fear deep into the recesses of his mind. But as he faced down the manifestation of everything he had been preparing for, he was reminded that when the stakes were life and death, fear hung heavy.

His objective in this moment was simple: retrieve the book. Turner knew he had two options: persuasion or force. He hoped for persuasion, but he feared it would be force.

He assessed the pedestrian bridge on which he stood. The bridge was approximately forty feet long and the white plaster ceiling fifteen feet high. The bridge offered four alternatives. Retreat down the very hallway he had just come; head left and climb the stairway to the roof that Ying had just taken; press forward across the bridge toward General Moloch, standing like the grim reaper guarding the gates of hell; or head right and drop twenty feet over the railing, into the training room below. None of these options seemed appealing.

Turner tiptoed toward Moloch, holding his palms open to minimize the threat. "General, it doesn't have to end this way. You don't have to throw away everything you've accomplished for this woman. She's a mirage. You can hand me that book right now, and we can work together."

Moloch sniggered. He had foreseen this tactic from Turner. "A mirage? That's your problem, Turner. You somehow view the current world as acceptable. It is not. It *is* the desert. Cristina isn't a mirage, she's the water. Now, why don't you just give us the key to this book, and stand aside? I've made my own little game tree for this moment, and it doesn't end well for you." He shook the soft leather journal in the air for emphasis and clicked off the gun's safety.

Turner crossed out the persuasion branch of the Tree in his mind. It was to be force. Normally, this wouldn't be a problem. Turner would simply bring a gas mask and some tear gas, and the rest would be history. But thanks to the early arrival of the FBI, Turner had nothing more than a bulletproof vest that Brick had snatched before they left and his knowledge of the Tree. Turner's one advantage was that Moloch wanted him alive. He needed the key. Moloch could shoot him to disable him, but he couldn't kill him. From Moloch, Turner needed nothing other than the book.

Moloch stood twenty feet from Turner. Seven strides. Turner eyed the general's pistol. This model carried ten rounds. Moloch would have ten shots to put him down. Ten shots in seven steps. The vest would protect his midsection, but his extremities were exposed. If Moloch caught a leg or an arm, he would be vulnerable.

Dodging bullets would be the easy part, though. Once Turner reached Moloch, it would be hand-to-hand. Hand-to-hand with someone skilled in fighting and with some knowledge of the Tree, and ten years younger.

One branch at a time, thought Turner.

"I'm going to give you until the count of three to give me the key to this book. One . . ."

Turner visualized the future. Moloch was right-handed and a skilled marksman. The first shot would be to Turner's upper thigh. Enough to drop him, but not enough to prevent him from giving up the key. In this moment, Moloch's accuracy worked against him. Turner knew exactly where the bullet would be.

"Two . . ."

Once he avoided the first shot, Turner estimated he could take two steps toward Moloch while he recovered from the shock of missing. The general wore his dress uniform, so he would be a step slow.

"Three."

Turner watched Moloch's eyes narrow and saw him focus on his target. Time slowed to a trickle under Turner's focus. In the split-second before Moloch squeezed the trigger, Turner pivoted his body sideways and shuffled forward like he was squeezing in between two tables in an overcrowded restaurant. The discharge of Moloch's gun reverberated through the cavernous room, and Turner heard the bullet skitter by him as he took two long strides forward, accelerating with each step.

Five more.

Moloch paused for a moment, temporarily stunned by Turner's nimbleness. He had miscalculated. He stepped back as Turner stepped toward him, steadying his aim on the target.

Turner watched the barrel of the gun tracking him like prey.

This shot would be at the midsection. He needs a bigger target. Now!

As Moloch squeezed the trigger, Turner dropped into a baseball slide. He groaned in pain as his arthritic hip slammed against the tile. One, two, three quick shots buzzed by his head.

Three more.

He rose from his slide and resumed his approach. His eyes met Moloch's. The general's cockiness had morphed into confused desperation. He could see Moloch running his decision tree back in his mind wondering where he had gone wrong, how he could correct. He would go for the head this time. The book's cipher be damned.

Turner watched Moloch's pistol rise two inches toward his head, as he lunged forward into the general's body. Bullets pinged and ponged off the walls of the room. The two men tumbled to the ground, sending the journal to the floor and Moloch's pistol to the training floor below.

Turner shuffled to his feet. His hip and shoulder throbbed from the impact. His lungs swelled as if they'd been shot full of fluid. He had underestimated the effects of his age. He eyed the exits and felt his hip. The hip was almost certainly fractured, and the exits were too far away. It was him or Moloch. No other way.

Turner watched Moloch rise, and from one look, it was clear he had made the same calculation. Moloch assumed a fighting pose and took two controlled steps toward Turner.

The punches are coming.

Turner eyed Moloch's pose. His left foot was forward and his right hand back.

The first punch will come from the right.

Turner struck the same pose to convey the same intention to Moloch. A feint.

I'm old. He'll expect me to lead with my right hand. He won't expect me to kick.

But Moloch knew better. He threw a swift jab with his left hand at Turner's nose. Turner heard what sounded like the snapping of a twig and stumbled backward. Blood poured from his nose, and a sickening, metallic taste filled his mouth. He was now five feet from the edge of the bridge. He would need to adjust quickly.

Moloch sensed his advantage and attacked. His eyes widened, and he reared back on his haunches.

Here comes the right.

Moloch launched a fierce right-handed uppercut at Turner. The professor calmly limped aside, took one step forward, and slammed both hands on the general's ears. Moloch growled in pain and dropped to his knees. Turner saw the opening and unleashed a fierce kick toward Moloch's head with his right leg. As Turner pivoted, his fractured hip gave way.

Moloch grabbed Turner's leg in midair and spun him to the ground. He fell face-first to the floor, his right check smashing on the cold white tile. His eye blurred, and he could feel the pressure steadily crushing his vision. Blood dropped on the tile like paint on a canvas. He crawled up to his knees. He was now at the edge of the walkway, staring twenty feet down into the abyss. Nowhere to go.

As Turner tried to visualize the next branch of the tree, Moloch's arm circled his neck, choking the fuel to his mind. Turner clawed at the general's arm. The smell of stale smoke thickened the choking sensation. Turner felt Moloch slide his other arm behind his neck, creating a vise compressing against his artery. Ten seconds, and he'd be gone.

His brain pounded, searching for oxygen. He should have panicked, but instead, Turner found serenity. All the branches of the Tree faded away, and one choice stood out to him. Glowing like the last leaf on the tree of life.

Turner slowed his heart rate, stopped clawing at Moloch, put his hands to his side, and drew one last breath. The general smiled as he watched his opponent's will collapsing.

Turner summoned every ounce of his strength and, with one powerful move, threw his shoulders forward and down to the floor. As he dropped toward the floor, he could feel the general's weight shift from pulling behind him to tumbling over him. Moloch's grip released, and he rotated over Turner and off the edge of the walking bridge. The hard, slim frame somersaulted off the bridge to the floor below. Turner heard a hollow thud as Moloch's body hit the epoxy floor.

Turner looked down to see a blank expression and blood pooling from Moloch's head.

He needed to go.

The cadets would be coming soon.

CHAPTER 12

A lbert exited the elevator and refocused on the entrance in front of him. *It was time. Time to flip the switch.*

He closed his eyes for a moment and saw his decision tree in all its splendor. At its center was a simple phrase: "Find the book". From that simple statement sprung an endless set of branches expanding in infinite complexity. *Get past security. Steal relevant evidence. Escape.* Each branch detailing an action was matched by a counteraction. The number of scenarios was overwhelming, but Albert felt he had been preparing for this his whole life. All his life, he had felt like a puzzle piece that had been forced into the wrong spot, but when his mind was inside the tree, everything seemed to fit. He was where he was supposed to be. Albert took a long breath, and just as he had in the boxing ring, his mind filtered through the deluge of data and potential scenarios and zeroed in on the one path that mattered . . . the one that would work.

"I'm ready," he said to himself.

Albert pulled a pen and notepad out of his pocket. The empty white pad gave him the same sense of clarity he experienced back at Princeton with a blank chalkboard.

He stepped up to the door and with a quivering hand swiped the key card.

The room around him was nothing he could have imagined. Floor, walls, and ceiling were all one giant 3D screen, like being inside of a cube made of LCD. All around him stood a virtual forest, and in front of him, a rickety wooden bridge swung over a violent river bubbling below. A holographic troll stood before him wielding an axe. Drool covered his gray skin, and his gnarled teeth jutted in every direction as he smiled. The troll's image jumped from the screen with such clarity that for a moment Albert questioned whether he was real.

The troll spoke with a deep Welsh accent coated in phlegm. "You have reached the valley of half-truths. I am the guardian of the bridge. One man may cross. The man who speaks neither truth nor lie. You may speak but once to me. If what you say is true, I will strangle you. If you what you say is false, I will chop off your head with my axe. You have one minute." And with that, the troll wound a gigantic clock that hung from his neck.

Albert paused a moment, attempting to absorb the bizarre reality into which he had been thrust. The screens surrounding him left and right, top and bottom, produced such vivid graphics that Albert couldn't help thinking he had been teleported to another dimension. Cristina Culebra's dimension. If he failed to answer this question correctly, the police, FBI, Cristina, Eva, and everyone else he feared would find him. Everything that Turner's army had been fighting for would be lost. Albert stifled the most potent desire that ran through his mind and his chest: the desire to run.

To orient and steady himself, he began scribbling the troll's riddle furiously in his notebook. His mind knew that the troll wasn't real and wouldn't strangle him or chop off his head, but his heart and stomach felt differently. The ticks of the troll's clock pounded mercilessly as if to remind Albert that his freedom was dripping away. He took a deep breath and told himself that this was just a show. A show to distract him from the logic at the core of the riddle.

After a few seconds, Albert spoke. "OK, if I say something true, you'll kill me. If I say something false, you'll kill me. So, I have to say something that is neither true nor false? That's impossible."

The troll gurgled, sensing that he had found his next victim. "Is it? Or is your mind too puny for the great troll?"

The troll's insult snapped Albert's mind to attention. His eyes brightened.

"Alright, I've got it. What is your name?"

The troll chuckled and shook his head. "You may not pass."

"Why? That was neither true nor false," said Albert, complaining like one of his students over a bad grade.

"Yes, but it was not a statement. It was a question." The troll sharpened his axe with his teeth.

"But a statement has to be true or false."

The troll gurgled out another foul chuckle. "Quite the paradox, isn't it, simpleton?"

Albert stared at the troll's clock. Twenty ... nineteen ... eighteen.

Suddenly, he slapped his notepad in his hand. "That's it! It's a liar's paradox. I just have to say something that contradicts itself."

He steadied himself.

"OK, troll, this is my statement: 'You will chop off my head.' If you chop off my head, then that makes my statement true, which means you should have strangled me. If you strangle me, then my statement is false, and you should have chopped off my head."

The troll sighed and dropped his axe by his side.

"You may pass," said the pouting troll. A door opened where the bridge used to be.

Albert smiled and moved on to the next room. He could sense his logical faculties overpowering his racing pulse and coursing adrenaline.

Like the room before it, this room was composed of wall-to-wall 3D screens and nothing else. Beneath Albert and on the screens to the left and right were blue sky and clouds, which gave Albert the sensation that he was floating weightless in the sky. Four massive figures dressed in white robes hovered on clouds before Albert: a giant bearded man and three gorgeous, powerful-looking women. The man spoke first.

"I am Zeus, and you have entered the realm of the gods." The power of Zeus's voice shook the room.

"You stand before three goddesses. One goddess is Apate, the goddess of treachery and deceit. Another is Veritas, the goddess of truth. The last is Eris, the goddess of chaos. Apate will always lie to you. Veritas will always tell you the truth, and Eris will answer according to her whims."

Albert nodded, prodding Zeus to continue.

"Only gods can see the true nature of other gods, and only gods can pass through my realm. So, if you hope to pass, you must tell me: Who is whom?"

"This is like the riddle of the two guards. I can do this," shouted Albert to no one in particular.

As if Zeus could hear him, he added, "The gods speak in the language of the gods, which no human can understand. They will answer your questions with the words 'Po' or 'Ko,' but you will have to figure out for yourself which means yes and which means no. You have two minutes."

Zeus flipped a person-size sand timer to signify that Albert's time had begun.

Albert thought back to his days in Professor Turner's logic class. He remembered how Turner had taught him that the easiest way to obtain information in yes-or-no scenarios was with an embedded question because you could create a situation where answers were either double negatives or double positives, and therefore it didn't matter if "Po" meant yes or no or if the person were lying or telling the truth because the answer was the same. That's how he had solved the riddle of the two guards.

If I pose the question like a hypothetical about what the other person would do, I can just assume "Ko" means yes. So, the first thing I have to do is figure out which one is the random god, Eris. Then I can focus on Veritas, the truth teller, and Apate, the liar.

Albert took a deep breath and turned to the dark-skinned goddess in the middle.

"If I asked you if the goddess on my left is Eris the Chaotic, would you say 'Ko'?"

She smiled and answered, "Ko."

"OK, so now I can assume that the goddess on the left is Eris the Chaotic or the goddess in the middle is Eris, but definitely not the one on the right."

Albert then turned to the blonde goddess on the right, whose smile seemed to mock Albert. "If I asked you, 'Are you Apate the Liar?' would you say 'Ko'?"

The goddess on the right smiled and answered, "Ko."

"Good, now I know you are the liar because if you were Veritas, you would have said 'Po.'"

Albert rubbed his hands together and smiled at the blonde goddess, whose smirk had now faded.

"So, Apate the Liar, I have one more question for you ... Is the goddess on my left Eris?"

Apate scowled and said, "Po."

"Well, since you are a liar, then the goddess on my left is Eris. And that means that you, lady in the center, are Veritas."

Veritas smiled a warm smile and stepped out of Albert's way as the door opened behind her.

Zeus chuckled. "You have proven yourself worthy of the gods. You may pass."

Albert exhaled and proceeded.

The third room he entered was even more striking. Albert could feel the great woman's presence in the stark power of her office. The lights of Long Beach harbor shimmered through the expansive window. The clear white walls and minimalist furniture captivated and seduced.

But, upon tiptoeing farther into the office, Albert knew his effort had been a waste . . . for there was nothing in it. No book. Not one potential piece of evidence of what Cristina Culebra had done or was planning to do. Not a file cabinet, not a piece of paper, not a computer. As he scanned the room, Albert heard footsteps from the passageway he had just left behind him.

"Did you find it?" whispered Ying.

Albert flinched and grabbed his chest. "Jesus, Ying. You nearly gave me a heart attack. What are you doing here?"

"Turner found Moloch and the book. He sent me to come get you."

"Well, then he's doing a lot better than I am," Albert whispered. "There's nothing in this office. This woman is a ghost."

Ying tiptoed around the empty office, squinting and looking for some piece of evidence.

"You're wasting your time. There's nothing in here—"

His sentence was interrupted by a loud clap and the hum of the overhead lights being turned on.

Albert squinted and looked toward the doorway.

He could not stop staring at the woman who stood before him. Cristina Culebra was magnetism personified. She seemed superhuman. As though God had taken a human being and enhanced every feature. Her skin gleamed with a tanned but somehow youthful vibrance. The gentle scent of her perfume massaged Albert's nostrils. Her strong, thin frame carried a sleek power. *And those eyes.* The deep darkness held sparks of flame. With one look, Albert knew Eva had been the cub. This was the lion.

Her appearance was rendered even more striking against the blank expanse of her office. A magnificent contrast of black against the shoreline lights. The three adjoining walls held nothing but were composed of a hard-coat white laminate that glowed from the overhead light. *Giant dry-erase boards,* thought Albert. *This is where she draws her decision trees.* A desk and three chairs anchored the center of the room. Nothing else.

"Bravo, Dr. Puddles. I must say, I gave you some of my better puzzles, which I didn't think anyone would be able to crack with so little time. Anyone but me, of course. Please sit down. You too, Ms. Koh."

Albert limply sat in the chair opposite her. *What is she doing here? How did she know we were coming?*

"It really is a pleasure to finally meet you," exclaimed Cristina, unveiling a row of bright-white teeth.

Every aspect of Cristina Culebra made Albert feel inferior. With one look she exposed every insecurity he had buried under his logical exterior. Like a wave smashing against rock and splattering into a thousand droplets.

She squinted her eyes and said, "Not bad for a beginner."

Albert thought he had misheard her. "I'm sorry, what was that?"

Cristina rose from her seat, grabbed a marker from her desk, and repeated, "I said, not bad for a beginner."

"I'm sorry, I'm not following," said Puddles, attempting to block out Cristina's condescension.

"Well, let's see if this rings a bell." She uncapped the marker and began drawing a game tree on the whiteboard behind her. "Hmm, the aim of you and your partner-in-crime here is to obtain the book and clear your name." She drew two branches of the tree.

"In order to clear your name, you must do one of two things: prove that, A, you could not have committed the crime, or B, someone else did. Since you have no ability to prove that you didn't kill the security guard and attack the police station—in fact, quite the opposite, since you are the man on the video right before the attack—you must choose route B."

She crossed out one branch of the tree.

"So, if you need to prove that it was Eva who, in fact, committed the crime, you must find evidence, specifically the journal. You believe that evidence to be here at Fix Industries, and thus you must determine how to obtain it." She drew additional branches on the tree. "You can obtain the evidence by force, by manipulation—i.e., blackmail or bribery—or you can obtain it by stealth. Presumably, you've considered that you are up against one of the most powerful women in America, who controls a defense company and her own private army, and, therefore, determined that force was unlikely to yield positive benefits."

She crossed out the branch of the tree entitled "force".

"Likewise, you considered that I'm one of the richest and currently most popular women in the world, while you are poor and not particularly likeable, and therefore ruled out manipulation. That leads us to stealth. The question is how?"

She drew several branches illustrating different pathways to finding evidence: daytime, nighttime, break-in, stakeout, etc.

"Of course, you can't do anything in broad daylight, so it has to be at night. You won't be able to get to me or Moloch in public. We're too protected. So, your best chance was to break into our offices at night. To make matters worse, thanks to my friends at the FBI, time is not on your side."

Cristina began furiously crossing out the remaining branches of the tree. "So, with that knowledge, I could say inevitably, indubitably, and irrefutably, I knew you would end up here in my office."

Albert and Ying sat in motionless silence, unable to move a limb or lip.

"As I said, not bad for a beginner. In chess, this attempt to distract and trap an opponent from a losing position would be known as a swindle. Am I right, Professor?"

Albert nodded.

"And swindles often work against inferior players. Unfortunately for you, I am not an inferior player. And because I am not an inferior player, I know I am in a position of immense strength. As I look across the table at you, I feel as though I have a board full of chess pieces and you merely a king and a pawn. And so, when you threaten my queen with your pawn, I know it is irrelevant because there are ten different ways for *me* to put *you* into checkmate."

She steadily erased the whiteboard and began drawing an alternate game tree of her own. "I could kill you, but that would be messy and inelegant. I could counter your threat with a threat of my own. For example, Ms. Koh, I'm sure your parents would be interested to hear of your recent criminal activities. But this seems like an unnecessary amount of effort. Rather, I think it makes much more sense to pursue the route that I decided on a few days ago when I realized you would eventually find your way into my office."

She paused and transferred her gaze to Ying and then to Albert, letting the full impact of her foresight set in. "I'm going to simply reclaim any materials that you may have gathered tonight, and have you arrested and discredited so that no one cares what you have to say about me—or anything else, for that matter. And if you resist, then these gentlemen will dispose of you. The choice is yours."

She pointed behind them to reveal two Red Army guards patiently waiting beside the exit from her office.

"You see, I play the game at a much more advanced level. It's something to which you should both aspire."

With that, the lion pushed a button behind her desk, and the massive whiteboards on each wall retracted down to reveal three additional whiteboards behind them. But unlike their predecessors, these whiteboards were covered in one massive, hyperactive game tree. Branches extended endlessly in every direction, creeping and crawling across the board like an insidious vine. Each branch carried an encoded text like the tree that Eva had left behind that night in the Princeton rare books collection. But at its center were two words in plain English: "ABSOLUTE POWER."

Albert and Ying stared, mouths agape. In minutes, Cristina Culebra had summarized and dismantled a plan that they had spent days preparing. She had revealed a previously unknown world, one for which Ying and Albert had been staggeringly unprepared.

CHAPTER 13

Angus Turner *was* prepared, and now, so, too, were his students.

The guards ushered Ying and Albert into the elevator. The two academics glanced at each other and nodded. This was the moment for which Turner had been training them for the last two weeks. Simultaneously, they reached into their pants pockets and removed the one tool that could extricate them from the trap into which they had just walked: Gabe's combat glasses.

Crossing the threshold of the elevator, Albert placed the spectacles on his face and turned to Ying, whose glasses were perched gently on the small bridge of her nose. He noticed her spectacles sat slightly askew on her face and carefully adjusted them.

"Seriously?" said Ying, mystified by Albert's OCD.

Albert just shrugged and gave Ying a final nod. *It's time.*

Albert turned first, eyeing the two guards who had walked them into the elevator. Over their shoulders, he watched Cristina, carrying a smug smile on her face. She leaned her head back upon seeing her guests' strange eyewear.

"According to my calculations, at this moment, there is a twenty-five percent chance that you two are going to try to escape," said Cristina. "Lest you feel that compulsion, I've taken the liberty of assigning my two best guards to escort you to the lobby, where you will find the Los Angeles County sheriff waiting to take you into—"

But before she could finish her speech, Albert shouted, "Now!" and hurled a vicious strike to the first guard's groin. The security officer doubled over. Through his glasses, Albert could see a green halo above his head with "90%" floating above it. He shoved his palm against the guard's forehead and slammed it against the stainless-steel elevator wall. The give of skull against metal sickened him. He spun to counter the guard on the left, only to see Ying striking him down with a measured chop to the neck.

Cristina Culebra looked on in bemusement.

Albert's hands trembled with rage and fear. He saw the great, devious woman in front of him and wanted nothing more than to lunge forward and grab her by the throat, choking back the life that she had stolen from him. But Turner's voice rang in his head: "Follow the Tree."

He grabbed Ying by her sweat-soaked hand and dragged her through the elevator doors toward the stairwell. Albert burst through the door beneath the illuminated exit sign. He could hear Cristina screaming, "Get backup, they're headed for the roo—"

As Albert and Ying leapt up the steps two at a time, combat glasses affixed to their faces, Albert felt the same sensation he had in the ring with Brick. Time had slowed. He was no longer an animal reacting to the world as it came to him. He was on a higher plane; he was in the Tree of Knowledge, a place where he knew the future, and he was playing the part in events that he had already foreseen. He sensed Ying's grip loosen and her breathing slow, and he knew she was there with him.

Albert and his sidekick leapt through the rooftop's emergency exit to see the clear sky that he had witnessed so many times before in his plans. Except in his vision, Angus Turner was there to meet him with a proud smile on his face and a calming word.

"Where's Turner?" screamed Ying, searching the speckled white roof for a sign of him. Her voice was carried away by the wind whipping across the rooftop. In the distance, the ocean danced and sparkled as the sun hid just below the horizon.

"Shit! I don't know," screeched Albert.

"What do we do?"

"Give me the rope."

Ying removed the long black rope that Brick had given them and tied it securely to a metal post along the roof's edge. Albert looked over the edge to the parking lot below. It was empty. *Where are Brick and Gabe? They should be here by now to pick us up ... Something's wrong.*

He attempted to collect himself, but could hear the slamming and banging of doors opening and stairs being climbed. *They're coming.*

"We can't leave without him," said Ying, anticipating Albert's thoughts.

Albert spun and looked at her. "That's not even an option. Brick and Gabe aren't here, yet."

Ying's eyes widened. The assured calm that had possessed them as they ascended the stairwell had vanished amid the swell of the unexpected. The steady lines of the tree in her mind's eye turned to dust.

"Get next to the door. We'll take them as they come," shouted Albert as he shoved Ying next to the rooftop entrance.

Two guards clad in red body armor slammed through the door, each carrying a high-powered gun, but the sight of the two massive soldiers paled in comparison to what followed: Eva.

Channeling Angus Turner, Albert sprung from behind the door and grabbed the first guard's gun. As he did so, his glasses once again illuminated green above the man's head. He slammed the butt of the gun against the guard's face, momentarily disabling him. Albert then turned to the next guard, whose stomach glowed green through the glasses. He jabbed the man in the gut and encircled his arm around his neck, depriving him of oxygen.

Ying watched as the other guard quickly grabbed Albert by the neck and shoulders and attempted to peel him off their partner.

Seeing both guards' legs glowing green, Ying dropped to a knee and delivered two measured blows to the men's knees, sending them tumbling to the ground. Albert kicked their guns away and body-slammed one of the guards, ramming his head against the ground.

The next thing Albert heard was the crack of limb against limb. His eyes shot upward to see Eva thrashing Ying with her black-gloved hands. She had dislodged Ying's glasses, and she tore at her hair, aiming furious blows at her face and body. Ying fell to the ground. Albert saw blood streaming from her lips and nose as Eva kicked her relentlessly.

"Stop!" screamed Albert with a newfound power. The plea reverberated throughout the empty rooftop. Eva turned. Ying crumpled to the ground, moaning.

Eva pivoted to him. Her face simmered with rage. She locked eyes with Albert, and her rage turned to despair. She was gone, now. She had chosen her fate, and Albert had lost her. There would be no bringing her back. Now she was Albert's enemy, and she knew it.

Albert rose to face her and assumed his fighting position.

Eva scoffed.

"I didn't want this, Dilbert," said Eva as she unleashed a series of blows that Albert attempted to block.

With the vibration of each blow, Albert's glasses fell farther down his face. Panicked, he covered his face to secure them.

Eva's eyes followed his movements.

She knows about the glasses, he thought.

Albert could hear footsteps rumbling up the stairwell like a growing fire. *More guards are coming. I need protection.* His mind quickly raced through the likely scenarios. He could stall Eva by herself, but once the guards arrived, it was over. *I've got to back her up against that door.*

"Turner's been training you, I see," exclaimed Eva with a sardonic smile. "Let's see what you can do."

Albert jabbed with his right hand. She dodged left. He jabbed with his left. She dodged right, almost imperceptibly, to highlight the minimal effort required. He kicked with his right leg, attempting to throw his opponent off guard. This time, Eva's hand sprung from her left side and swatted Albert's face. He reached for the glasses, but it was too late. They clinked against the ground. Before he could recover, a devastating kick to his knee dropped him to the ground, followed by a jaw-smashing blow to his face.

As Albert fell to the ground, the roof door burst open, and Angus Turner limped onto the roof. Dried blood covered his nose. With one forceful arc, the aging professor swept Eva's legs out from under her with his walking stick, sending her tumbling to the ground.

"I think you've caused enough trouble for the day," said Turner. He snatched one of the guard's pistols off the ground and pointed it at her head.

Albert rushed over to Ying, who was curled up on the cement roof.

"Are you alright?"

Ying smiled, her mouth caked in blood. "Yeah, you should have let me take her. I had her right where I wanted her."

"Attagirl," exclaimed Turner as he dragged Eva away from the rooftop entrance and toward the rope hanging from the roof's steel edge. Eva's face seethed.

"Dr. Puddles, Ms. Koh, I believe it is time for us to make our escape," said Turner, gesturing to the rope. "Ms. Koh, do you think you can make it?"

"Yeah, I'll be fine," replied Ying, lifting herself off the ground and limping toward the roof's edge. As she passed Eva, she stepped on her hand.

"Ahhhh," screeched Eva.

"Oh, I'm sorry, did I step on you?" said Ying with a grin.

Albert frowned and gestured to the empty white-lined parking lot below. "Bad news, Angus. Something happened to Gabe and Brick. They're not here."

Turner closed his eyes. Albert could see that the events of the past few weeks had taken their toll on the old man.

"Onto the next branch of the Tree. We go by foot," cheered Turner, attempting to convince himself as much as Albert and Ying. He handed Albert a yellow envelope with something thick inside.

"Is this . . . ?"

Turner nodded.

Albert slipped the envelope into his jacket pocket and followed Ying down the rope, all the while looking up at Turner.

"Are you coming?" asked Albert.

"Yes, and so is Ms. Fix here," said Turner, gesturing with the gun for Eva to grab the rope.

"I'm afraid I can't allow that," came the voice of Cristina Culebra. From the sound of her voice, Albert could tell she was standing behind Turner.

Albert watched from below as Turner quickly slid his body behind Eva and brought his pistol to her head. Panicked, Albert began scaling back up the rope. Without looking back, Turner pointed his finger downward, signaling for Albert and Ying to keep descending. Albert kept creeping down the side of the building but could see the professor's silhouette. Turner stood at the roof's edge, using Eva as a shield.

"It's been a long time, Cristina," said Turner.

"Yes, Angus ... too long." Albert heard Cristina's heels crunching toward Turner on the rooftop gravel. He looked down. Ying was nearly at the bottom, now.

"Don't move any closer," said Turner. Albert could hear the rooftop door open again and the shuffle of numerous footsteps. *The backup has arrived. I can't leave him.* He began climbing hand over hand back up the rope. The fibers of the rope tore at the skin on his hands.

"Come now, Angus. You're smarter than that. You're cornered alone on a rooftop. Ten armed guards have pistols pointed at you. Even your precious Tree of Knowledge won't do the trick. Why don't you put down the gun, and we'll discuss this like civilized adults?"

From his vantage point, Albert could see Cristina approaching Turner. She was carrying a gun. *What is he doing? She's getting too close.*

Behind his back, Turner again motioned for Albert to stay put.

"Now, Cristina, don't do anything rash, or I may hurl myself off this roof, and you'll never be able to crack the code. Or worse yet, I may be forced to do something unpleasant to your daughter," said Turner, his voice breaking.

Cristina Culebra smiled. This was her moment. She cocked her head to the side and delivered the words she had been waiting to speak to him since the beginning. "Don't you mean *our* daughter, Angus?"

Turner slouched and staggered to the left, looking at Eva as if he were seeing her for the first time. His eyes carried the pain of a man who realized he'd chosen the wrong road in life.

Albert glanced at Eva and could see she felt all of this and more. Hope filled and softened the face that had been so hard a minute ago. This was the girl that he had known, the girl he had cared for. She reached out to her father and grabbed his hand as if to restore a connection that Cristina had taken from them.

Their connection was broken by a gunshot.

Cristina and Eva both turned in panic to see the bloodied presence of Isaac Moloch, arm extended, gun in hand.

Turner grabbed his chest and staggered backward, attempting to find his footing.

Albert looked on in horror as Turner's foot caught on the edge of the roof. He reached and strained with his free hand. His pant leg slid in and then out of Albert's hand as his body tumbled off the building.

"Nooooo," screamed Ying.

Turner's body descended earthward and slammed against the remorseless concrete below.

CHAPTER 14

Albert walked out of Fix headquarters side by side with Ying and an escort from the Los Angeles County sheriff's office. The morning sunrise shined a harsh beam, an interrogation light, stripping Albert of pretense, exposing him for what he was, mocking him for what he had lost. Every few steps, he looked behind him toward the ledge of the cruel glass building where Turner had fallen. He wondered: If he looked hard enough, could he prevent it from happening? One look at Ying, and he knew she thought the same.

Ocean air brimming with expired fish and thriving industry lilted in front of him, carrying the chatter and laughter of officers in the parking lot. Handshakes. Pats on the back. Bullies at the playground. In one of the squad cars sat Brick and Gabe, handcuffed and complaining vehemently to anyone who would listen.

As he walked toward the blue-and-white sedan that would carry him to confinement, Albert's mind flitted from one feeling to the next. With each step, sentiment bubbled and burst like water in a cauldron. Grief at everything that Cristina took from him. Turner, his job, his home, his life, his comfort in knowing what each day would look like ... his hope. Wonder at how his calculations had gone wrong. How the Tree had let him down. Guilt for bringing Ying into this chaos, for not having the foresight to protect Turner. Isolation at the realization that he was the guardian of the Tree now, that his mentor wouldn't be there to teach him, to protect him. Responsibility for the Book Club, for those who would be harmed by Cristina Culebra, most important, for Ying. Anger at himself for allowing emotions to corrupt the order that he had built in his life, blinding him to Moloch's gun and Turner's weakness, keeping Eva forever in his mind. Demolishing routine, organization, predictability.

Confusion that those same emotions made him feel alive.

Alive.

Something stirred inside of him. He understood now. His back straightened. He looked at the sun again. The harsh spotlight was gone, and in its place a new beginning. His steps quickened. Ying and the deputy started scampering just to keep up.

Emotions were water.

It was his choice how to deal with them. He could do what he'd been doing, shoring up a wall to keep the water out, inevitably crumbling as the sea wore down the rocks and seeped its way inside. Or he could harness it like a waterwheel and use it to give life to something greater than himself. To fuel his resolve. The Tree. The fight against Cristina, the—

"Tim! Not that car."

Albert snapped back to reality. The deputy had opened the back door to the squad car, but another officer interrupted him.

"These guys are apparently suspects in a case back in Jersey. They need to be transferred. Put them in the navy unmarked Crown Vic over there." He pointed to a car inconspicuously parked in the back of the visitors' circle.

Albert squinted at the officer, trying to glean meaning through his mirrored aviators. *Transferred? How would they already know we need to be transferred? Does Cristina Culebra control the sheriff as well?*

The sheriff's deputy pushed Ying and Albert through the crowd of cars and toward the dark-blue sedan. Through the tinted windows Albert could see there was a driver in the car waiting for them.

"Where are we going?" asked Ying to the deputy.

"You're going to jail, ma'am," said the deputy triumphantly. "This gentleman here's going to take you back to Jersey and make sure justice is served."

"Who is he?" asked Albert.

"No more questions," said the deputy and shoved them into the mysterious car.

Albert and Ying tumbled into the dark vinyl seats. The creaking sound of the material reminded him of a New York City taxicab. A thick black cage separated them from the driver. Albert peered through, but the driver kept his head and his eyes forward.

"You've come a long way from solving logic puzzles, haven't you, Professor?" said the voice.

Albert grabbed the cage. "Detective Weatherspoon?"

The bearish detective turned and flashed a sly grin. "The one and only."

Both Ying and Albert leapt forward in their seats and pressed their faces against the divider. Weatherspoon reminded them of home.

"Wait, so you're here because you know about Cristina Culebra? You know that what I told you was true? I knew it. I knew you'd see that this whole thing was a scam. Oh, thank God you're here. She killed him. She killed Turner. We need to get her!"

"Whoa. Slow down, Puddles. Don't get too excited. I'm still not convinced you aren't a part of something, but I know for sure that this mess is a whole lot more complicated than it looks. First things first, let's get the two of you out of here and back to New Jersey in one piece, and then we can go about figuring out what's really going on."

The detective started the car and crept out of the parking lot. Albert could hear the pebbles trickling out from behind the tires as they left. Ying looked behind them. No one followed.

"Since we've got a little time, why don't you start at the beginning," said Weatherspoon.

Albert leaned his head back, closed his eyes, and gathered himself. He was exhausted, and the man who had been his father for the last sixteen years was dead. All he wanted was to sleep. But he knew he couldn't. He had listened to the serpent and taken a bite from the apple. He was no longer ignorant. He was awake. His life was no longer a life; it was a cause. Ying—and hopefully Weatherspoon—would be his partners in that cause.

He took a deep breath and began, "It all started when you came to my office with a piece of paper . . ."

CHAPTER 15

Angus Turner would have loved his funeral, Albert thought. The man of tradition now rested center stage in the most traditional of funerals. Hundreds of professors, dignitaries, friends and family walked through the green funeral grounds of Princeton Cemetery toward the dark wood casket to pay homage to the legend. As they walked, they passed the weathered gray headstones of Nobel Prize winners, Pulitzer Prize winners, presidents, and vice presidents—an exclusive club to which Angus undoubtedly belonged. The heartbreaking whine of bagpipes rippled through the fall air. The faint smell of burning firewood appeared and then vanished. The trees were turning color as if even they knew that this was the end of something that needed to be marked in time.

Albert stood with Ying outside the cemetery gates, watching from afar. They both wore black. Weatherspoon had told them not to go. They were under investigation for Turner's death, among other things, and Cristina still loomed large. Not the time to make a public appearance. But Albert ignored him, and so did Ying. It felt wrong to be anywhere else.

Now that he was here, he wasn't so sure he had made the right choice.

Not only had Cristina taken his mentor—his friend—from him, but she had taken away his right to mourn him as well. He wanted to meet Turner's family and tell him what the man had meant to him. He wanted to share stories with his colleagues of who Angus really was. He wanted to compile and revitalize the memories of a man he felt was already slipping away. The funeral had made Albert realize that he had only known one side of Turner, but there was so much more to learn. What were his dreams? What were his regrets? His idiosyncrasies? His hopes? His fears?

Now, all Albert could do was watch as people who barely knew Angus pretended to grieve, while he and Ying, two people who had been in the fire with Angus, stood watching like curious passersby. Angus may have loved it, but to Albert, it was a fraud. A show.

"What do you think we should do now?" asked Ying.

Albert turned to her, but she looked straight ahead, unable to take her eyes off the casket. Ying had grown so much older and wiser in their time together, but he could see that right now she still hovered in the fog between shock and grief. He looked on with her.

"I don't know. I don't think it's safe for me here." He hated the thought of leaving Princeton. Of leaving Ying. It was home, now. But there was nothing for him here. Only hiding. From the police. From Moloch. From Cristina. From Eva.

"Where will you go?"

"Somewhere abroad. Somewhere quiet. Where Cristina will forget about me. Somewhere I can think. Try to figure out our next move."

"I could come with you, you know." Ying dipped her shoulder into his and gave him a friendly bump.

He looked at her and smiled. He wanted to say yes, but he had done enough to derail Ying's life already. He refused to drag her down whatever path he was about to take.

"I couldn't do that to you Ying. Your place is here."

He turned to watch the funeral as it was about to begin. The assembled mourners quieted down and gathered around the casket for the start of the service. The minister held up his hands and opened his Bible, preparing to speak. As he was about to begin the service, a black motorcade of three SUVs rumbled into the curved entrance to the cemetery, their engines sending crows cawing into the gray fall sky. The minister closed his Bible and looked down, waiting for the interruption to cease.

A man in a black suit and red aviators emerged from the front seat of the middle SUV and opened the back door. Cristina Culebra stepped out, followed by Moloch and Eva. A murmur made its way through the funeral gathering. Everyone turned to see the spectacle that was Cristina. She had stolen everything from Turner. And now, he was no longer even the focus at his own funeral. Cristina and her entourage walked toward the mourners, giving solemn handshakes and hugs as she made her way through the crowd. The group parted around her until she reached the front. Cristina nodded to the minister as though he needed her permission to speak.

The minister began the service. Albert and Ying stood too far away to hear it.

"It looks like she outplayed us again, huh?" said Ying, turning her back on the funeral. "I'm sorry Albert, I can't watch this." She clutched his arm.

Albert saw tears welling in her eyes. He stared at his feet. He wished he could find the words to comfort her. But what could he say? The man who had shot Angus stood footsteps away from his body while Albert and Ying hid behind a tree.

Ying pulled her keys from her pocket and pushed the keyless entry button to her gray sedan.

"Well, it's been one hell of an adventure, Albert. I just wish there was something we could do to honor Angus, you know? To make sure he didn't die for nothing. But how do you fight a four-star general?"

She started walking to her car.

"Ying," Albert called.

She turned. "Yeah?"

He smiled a worn smile and pulled a small, tattered leather journal from his jacket pocket. "Maybe there is something we can do."

Ying's eyes popped wide open. "Is that? Is that it?"

"Yeah, it's Turner's journal. The Tree itself. He recovered it from Moloch and gave it to me on the roof before he died."

"Ah, that's what was in the envelope he gave you. Have you cracked it? Have you cracked the cipher?"

Albert shook his head. "No, this one's going to take some time."

"I can help you. We can do it together."

"Thanks, but I think I need to do this on my own. I think that's how Angus would have wanted it."

"You sure?"

"Yeah. I'm sure."

Ying stepped back to her car and opened the door. "OK, but you know that if you ever need my help, I'm here. I won't sleep until Moloch pays for what he did."

Albert smiled. "Thanks, Ying." He gathered himself. His voice was leaving him. "I mean it. Thanks for everything you did. For me. For Turner. You really are incredible."

Ying blushed and pushed her glasses up on her nose. "You're very welcome, Albert. But this isn't goodbye, you know. I'll come hunt you down if I have to." She shook her tiny fist at him.

He chuckled. "I know you will."

Ying slid into the driver's seat, closed the car door, and turned the ignition.

Albert watched her every move, knowing that once she drove away things would never be the same between them. They had been on a life-changing adventure, and now the world was different. They were different.

"Ying!" Albert shouted, as she turned the car onto the street.

She rolled down her window. "Yeah."

"Be careful, OK."

She pursed her lips and let her hair fall down in front of her face. "You too, Albert."

Albert watched Ying turn onto the street and drive away. He could see from the way she tilted her head that she was crying, just as he was. He turned back to the funeral and stifled the tears. Tried to push it all down.

He took a long inhale through his nose. He opened Turner's journal. An indecipherable code rolled from page to page. Holding the keys to something magical. He took one last look at Cristina Culebra and slammed the journal shut. He buttoned his jacket and started walking. There was work to do.

EPILOGUE

This is a celebration, not of my election but of our independence," called Cristina Culebra into the gleaming silver microphone.

A crowd of one hundred thousand Californians rocked and jostled like a single mindless organism, hoping to glimpse the newly elected governor. Red banners and T-shirts gleamed in the sunlight. Drumbeats rippled through the crisp fall air and echoed around the state capitol.

"For too long, bureaucrats in Washington, DC have held us down.

"For too long, your hard-earned money has been sent to other states and wasted by corrupt local officials.

"For too long, our elected leaders have ignored us and abandoned us.

"For too long, the Golden State has been cloaked in darkness.

"Today, we say: No more! No more income taxes. No more federal regulations. No wasteful spending. Today, I am here before you to proclaim California's independence from the Union."

The assembled throng screamed with delight, oblivious to the impact of the newly elected governor's words. They were hers. They would follow her anywhere.

"From now on, we are not Americans, first; we are *Californians*, first. From now on, we rise and fall together. From now on, our destiny is our own. And as your president, I will promise you that our future will be bright."

Cristina paused, adjusted her crimson scarf, and pointed a long, tanned finger at General Isaac Moloch, who stood over her left shoulder like a ghost. "And to those who would try to stop us, I would say one thing. There's a four-star general and a RED Army that's got our back."

Cristina Culebra's final words were drowned in chants of "Cris-ti-na, Cris-ti-na!".

The self-proclaimed president stepped back from the microphone and waved to the crowd, delighting in the power that was finally hers. She kneeled down on the edge of the stage and shook hands with the screaming, crying citizens reaching up to touch their newfound savior.

From the side of the stage, Eva looked on, attempting to grasp the magnitude of what had happened and what was about to come. She had committed herself entirely to her mother's cause, seen it come to fruition...and had, somehow, entirely lost her belief in it.

When she stared at her mother now, she could only see a jumble of images, flashing before her eyes in a relentless loop: her mother, stalking toward Angus Turner, the professor falling, his eyes meeting Eva's one last time...

"Was it true?" she had asked her mother, as the police hauled Albert and his assistant away. "Was Professor Turner really my father?"

Her mother had only given Eva one of her pitying looks. "Evalita," she said, in a tone of censure.

It could have meant anything, but to Eva, it had been like a spark to tinder. She realized it almost didn't matter if it was true. Her whole life, she had mourned the father she never knew. At fourteen, she had known a man who had been her match in wits, who had delighted in how far her mind could go—a man who could have, *would* have, been the father she had always wanted...if her mother had allowed it. Now, Eva remembered just how closely her mother had watched her for signs that she might be growing too close to Professor Turner—and how quickly Cristina had pulled her daughter away once she had what she wanted from him.

Eva had gained and lost a father in a moment, had realized she had gained and lost him once before, and her mother didn't even care.

Eva stared with a nauseated air as her mother smiled and pressed the flesh of her unwitting victims.

She took one last look and walked away.

Thank You

Thank you so much for reading *The Tree of Knowledge*. I hope you enjoyed reading it as much as I enjoyed writing it. You can find out what happens next to Albert and the Book Club by downloading *Of Good & Evil*, Book 2 in The Tree of Knowledge Series. You can also sign up for my newsletter and get updates on upcoming novels and deals at danielmillerbooks.com.

If you enjoyed the book, I also encourage you to leave a review on my Amazon page and Goodreads page. Reviews from readers like you are the fuel that keeps authors like me going, so even a one sentence review can make all the difference. Thank you so much for your support!

Acknowledgments

To my publishing team—Bethany Davis, Clete Smith, Georgie Hockett, and Christina Henry de Tessan—for taking a raw piece of clay and molding it into a finished product.

To all of the readers who have taken the time to read the book and enjoyed it. And even the ones who didn't enjoy it. You've given my writing meaning.

To the independent booksellers who take chances on new authors like me. Your commitment to creativity and diversity enriches the world.

To my family, for always supporting my crazy dreams, no matter how far-fetched they may seem.

To my friends, who have always provided the steady humor and intelligence that I hoped to infuse into this novel.

And finally, to Lexi, my perfect match. Your relentless positivity and love gave me the strength and courage to finish this book.

About the Author

Daniel G. Miller is an entrepreneur and former business consultant with a master's degree in public policy and economics. In his work in economics and consulting he witnessed the power of complex decision trees and mathematical models in predicting real-world events. The experience with prediction in business inspired the question, "what if we could use math to predict everything in our lives." From there, Albert Puddles was born. He currently lives in Florida with his wife Lexi.

Made in the USA
Columbia, SC
26 April 2023

451af1e3-e298-4355-b202-4fa3881c780dR01